THE HAUNTING OF ASHLEY HALL SCHOOL

Jim D'Andrea

Published by Crystal Cove Press

www.crystalcovepress.com

Copyright © 2025 Jim D'Andrea

All rights reserved.

ISBN: 978-1-968532-21-5

Cover art: Michael Squid

Cover Design: Ben Baldwin - www.benbaldwin.co.uk

Crystal Cove Press is the young adult imprint of Crystal Lake Publishing.

Sign up to their newsletter today!

For Steve and Linde — They would have loved this.

1

Emily learned what death smelled like at an early age. She would become a "smell" person, remembering things by their scent. If she experienced that aroma again, even years later, it would transport her back to that place and the feelings associated with it.

One of her earliest memories was visiting a nursing home and getting a putrid stench trapped in the back of her nose, as if it was sitting on her throat. She may have had a couple of moments in life that she recollected prior to that, but they were more like fleeting snapshots than full memories.

On that day at the nursing home, it stunk—big time. That's what she would remember, and it stayed with her.

Five years old seems to be when memories begin to become clearer and more developed, albeit through the lens of a young child's capacity to understand the situation.

Emily remembered the bad smell, and she nailed that one. *What was the source of the odor?* she wondered. Yes, most everyone was wearing diapers. That certainly played a role and served as a bumpy start for the fragrant sensitive. *Could it be the food? Too much heat? Lack of fresh air?*

Or could it have been decay? Specifically, the rotting away of the human spirit—the odious stench of death.

Smell a puppy's breath, a baby's head, or a freshly cut flower—all wonderful. Youth teems with optimism. It knows no boundaries. The human spirit, when new and unfettered by failure, illness, or depression, is the most potent force in the universe. It looks good, it feels good, and it *smells* good.

But with experience comes pain: burying people you love, failing at things you thought you'd succeed at, getting sick, losing optimism. It's like buying a new car—so shiny and unblemished. It doesn't become tainted quickly enough for you to notice. It starts with a ding, then a stain or a scratch. It sneaks up on you—the little imperfections that add up over time, like the gray hairs on your head. Then one day, you realize you're driving a jalopy.

Time is cruel. That was Emily's very astute observation that day at the nursing home—an impressive extrapolation for a child so young.

She wanted to escape the rotting human spirit surrounding her as quickly as possible. Instinctively, Emily clung to her mother's leg for protection from whatever was causing all the death. Mom tolerated the grasping child but did not reciprocate with warmth, a dynamic that defined their relationship.

They were there visiting her mother's grandmother, a woman in her nineties who looked every day of it. Emily had never met her before. She was told that this was her "great-grandmother"—an impressive title for such a fragile, petite person. She was missing most of her teeth, and her hair looked like a pen-and-ink drawing of a tumbleweed resting atop her tiny head. She also had dementia, which left her lying in bed, playing with a cloth doll, making it dance while she sang songs in Polish. Emily found it all spooky and wanted to go home.

"Wait, we're staying *here?*" was the first thing Emily said to her mother after spending an interminable hour in the place.

"Yes," her mother replied. "I told you that last night. It's too far to drive back home."

A hotel! she thought, not *here.*

She did recall her mother mentioning they'd be staying. The long trip wasn't one she wanted to make twice in the same day. In fact, Emily was excited. She loved hotels, at least from the few times she could remember staying in one. She enjoyed the fuzzy white robes, the tightly made beds, the vending machines filled with candy, and those long hallways for her to run up and down. She hoped this place would have a restaurant, like some do—maybe an Outback Steakhouse with honey butter for the dinner rolls.

The communication breakdown was becoming clear now. They would be staying right here, in the old folks' home, in an unimpressive apartment that could be rented for fifty dollars per night by visiting family members. Terribly convenient. Emphasis on the word "terribly."

Even their rented apartment smelled, which wasn't surprising, as it was just another room, exactly like the one her great-grandmother occupied.

The residents of the facility—also known as the old people—scared her. She felt guilty about that, figuring it might be a sin to think that way. So be it. They were damn creepy to be around: the lack of color in their skin—the way it hung so loose and sloppy off their skulls, their cataract-clouded eyes, their big, cumbersome-looking false teeth, their veiny little hands. Even the way they sat silently and stared. It all made Emily feel uneasy. She didn't need to reason through it; she just wanted to be away from it. Away from *them*.

But here she was, in this pint-sized apartment within a smelly nursing home, where she and her mother would apparently be spending the night. There would be no fuzzy white robes, no tautly pulled sheets, and no lobby restaurant to get excited about. On the contrary, she begged her mother not to make her eat the flavorless, unappealing food served in the cafeteria. She wanted to go to McDonald's. Her plea fell on deaf ears, of which there were many.

She pushed a few bits of chicken around her plate, sniffed the tapioca-colored dessert, and ultimately went to bed hungry. She couldn't sleep, though, with the room being so warm and stuffy and quiet. Dear *God,* was it quiet.

Then, in the near blackness of the night, Emily heard a noise—a gentle squealing sound. It started off faint but steadily grew louder, coming closer. It was a squeal, not a squeak, which was important to differentiate because she wasn't psychologically prepared to confront a mouse, or a bat, or whatever else might squeak. No, this was definitely a squeal—a gentle squeal, nothing pig-like.

A loose bolt in an air conditioning unit? she wondered. That would explain why it was so warm and stuffy. *Could it be from the refrigerator in the kitchen?* Probably nothing to worry about, she figured. So why was she feeling alarmed? *Is it growing louder? How much closer will it get?*

She raised her head off the pillow in the first act of real concern.

Squeal, squeal, squeal. Louder, closer, louder. Her mom was snoring next to her, occupying the bed while Emily was on a pullout couch with a mattress built into it. A hard metal post ran laterally across the middle of her back, making it supremely uncomfortable. *Who missed that design flaw?*

The room was so dark that Emily couldn't see anything at all, no matter how wide she opened her eyes. But the sound kept growing louder, coming closer, until Emily decided she had to take a peek outside to find the source. She needed to know.

She crawled out of her awful faux-bed and tiptoed to the door. Gently, she turned the lock, which thumped heavily as the metal deadbolt slid back into the wooden panel.

She grasped the handle, feeling the heaviness of the door as she pulled on it. She wouldn't open it all the way, though, for fear of waking her mother with the hallway lights. Instead, she peered out through a tiny crack. A few dim fixtures in the hallway provided just enough illumination for her to see the area.

She heard it approaching, the soft squeal. Oh yes, it was coming closer. Squeal, squeal, squeal, and then something appeared around the corner where the hallway turned. A metal bucket with a mop in it, being pushed by someone. And when the person at the back of the mop turned the corner, Emily's heart skipped a beat. The man was *huge*—both round and tall. His head was shiny, like it had been waxed. His skull was laced with pink scars that looked painful. He was blubbery, with a stomach that jiggled through his uniform as he walked.

He looked goofy, she thought. Goofy and *scary*, like a gigantic baby, but not a cute one. He was missing a front tooth and had dark purplish circles under his eyes. She figured he had something wrong with him but couldn't quite place what. She sensed danger, and so she closed the tiny crack in the door to an even tinier one, just barely enough for one pupil on one eye to see out of.

Emily assumed the man was a custodian, wearing a blue jumpsuit that zipped down the front to his beltline. A white nametag was sewn into the chest pocket.

He stood in the dim hallway, fumbling with his keys outside a residential room. Emily had walked past it earlier and could see inside. There was a man living there. Residents seemed to keep their doors open during the day, likely out of boredom or perhaps the fear of dying unnoticed.

The big, goofy "possible" janitor pointed a small flashlight at the doorknob as he found the right key and unlocked the room. He entered, leaving his bucket and mop outside. After about sixty seconds, he reemerged, pushing a wheelchair with an elderly man in it. Emily began to feel uncomfortably warm in her pajamas. She wanted to close the door now, but she was afraid its heaviness would cause it to make a sound. He might hear her. She could get in trouble. So, she stood there, paralyzed, growing warmer by the second.

She glanced away for an instant to check the alarm clock—2:15 AM.

Looking back through the sliver in the door, she watched as the janitor leaned down toward the sickly man in the wheelchair and smiled. The old man appeared disturbed by the expression on the custodian's face. He looked frightened.

Then, the custodian pulled a clear plastic bag from his pocket and, in one swift motion, slipped it over the old man's head. With one hand, he yanked the bag tight around the man's neck to stop the flow of air.

Emily gasped at the aggression but covered her mouth with her hand to muffle any sound. She was too scared to move. She could see the old man's face as he sat helplessly in his wheelchair. The clear plastic bag expanded and contracted slightly as he struggled to breathe.

He reached his hands out in front of him, as if searching for something in the dark. She recognized it as a last-ditch effort from a vulnerable person no longer capable of defending himself. The assault lasted no more than forty-five seconds, but it felt like ten minutes to watch. Witnessing the life leaving a person was the worst thing she had ever experienced. The tiny bit of response he could muster—how inadequate it was—followed by his sad fade into a merciless death at the hands of this bully was traumatizing for the young girl.

Just as the man was about to suffocate, the janitor retrieved a small handheld mirror from the side pocket of his pant leg and held it up to the old man's face, forcing him to see his reflection through the clear plastic bag.

Emily saw the old man's eyes widen for a brief instant of horror. His face was a mask of visceral fright. A moment later, he died. His own mortified image would remain emblazoned in his mind for eternity, Emily thought. What a terrifying way to die, being forced to watch himself wilting in the reflection of a cheap mirror.

The custodian watched with glee until there was no life left in his victim. He was dead, with his eyes wide open, frozen in panic.

The custodian put the mirror back into the side pocket of his pants and then paused.

What was he doing? Emily wondered, feeling a droplet of perspiration rolling down her back into the crack of her buttocks. It tickled but felt uncomfortable. She wanted desperately to close the door now.

Then, unexpectedly, he turned and looked right at her. He could see her, she thought, through the tiny crack in the door, which was no wider than a centimeter. Their eyes locked. Her body felt icy cold in one instant, and an inexplicable warmth flowed from her crotch down the legs of her pajamas, drenching them.

She closed the door as carefully as she could, heavy as it was. She clicked the deadbolt and chained the door as well. She closed her eyes and stood in the blackness of the room, shivering with fear, pressing her back against the wall, trying not to breathe too loudly.

Was he out there?

Tears rolled down her cheeks, but she was too afraid to make a sound—afraid of waking her mother, afraid of getting in trouble, afraid of being killed by the man in the hallway just outside her door.

Eventually, she tiptoed to the bathroom and clicked on the light, but not until the door was almost fully closed so the light wouldn't shine out. She locked the bathroom door and peeled off her pajamas, which were soaked with urine and sweat. Her body felt moist yet chilled, despite the excessive warmth of the room.

She grabbed a small towel and ran warm water over it, careful not to turn the pressure up too high for fear of waking her mother. She wiped her body up and down and then dried off with a larger, softer towel. Wrapping it around herself, she turned off the bathroom light before opening the door and quietly making her way back to the sofa bed with the uncomfortable metal bar.

That metal bar wouldn't matter tonight, though, because she just sat on the end with her feet hanging off, waiting for the night to pass as she stared straight ahead. It felt like it took a full week for the sun to rise, but when it did, Emily sure would have a story to tell.

The next morning, there was activity in the hallway. Emily managed to fall asleep after all, though she didn't remember when. It must have been around the time the sun began to creep up because she recalled the relief she felt seeing a hint of light appearing through the blinds, however negligible it may have been.

Her mother was awake now, getting dressed and simultaneously packing—always an efficient woman. There were things that needed to be done, always.

But there was noise in the hallway—men's voices. In Emily's experience, that meant something serious. She associated males with authority because that was how her father behaved. For women, it was acceptable to discuss trivial matters, but not so for men. She'd heard him say that, and so she assumed it to be true.

Not that her mother was convivial and merry, mind you. She wasn't—at least not with her daughter. Mom was mechanical, performing her routines with exactness and without emotion.

Emily was reminded of this when her mother finally said matter-of-factly, "What in the world?" as she looked toward the ruckus happening in the hallway behind the closed door.

She didn't finish her sentence, always the queen of truncated thoughts. People knew what she meant.

Mom pulled open the heavy door to see what all the chatter was about. She had to give it a hard tug, which made Emily proud that she had managed to open it herself just a few hours earlier.

Emily hopped off the sofa bed and scampered across the room to get behind her mom for a protected look into the hallway.

What would they find?

She clung to her mother's skirt, more toward the back this time, needing more protection than she had from the senile woman playing with her doll and singing Polish songs. This was graver.

Her mother swiped at her without looking back.

"Oh, Emily, you're always right *there*," she said, sounding annoyed. The comment made Emily feel bothersome—like maybe she was a burden. Too needy. *Was she?*

In spite of that, she still clung on. She needed her, and mom didn't actually push her away—just made a shooing gesture. That was enough.

Emily was right, though. There were men in uniforms having a conversation in the hallway. They weren't police, but something similar. Something official.

"Who are those men?" she asked her mother, who now seemed interested in the hallway kerfuffle as she peered out the door. Mom didn't answer.

A moment later, Emily tried again. "Who are those—"

"I don't *know*, Emily. I don't know what's going on," her mother replied in the curt manner she'd perfected.

Emily stopped talking and watched along with her. A moment later, two men in white jackets and blue pants wheeled a cot out of the room. There appeared to be a body on it, covered by a blue plastic sheet.

Her mom stepped backward into the room, seemingly stunned by what she was seeing. Emily noticed; her mother was not one to react without real cause. Mom shut the door quickly to keep the child from seeing anything further.

"What was that, mom?"

"Nothing. I don't know what they're doing," her mother replied, uncharacteristically picking Emily up and carrying her further into the room, away from the closed door.

"Let's go ahead and pack your things, okay? We can go home now," her mother said in a soothing tone, perhaps to ease her own anxiety as much as her daughter's. Whatever her mother's motivation was, Emily was on board to get out of Stink-ville as fast as possible.

"Okay," Emily responded enthusiastically.

Duh! That's what I've been saying since we got here, she wanted to add.

Finally, they were making progress. Clothes were being packed, they would be on the road soon. Maybe they'd even stop at a quaint country diner for a proper breakfast. Emily was starving, having had virtually nothing for dinner the night before at the tapioca tavern. The end was so close—until a knock at the door derailed her plans.

Her mom opened the door to find a staff member standing there. He was a tall, thin young man dressed in white. He glanced at Emily, then at her mother, and quietly asked her something. The two of them stepped out into the hallway, away from Emily.

Through the half-open door, Emily could see into the hall. People were gathered around a body resting on a cot under a blue sheet. Emily poked her head out, curious about the interactions. Was there a person under there? Was it…the guy?

"Is that a dead person?" Emily asked, prompting her mother to pull the door closed, leaving Emily alone in the room. She waited, ready to leave but also eager to share her story. She had information the adults might find important, and that excited her.

When her mother returned, Emily went straight to the point.

"Mom, was that the man from that room lying under the blue sheet?"

"Emily, grab your things, brush your teeth, and let's get ready to say goodbye to your great-grandmother."

Record scratch! She had to say goodbye???

She thought they were headed straight for the car. But there was also something more pressing at hand and she was going to address it.

"I saw him," she said.

"You saw who?"

"The man from that room. He was in a wheelchair. Someone killed him."

"Emily!" her mother exclaimed, kneeling in front of her and gripping her shoulders. "Don't ever say something like that again."

Emily pulled away slightly, careful not to upset her mother. "But I did," she said softly.

"Stop," her mother told her, ending the exchange.

There was a brief silence before her mother stood up and began collecting their belongings. The conversation was over. They left the room without another word. In the hallway, men in uniforms were wheeling the cot with the presumed body on it.

Emily walked past his bedroom, now empty except for a wheelchair.

As she and her mother approached the men rolling the cot, one of them smiled at her. He was tall, handsome, and young, and he looked easy to talk to, Emily thought.

"I saw him," she said to the young man. She felt the urge to share this important information.

"Pardon?" he replied with a polite smile.

"The janitor in the blue suit killed him last night."

"Emily!" her mother said, grabbing her arm and pointing a finger in her face. "I said stop."

Her mother then turned her attention to the men.

"I'm sorry. She's five."

The men nodded as if to assuage her mother's concerns, and then went about their business. Her mother dragged her by the hand to the senile woman's room, whom she apparently was related to. They all said goodbye. Her mother made her kiss the woman on the cheek, which tasted awful. She couldn't get the disturbing flavor off her lips despite spitting multiple times in the parking lot and wiping her mouth with the front of her shirt.

When they reached the car, Emily felt a sense of relief in its familiarity. Still, she knew her mother was angry with her.

"Why did you say those things in there?" her mother asked, as if Emily had done something wrong.

"Was that man dead?" Emily inquired.

"Yes. He was old, and he passed away, Emily. People pass away. Especially old people."

"I saw a man kill him last night."

"Stop saying that," her mother snapped, looking miffed enough that Emily was afraid to repeat it.

"You just had a bad dream. That's all. That man died of old age. Now, I don't want to hear another word about it, understand?" her mother said.

Mom didn't wait for a reply. She climbed into the car and started it for the long ride home. There would be no breakfast at a quaint country diner, Emily realized. Not now.

As they drove, Emily gazed out the window. She knew what she had seen back there. She was young, but not stupid, and could clearly tell the difference between a bad dream and reality. She resented her mother for not believing her.

It didn't matter now, anyway. She was out of that Godforsaken stink-shack and hoped to never return.

More importantly, she was relieved to know that the hideous custodian was left behind, far away from her. With each mile they drove, he grew smaller and more distant. She would never have to see him again—that horrible monster. That thought comforted her tremendously.

Unfortunately, she was wrong.

2

shley Hall School was an all-girls school for grades K-12. Most students commuted, but high schoolers had the option to board. About sixty percent of the students lived at home, requiring their parents to provide transportation, while the remaining forty percent resided in dormitories on campus, Emily being one of them.

Emily arrived as a fourteen-year-old freshman, having previously attended Catholic schools for her earlier education. Her mother encouraged her to enroll at Ashley Hall and ultimately insisted that she board, as commuting would be too inconvenient and complicated. Things were always complicated with her mother. Emily had grown used to that.

She'd been nervous about coming to boarding school, but truth be told, she didn't miss her mother very much. It was her friends and the comfort of her own home that she longed for. Living at a boarding school felt prickly; nothing seemed warm or familiar.

She had hoped that living away would be fun, sort of like being in college. As it turned out, the administration were sticklers for rules. Her schedule was structured and closely supervised. Ashley Hall School earnestly promoted the tenets of Christianity to its pupils, which was a diplomatic way of saying they were strict.

She met a lot of people, but they never quite felt like friends—not like the kids she had grown up with.

Weeks passed, and her life settled into a routine: wake up, put on her school uniform, pull her hair back, avoid makeup, have breakfast in the cafeteria—always cereal, eating in silence. Classes. Reading. Lunch. Physical education. Religious studies. Homework. Bed. Repeat. The food was terrible, the dorm rooms were small, but the weather was nice. Autumn in the Deep South rarely disappoints.

Even the weekends felt stale. There were no parties to speak of, not much fun, and definitely no boys. There were some male staff, but they were grown men, and most of them weren't attractive. The nearest boys were at a school across the pond, where the "sister school"—or perhaps it should be a "brother school"—was located. It, too, was K-12, all male. Uniforms. Boarders. Same routine. The girls could see it across the pond, but it might as well have been across the ocean.

Emily felt like she was counting the days, but it wasn't clear to what end. She mentioned this to a teacher she liked—Mister Cogswell. He could be funny sometimes.

"Miss Cox," he said to her one day as they passed each other in the hallway.

"Yes?"

"How's it going this year?" he asked.

Emily shrugged a bit. "It feels like I'm in jail sometimes."

He laughed at her candor—a good, sincere laugh that made his face turn red. "We're all doing time, kiddo. In one way or another," he said as he walked off, still smiling from her comment. She heard him repeat the word "jail" with an audible chuckle.

In mid-September, it finally happened—seven weeks into the school year.

Emily was walking down the hallway of a dormitory she did not live in. She had gone there to return a book to the library, which had a return bin in the building.

After dropping off the book, she headed back toward the exit when she noticed a dorm room door was open—nothing unusual.

She glanced inside and saw Gia—that was her name. Emily remembered because she had seen her earlier in the school year when they all had to wear nametags for the first three weeks and hers said "Gia" written by hand in fancy calligraphy.

Emily paused to admire the room, specifically the artwork. Gia seemed to be decorating for Halloween, or maybe she just liked creepy stuff. Either way, it worked.

"Whoa, it looks like the set of a horror film in here," Emily said with wide eyes as she poked her head through the doorway for a closer look.

"Thanks," Gia said, flashing a flattered smile.

"I did these in pen and ink," Gia continued, pointing to a drawing of skulls that she had framed and hung on the wall. The tour had begun. "I bought this grim reaper at a yard sale when I was seven," she said, both girls looking up and down at the six-foot-tall wall sculpture of a human skeleton draped in a hooded black cloak.

"Holy crap," Emily exclaimed.

"It lights up," Gia said, clicking a switch to prove it.

"Nice," Emily replied.

"Right?" Gia said, locking eyes with Emily and smiling. "I also set up that whole graveyard in the corner using gray cardboard to make the headstones. The bones are plastic," Gia said, pointing to a section of her room that was cordoned off.

"That is cool," Emily confirmed.

"Thanks. All the witches, vampires, and stuff on the walls are mostly paintings I've done over the years," Gia said, gesturing at the collection of artwork covering nearly every bit of the room.

"What about this?" Emily asked, pointing at a mural of a vampire painted directly onto the wall.

"I just finished that. I'll have to paint over it after the year is over, or they'll charge my parents for damage to the room," Gia said with a hint of glee.

The two girls paused to give each other a looking over. Emily wasn't the type to be intrusive, but Gia had a way about her that felt approachable, at least to Emily. She wasn't like the other girls; she was an outsider.

"The rest of the stuff I bought at flea markets. I love flea markets," Gia said with a little shrug.

"So do I," Emily responded, inspecting the craftsmanship of the vampire mural more thoroughly. "So cool," she said with heartfelt approval.

"Thanks," Gia said. "Do you Ouija, by chance?" she asked, prompting Emily to turn from the artwork and look at her directly.

"Ouija?"

"Yeah."

"Is that a verb?"

They both smiled and chuckled. Gia's laugh was genuine and nicely contrasted with the macabre image she seemed hell-bent on promoting on the outside.

"You have a nice laugh," Emily told her. Gia looked flattered.

"Thanks. You do too," she replied.

"I'm Emily."

"I know. It's nice to officially meet you. I'm Gia."

Friends aren't made; they're discovered. Emily always believed that to be true. When you meet one, you just know. It isn't work; it happens fast. It's easy. That's how she felt about Gia. She could have tossed her backpack down and plopped on the couch to chew the fat for hours.

"So, how does one Ouija?" Emily asked, her curiosity piqued.

"It actually takes practice," Gia said, already pulling a Ouija board from a footlocker at the base of her bed. "Most people think it's just for fun—a game, sort of. Which is fine. But if you work at it, it can become real."

"Real how?" Emily asked. "Like, you talk to spirits?"

Gia shrugged her shoulders. "You can, but not always. And not easily. It's like anything else in life; you have to put in the time. Nobody gets great at something without lots and lots of practice," she explained, clearing off a small coffee table of various trinkets and trumpery.

Emily liked the way she spoke. She made sense. She had conviction.

Gia continued to speak without looking at Emily, a side effect of her shyness. She busied herself with the task of setting the board up perfectly on the coffee table. "I made this board myself. I used a chisel to whittle the letters and then put a nice shellac on it. After that, I painted it with all the details. Most Ouija boards aren't certified by the Association of Wicca. This one is," she said as she looked at Emily with a nod.

"Seriously?"

"Yuppers."

Emily examined it with admiration for the craftsmanship and beautifully painted details that she could have spent an hour admiring.

"You're really creative, huh?" she said.

Gia shrugged a bit, looking slightly uncomfortable with the compliment.

After Gia laid the board out, Emily could see this was no Amazon Ouija board; there was love involved in its creation. She couldn't help but smile.

"It's so impressive," Emily said.

"This is my Frankenstein," Gia said. "I gave it life. It was a charcuterie board originally. My mother planned on tossing it," Gia told her, stroking the surface of the board with loving hands.

The artwork on the board was haunting and gorgeous. Emily had seen Ouija boards before, but never one like this. The lettering made it look Middle Eastern and perhaps unholy. There was an eeriness about its beauty that felt almost sinful. The board was thick, too—not some flimsy piece of wood.

"I like how passionate you are," Emily said.

"Thanks," Gia said, looking away from the compliment.

Emily remembered her first encounter with Gia during their orientation. Gia had looked so alone and out of place at this uppity private boarding school. She was dressed differently—lots of black, medieval-style jewelry, and numerous piercings.

The school administration had forced her to make some adjustments to her attire that they deemed violations of the Christian values the school purported to espouse.

Emily recalled Gia standing alone, off to the side of the larger group. Even so, she had the air of someone who was unapologetic. Emily remembered some girls giggling at her. She was sure Gia heard them, but it didn't seem to faze her. She just walked past them without so much as a glance.

Emily was impressed by her independence and wondered if she could do the same. She often felt too quick to conform. That instinct for self-preservation among the pack was powerful—fit in, don't make waves.

But now, here was Gia, showing off her artwork, allowing herself to be vulnerable with Emily. She looked less fierce, less defiant, and less comfortable being alone.

Gia placed the planchette on the board. Emily always called it the "floaty thing," the little triangular object that looked like a computer mouse. Participants in a séance place their fingers on it to help guide it to respond to questions.

It had a small hole in the middle to read the letters through, a kind of looking glass. The whole thing resembled a sliced-open avocado floating around the board with just the lightest of touches. Thus, the moniker 'floaty thing.'

"There are Ouija boards that are games, and there are ones that are certified. A *true* Ouija board needs to be certified by the Association of Wicca. That's my religion, Wicca. My parents say I'm a Christian. I'm not."

"Maybe we can play sometime," Emily suggested.

"Play?" Gia replied with a twinge of disapproval. Their eyes locked for a moment, a discernible pause hanging between them.

"Well, maybe we could Ouija sometime," Emily corrected herself, offering a gracious smile.

Gia smiled back.

"It sounds like *wedgie* when you say Ouija," Gia said, smiling wider now, showing her full white teeth.

"Yeah, let's give each other wedgies sometime," Emily chuckled. "After all, this is an all-girls school."

They both laughed.

"If you'd like to try it, we can. I haven't used it since I got here. I haven't had anyone…" Gia's voice trailed off. She continued a moment later, "I just don't have…" she paused again, her face growing serious. She looked embarrassed.

Emily interjected, "I'd definitely like to try it with you. The Ouija, not the wedgie."

Gia nodded. "Okay, we'll pick a good, dark night to try it together. It doesn't always work, but if we get a third person, it will help. More people equal more energy being put out to the universe. There's a lot that needs to fall into place, and if the juju isn't right, nothing will happen."

"Well, what if something does happen?" Emily asked. "I mean, do you really think you can connect with spirits?"

"Absolutely," Gia replied without hesitation, her tone firm and convincing.

"Have you?" Emily asked.

"Yes," Gia said, her voice softening slightly, as if the answer required some reverence. "There are people who have the ability to interact with the transcendental world, and most of them aren't even aware of it. They miss the signs."

"Signs?" Emily replied.

Gia nodded, moving a bit closer, as if she was about to share important information. "We get signs. Life is full of them. People sometimes call them coincidences, which is complicated by the fact that coincidences *do* exist. Often, people confuse a sign with a coincidence. You have to look for the signs—they'll guide you. That's why they're called signs."

"What if I'm not one of those people who see signs?" Emily asked.

Gia looked into her eyes with a seriousness that was almost unnerving. "You are," she told her.

Whatever remained of Emily's smile melted away as they stared at each other, the mood growing heavy.

"I knew you were coming today. That's why I left the door open. I didn't do it consciously, but I did it because I'm so in tune with my subconscious mind. I felt you before you even left to walk over here. And here you are," Gia said, tucking her hair behind her ears. "It's a sign. You have to read it."

Emily opened her mouth to speak, but nothing came out. She saved face by nodding instead. Gia returned to her Ouija board and began the process of packing it up. Show and tell had ended. Emily made her way to the door.

"Nice finally meeting you," Emily said as she stood in the open doorway, ready to leave.

Gia looked up and smiled at her. "Yes, great meeting you, Emily."

Emily left the room and walked back to her own dormitory. She went through her nightly routine: dinner, homework, tending to her ablutions, and then off to bed. The whole time, she was distracted, deep in thought, reflecting on what Gia had said.

Was any of it true?

She liked Gia a lot and wanted to be friends with her. Emily needed friends too; she felt so lonely. Plus, Gia was unique, talented, and unabashedly genuine. There was something so appealing about that.

Just the same, something made her skittish about all the otherworldly stuff. She had that feeling people get in certain situations, the instinct they tell you to trust but you rarely do until you're looking back in hindsight.

It's probably nothing, Emily thought to herself.

Or maybe it was a sign.

Across the pond from Ashley Hall School was Porter-Gaud School for Boys. Martin Grabarz and his closest friend, Twerp, were surreptitiously making their way to the "beach"—a thin, rocky patch of hard sand at the base of a short cliff on the edge of campus. It was where the pond lapped up against the land. The area was off-limits, per school regulations.

Nevertheless, it was common practice for students to go there, and administrators didn't typically view it as a serious infraction.

What *was* a serious infraction—and one that could lead to expulsion—was attempting to cross the pond by boat, watercraft, or swimming. This rule was strictly enforced. Something about the administration not wanting any of the students drowning, blah blah blah…

The boys were there to check on a boat that Martin had discovered in the wooded area around the pond. The boat had pedals, allowing it to be ridden like a bicycle on water. It seated two, which was Martin's plan. He and Twerp would pedal to the other side of the pond after dark on a weekend night, heading to Ashley Hall School, and…

Well, he wasn't sure what. He hoped to meet girls. Martin wasn't great at that, and Twerp was worse. The only advantage Martin had in this situation was that Twerp was even less virile than he was. He figured if they did meet a few girls, they might be more likely to notice him first.

Not that either of them would be getting lucky, mind you. It just meant Twerp would strike out faster than Martin. Still, there was some pride in that.

"There it is," Martin said to Twerp, pointing with one hand and slapping Twerp's arm with the other.

"Nice!" said Twerp as he spotted the small, white boat.

The two boys grabbed hold of it and dragged the craft closer to the pond. They muffled their grunts, trying not to let the other know they were struggling. The boat had clearly been abandoned, evidenced by its state of disrepair.

"You think we can do it?" Twerp asked as he looked across the pond, assessing the task. They could see the lights of the Ashley Hall School campus in the distance. It looked like Oz.

"I think so," Martin replied with a tepid level of confidence. The pond wasn't particularly wide, but neither were Martin's legs—or Twerp's. A sense of potential failure—or even disaster—loomed over their effort. The only comfort was that it wouldn't be happening tonight; they were conducting a reconnaissance mission, a dry run. Martin figured Friday night would be the launch.

"If we get caught, my mother is going to kill me," Twerp said, his voice cracking a bit, more from puberty than fear, although it still made him sound scared.

"I know. Mine, too," Martin assured him. "But we're in high school now. We need to start asserting ourselves."

Martin knew Twerp's mother quite well. The boys had grown up together, and he'd spent many nights at Twerp's house. Twerp's mother was a staunch Catholic who insisted her son act accordingly. She considered it an embarrassment to her parenting skills when he misbehaved, taking it personally.

Martin remembered an incident from second grade when Twerp's mother caught him putting a potato chip on Martin's tongue like a Holy Eucharist. Twerp wore a black shirt, pretending to be a priest, and held out the chip between his fingers, saying, "Body of Christ…"

"Amen," Martin responded.

Twerp then placed said potato chip on Martin's tongue. Twerp was practicing; he thought his mother would be proud that he wanted to be a priest. Martin was just enjoying the chips.

"Blasphemer!" was all the boys heard as she burst through the door like an enraged version of the Kool-Aid Man. She didn't plan to beat him with paper towels necessarily, that's just what she had in her hand. If it had been a rolling pin, Twerp might have died that day.

"I'm sorry!" he yelled repeatedly, covering his head with both hands and running in circles around the small room as she chased him. It looked like a Benny Hill skit.

Martin wondered if he would be next, but she spared him.

"We won't get caught," Martin told Twerp about the boat trip. "There are girls over there—lots of them—and they haven't seen a boy in a long time. I like those odds for us."

"I do, too," Twerp confirmed. "If we're the only boys on their campus, they *have* to pay attention to us."

They sat down next to the boat like a couple of guys who'd accomplished something, even though they'd done little more than drag a small boat thirty feet. It still felt good.

"Ya know, Martin, I was thinking…" Twerp said reflectively.

"Uh-huh," Martin replied, obliging Twerp's lead-in.

"You mentioned earlier that we're in high school now," Twerp continued.

"Right," Martin said, curious where this would lead.

"Well, high school is a pivotal time in a boy's life."

Martin didn't respond, sitting in silence as he waited to hear what silliness Twerp was about to spew.

"So, anyway," Twerp continued after a brief silence. "My name—"

There it was.

"Go on," Martin encouraged, even nodding at Twerp like a therapist.

Twerp sighed and said, "I think it's time to put it to bed."

"What, the name 'Twerp'?" Martin asked incredulously.

"Yeah."

"But we've always called you Twerp."

"I know."

"Everyone *knows* you as Twerp."

"I know."

"Even your family calls you Twerp!"

"I've outgrown it," Twerp said, lacking any discernible conviction. It was like listening to O.J. Simpson telling reporters he was innocent.

Twerp's actual name was Roger Twerpinski. It lent itself beautifully to the nickname. The fact that Twerp was an actual 'twerp' just seemed to be one of those moments when you realize the universe has a sense of humor.

Twerp was skinny. Pencil-skinny. Dental-floss skinny, even. His arms, legs, and torso were all thin. He was short and pale, with soft features, although Martin would never articulate that in such candid and emasculating terms. Martin wasn't exactly the Hulk, but Twerp was worse off. He had a wimpy, almost whiny voice. He was a physical non-specimen. An *un-specimen*. Or perhaps a dys-specimen. Hard to diagnose accurately.

"So, what, you want to be called Roger now?" Martin asked, leaning back slightly and staring at Twerp for clarification.

"No," Twerp insisted softly, thinking Roger sounded dorky, too.

"What then?"

"I was thinking something like … Rocky," Twerp said, wincing even before Martin replied.

"*Rocky???*"

"Yeah."

Martin was shaking his head 'no' before Twerp had even finished.

"I don't think so, Twerp."

"Look, I need you to get on board or else nobody will, Martin. How about Lou? Or Butch?" Twerp suggested desperately.

"*Lou?*"

They stared at each other.

"Magnum?" Twerp croaked in a final plea.

Martin stood up, wiping the sand and dirt off the back of his pants.

"We'll have to see how things develop, Twerp. Let's circle back to this on Friday."

It was dead on arrival, as reflected by Twerp's defeated slouch as he stood up.

"Remember," Martin continued, changing the subject, "after dinner, Friday night. Wear shorts, but bring pants. Our legs are too skinny to show to the girls just yet."

"Gotcha. Good thinking," Twerp replied.

"She goes to school there, you know," Martin said as casually as he could.

"Who?" Twerp asked.

"Emily Cox," Martin said, unable to stifle his hint of giddiness.

"You think we can find her?" Twerp asked.

"I don't know. It sure would be nice, though."

The two boys walked back, off the "beach", up the small, rocky cliff, and headed to their respective dormitories, both quiet with excited thoughts of what might lie ahead this weekend.

Emily's roommate was a girl named Dahlia, who was quiet to a fault. She studied constantly, probably more out of boredom than a desire to excel. Her lack of a social life created a significant void that needed to be filled, so she did so with academics.

Dahlia was nice and harmless. Emily tried to forge a friendship with her, especially at the beginning of the year when she didn't know anyone and needed a friend.

However, that endeavor quickly ran its course, and they both understood it wasn't going anywhere.

Friends are discovered, not made, she often reminded herself.

Then, one day, a girl named Betsy showed up at the door. She was also a freshman and had a class with Dahlia. Betsy had borrowed some notes from a lesson she'd missed and came to return them. Dahlia was in the shower, so Emily and Betsy began to chat. Betsy was goofy, awkward, and funny, making a lot of little jokes and laughing at the end of each one—like her own personal laugh track.

Emily liked her right away, and before long, they were texting, eating meals together, and taking walks.

That's why, when Friday finally rolled around, Emily brought Betsy with her to Gia's room. They had decided to Ouija that night.

"Is that a verb?" Betsy asked, punctuating her question with her signature laugh.

"I asked the same thing!" Emily exclaimed, laughing.

Gia had said they needed at least three people for a session; she called it a quorum. "I won't Ouija with just two."

"You have your standards," Emily responded with a smirk and a nod. "I respect that."

Gia nodded back. "Damn straight."

Gia and Betsy got along just fine, but Emily was the nucleus of the friendship that the three of them would forge.

Without delay, Gia opened a two-liter bottle of soda and laid out bags of potato chips and other snacks. She set the ambiance with lit candles, burning incense, and relaxing background sounds that were part music, part nighttime nature recordings.

Her room felt isolated from the rest of the dormitory, like a cave. Every wall was adorned with artwork, creating an immersive experience that felt like an escape from the mundane routine of boarding school. There would be nothing soft, feminine, or gentle about tonight. This was going to be graphic, assertive, and fun—a perfect representation of Gia's personality, reflected in the pieces she'd crafted herself.

Soft, fat pillows were arranged on the floor for the girls to sit on, positioned around a low, round table that stood about a foot off the ground. The ornate Ouija board was centered on it.

"Shall we begin?" Gia asked, her face breaking into a giddy smile.

"Oh my God. I'm actually nervous," Betsy admitted, giggling.

"No laughing," Gia admonished. "The spirits don't like it."

"Sorry," Betsy said, giggling again, which prompted her to apologize for the giggle. "I'll shut up now," she finally said.

Emily could tell this was serious business for Gia, and her enthusiasm for anything supernatural was contagious. So, the three of them sat in the dimly lit dorm room, surrounded by Gia's gothic art collection, and got into a spooky mood together.

They played with the Ouija board for a couple of hours, starting with general questions to warm up before moving on to more personal ones. They asked about sex and boys, their lives, their futures, and more about boys. They shared secrets, dreams, and desires, discussing movies, TV shows, music, and celebrity crushes.

They munched on snacks and drank soda until they were wired on salt, sugar, and caffeine, laughing as if they'd known each other for ten years. It was the first enjoyable night Emily had experienced since arriving at the boarding school, and it felt therapeutic.

"It's not always like this," Gia said to them more than once. Emily wasn't sure how to interpret the remark.

"Isn't like *what?*" Emily asked after the third time she'd said it.

"This light and goofy. Sometimes it's heavy—even scary. The spirits are in a good mood tonight."

"Or we just have the happy spirits with us, and the mean ones don't know about it," Betsy added with a giggle.

Gia looked at Betsy.

"Do you want to try calling them? The dark ones?" she asked, glancing between Betsy and Emily. They exchanged uncertain looks, neither wanting to answer. *Did they?*

"I mean, is it like, dangerous or anything?" Emily asked, half-kidding.

Without a hint of jest, Gia replied, "Yes."

They fell silent for what felt like a full minute. Nobody was smiling.

Emily didn't want to ruin a good time by chickening out. She didn't want to seem lame or boring, either. However, she did have to walk back to her dorm alone in the dark, which made her less amenable to poking the hidden goblins of the night.

The silence continued. Gia took it as tacit acceptance, reaching out her hands toward each of the girls around the table.

Betsy looked at Emily, and Emily looked back at Betsy as they both held out their hands.

"Here we go," Gia whispered as they all formed a circle, holding hands.

Emily's lower back ached from sitting on the pillow for so long. She started to feel tingly, as if tiny beads of perspiration were forming on her skin, too small to appear just yet. She couldn't tell if her own hands were moist or if it was Betsy's and Gia's. Or perhaps everyone's.

Her pulse quickened, as silly as it seemed. The Ouija board was nothing but a game; she knew that. But with a caffeine buzz and Gia's insistence that it could all be real, Emily believed she felt something unnatural, and anxiety crept in.

Gia began speaking to the girls. "I will be here as the high priestess. In my religion—Wicca-Voodoo—any séance must be overseen by a high priest or priestess," she said with a smirk. "In other words, I'll do the talking."

This prompted a quick smile from Emily, a welcome break from her jittery state of mind.

With closed eyes, Gia began to chant, "Hounkou Bolokou Djavohoun Bohoun," repeating it again and again.

"What is that?" Emily asked.

Without opening her eyes, Gia answered, "It's an ancient Voodoo incantation intended to encourage the souls of the dead."

"What were we doing before?" Emily asked, wondering why this was just happening now.

Gia opened her eyes and looked at her. "We were swimming in the kiddie pool," she said, then closed her eyes again. Emily exchanged glances with Betsy, who looked nervous too. They closed their eyes as well.

"Hounkou Bolokou Djavohoun Bohoun," Gia chanted softly. A breeze blew through the room, flickering the candles. Emily noticed the window was cracked open, which reassured her, despite it being the first tangible movement of air she'd felt all night.

Gia sensed the breeze too, as she opened her eyes and said, "It's time."

She then let go of their hands and instructed, "Everyone put one finger on the planchette."

The planchette was the "floaty thing", Emily recalled, as she gently laid her index finger on top, alongside one from Betsy and one from Gia.

"Don't try to move it, but don't resist, either," Gia said. "Use no pressure. Let the spirits drive."

Together, they stared at the board, at their hands, at the planchette. Nothing was happening, but it felt strange to Emily. Her hand felt heavy the more she tried to make it light.

"It's moving," Betsy whispered.

Was it? Emily couldn't tell. It might have been, just a tiny bit. Were her eyes playing tricks on her?

Once more, Gia chanted, "Hounkou Bolokou Djavohoun Bohoun."

Then the planchette began to move. Emily could see her heart thumping through her wrist as she watched their hands glide around the board. Her chest felt tight. She wanted to pull her hand away from the planchette but feared it would ruin the moment for Gia. She couldn't determine if Gia was moving it intentionally or not. She knew she wasn't moving it herself, as best she could tell. Her hand felt so awkward at this point that she may have inadvertently been pushing it. Either way, the planchette was gliding. A moment later, it slid right off the board.

They sighed, one of relief for Emily—a much-needed break from the tension, as Gia placed the planchette back on the board.

"They're here now," she said, nodding to the girls.

"How do you know?" Emily asked, shaking out her right hand to get the blood flowing again.

"I can feel them. They pushed it off the board on purpose. Put your fingers back on it," she instructed.

They complied. And then they sat and watched.

Had it actually moved on its own? Emily wasn't sure now. Her hand felt heavy and numb, as if it had become difficult to not apply weight to the planchette.

"Identify yourself, spirit. I can feel you," Gia said, her expression growing weighty. She was in the zone. Emily thought she almost looked silly, acting as if all this was real. The "floaty thing" began to move again, unmistakably this time. Emily watched it glide, even as she tried to be careful not to press down on it.

"You guys…" Betsy said in a hushed voice, a quiver of concern in her tone that made Emily uncomfortable.

"Identify yourself," Gia insisted, louder this time, more forcefully.

The planchette floated across the board to the beautifully painted arc of letters. It stopped at 'B' for a brief moment, then 'A', and finally 'G'.

It became clear to Emily that nobody was pushing the planchette. She was officially spooked. She contemplated pulling her hand away and quitting the game but felt frozen.

The planchette glided to 'H', then 'E', then 'A', and finally 'D'. That's where it stopped.

"Baghead?" Gia said, her expression quizzical as she looked at Betsy and Emily for help.

Emily's hand felt as if it were cemented on the planchette. Her throat went dry, so much so that she couldn't speak. Her eyes grew watery, and her face flushed warm—the kind of warmth that comes when you're threatened. She saw Gia looking at her, and the expression on Gia's face told Emily she must have looked frightened.

"Oh my God, Emily, what's wrong?" Gia said, her eyes widening with concern, prompting Betsy to scan Emily hard as well.

"Are you okay?" Betsy asked, visibly upset by what she saw on Emily's face.

Emily was afraid to blink. She thought if she did, tears would streak down her cheeks. So, she sat there, trying not to cry, unable to speak, incapable of removing her finger from the planchette. Her chin quivered.

"Emily…" Gia said, leaning toward her.

Emily shook her head as if to say "no", even though it wasn't clear what question she was answering.

"Let go of the planchette," Gia instructed Betsy, who complied. "Emily," Gia said again, shaking Emily's leg to jolt her from her paralysis.

"I'm fine," Emily heard herself say, although it felt like someone else was speaking. A tear rolled down her cheek. She wanted the girls to stop looking at her. She couldn't lift her hand off the Ouija board.

Suddenly, a loud knock at the door made the girls scream in unison. Emily's hand was freed from the planchette as the door flung open, and in walked the dormitory monitor, a woman named Miss Warburton. She was tall and hippy, dressed in an outfit she must have bought in 1978. She was in charge of Campion Hall.

"You," she said, pointing at Betsy, "up to your room." Betsy was halfway out the door before the woman finished her sentence. "And you," she said to Emily, "come with me."

Emily couldn't feel her legs as she stood up. She was moving on autopilot. Things were happening so fast. She suddenly found herself in the brightly lit hallway, following Miss Warburton, barely registering what was transpiring. She was overwhelmed by the flurry of activity from the last several minutes; it felt like it had all passed in an instant.

Emily realized now that she was crying. At first, she barely noticed, but the salty tears were on her lips, and the taste helped snap her out of her daze. Miss Warburton noticed too, wearing a look of satisfaction. She had that 'I still got it' swagger in her steps, swaying her hips left and right as if she'd just served up an ace at Wimbledon.

Emily would be written up for being out of her dormitory past midnight. But that wasn't why she was crying. In fact, she couldn't quite pinpoint exactly what had upset her. Was it the moment? The Ouija board? The name? *Baghead.* She felt something so alarming. She knew it now, and it terrified her.

It was him.

3

Across the pond at Porter-Gaud School for Boys, Martin and Twerp were navigating the early part of their freshman year. Rule number one: don't get beat up.

As fourteen-year-olds, high school seniors looked like absolute goons. The transformation during four years of high school—especially for boys—was spectacular.

Fights did happen at Porter-Gaud, and although there was some consolation in the fact that there were no girls to witness the beatdown, it still sucked. Martin was small for his age. In fact, he was small for any age. Twerp was even smaller. They were the Batman and Robin of wimps. Neither of them was aggressive, assertive, strong, hairy, virile, or sexually active in any way other than waking up with an unyielding erection.

The boys and their friends knew that avoiding a public butt-kicking was paramount to getting through freshman year with their reputations somewhat intact.

"Be like water," Bruce Lee would say. Martin admired Bruce Lee. Bruce was small in stature, just like Martin, yet he was a famous warrior—a true American badass.

Martin had posters of him all over his walls. He knew his inspirational quotes by heart. "Be like water" was one of them. But what did it mean?

Water effortlessly conforms to its surroundings. It shapes itself like the bowl that holds it. It flows along the riverbed that guides it. It can disperse into millions of individual droplets or coalesce into a massive ocean. It's softer than cotton, yet it can break down mighty boulders over time.

Martin would be like water, too.

This was what he was thinking about that day at school—the Bruce Lee stuff, the "don't get beat up" stuff.

It started when he couldn't find his classroom.

"Where's P12?" he asked Twerp, almost rhetorically, not convinced it would yield any results.

"I don't know. I think it's the gym," Twerp replied, based on absolutely nothing.

"The gym?" Martin said, the doubt evident in his tone as he stared at his schedule on his phone. Twerp slammed his locker closed.

"I don't know, Martin. My classrooms don't have letters," Twerp pointed out. He had a valid point; none of Martin's classrooms had ever had letters either. This was a new class he had signed up for just prior to the drop/add deadline.

"It's an art class," Martin said.

"That's probably why it's in a weird location," Twerp confirmed.

That made sense. The classroom would be unconventional, and the teacher would be quirky. He'd dress poorly and look like an adult stoner—the most embarrassing kind. But Martin figured the class would be easy.

Until now, all of Martin's classes had been in the "Main Building," as they called it. It was the only building that resembled a traditional schoolhouse, with lockers and classrooms featuring old chalkboards and hard wooden desks. There was no P12 in the main building, which meant Martin would have to hustle to make it to class on time.

He roamed earnestly around the grounds outside. Three smaller buildings formed a triangle around a huge lawn, and after whiffing on the first one, he became anxious—especially when the bell rang, signaling that he was officially late. All the other students had vanished from the hallways.

He hated walking into a classroom after everyone was already seated and the teacher was lecturing. All eyes would be on him, awkwardly standing there in the pants his mom bought him for school, which he didn't fill out in any of the right places. He'd be holding his oversized bookbag, which was only a smidge smaller than he was, having to answer questions from the teacher, his voice likely cracking. Then he'd have to find a seat.

What if there weren't any? The embarrassment!

These were the things he fixated on. It took an out-of-place, yet familiar aroma to jar him from his mental preparation for catastrophe. He smelled smoke.

Yes, someone was smoking in the building, which was prohibited anywhere on campus, let alone indoors. Who would be so bold?

He followed the scent, which led him to the boys locker room. Twerp wasn't so dumb after all—Martin was in the basement of the gymnasium.

He pushed open the door and entered. The locker room was a sea of cement, metal, and hard tile—anything easy to clean. It appeared empty except for the smell of cigarette smoke. He followed the scent further, and when he turned the corner leading to a row of urinals, he saw him standing there like a pile of chipped bricks: Ricky Rude.

His first impression was that Ricky was big. He had to be six-foot-two and must have weighed two hundred pounds. He was a senior—again—having flunked out the previous year. His father was an alum and a donor who pulled strings to get Ricky another chance. Martin had heard his name before; they all had. Ricky was on the Mount Rushmore of high school bullies. Even amongst the meanest of kids, his reputation was prominent.

He was one of the few students who could grow a full beard. He wasn't just big, either, he was strong. Scary strong.

Ricky was smoking a cigarette, leaning against the wall, wearing a leather jacket and faded Levi's with torn knees. No dress code for this guy. He was surrounded by unused urinals. Martin froze, feeling as if someone was pouring cement into his legs.

He tried to think of something to say—anything. He couldn't. Using a urinal wasn't an option; he was too scared, which meant he wouldn't be able to pee. He'd be standing there with his wee-wee between his thumb and finger with Ricky Rude glaring down at him. That's no way to die. Ricky gave him a look as if to say, "What?" although he didn't actually speak. He didn't have to.

"Smoking, huh?" Martin finally chirped, his voice sounding the most feminine it ever had. His words got swallowed up in the echoey locker room.

Ricky took a final drag of his cigarette and said, "What the fuck does it look like?"

He then flicked his spent cigarette at Martin's face. It bounced off his nose. A direct hit! Touche, Ricky. It hurt, too, and the hot ash hadn't even touched his skin. The pain came from the filter doinking off the tip of his nose. Imagine what a punch must feel like.

There was some ash residue on Martin's face. He could feel it. Some had gotten on one of his eyelashes, too, obscuring his vision just a little. He tried to blink it away without looking silly. He didn't want to make a big deal out of it by rubbing his eye. Maybe Ricky would think he was cool and leave him alone.

What would Bruce Lee do?

He tried to conjure the spirit of "Little Dragon," as Bruce was known. But it had never been more clear to him that he most definitely was not Bruce Lee.

"You like hanging out in the boys locker room?" Ricky asked. It didn't seem like a genuine inquiry. Martin began to perspire. He was in trouble here.

Martin shook his head 'no' without speaking, looking down at the floor, the universal sign of submissiveness. And then Ricky Rude—so aptly named; the comical universe at work again—grabbed Martin by the back of his shirt and pressed his face into a urinal, flushing it four times.

Martin put up no resistance. His body was limp, as if Ricky were holding a ventriloquist puppet. His forehead rested against the cold porcelain of the toilet as water cascaded around his head.

I don't think this is what Bruce Lee meant when he said, "Be like water," Martin thought as he listened to the repeated flushing. Thankfully, it was clean. He'd give a nod to the janitor if he survived this.

"Frickin' geek," Ricky said as he dropped Martin's flaccid body to the floor and sauntered off.

Was it degrading? You bet. But there were a couple of victories here. One: he didn't get beat up. Two: nobody saw it. Most likely, that's why Ricky didn't punch him—no audience. Those two green check marks were as close to victory as Martin would get on this day. Plus, the cigarette ashes on his face had been washed away in the toilet as a bonus. He'd take it.

Martin spent the rest of the day walking softly and carrying a tiny stick. Then came the bad news, later that day, announced by Twerp, of course.

Twerp was that friend who seemed to relish delivering bad news. Not "horrible" news, mind you. He didn't want to tell someone their mother had been run over by a cement mixer. No. But he couldn't hide his giddiness when telling a classmate they'd gotten an F on a big test, or letting a friend know the girl he had a crush on was kissing someone else behind the football bleachers. Or that Ricky Rude was telling everyone at school he was going to kick their ass.

"Wait, what?" was all Martin could say, nearly coughing up the sip of apple juice from the tiny 8-ounce plastic Mott's bottle he'd bought from the vending machine. Even his beverage was small.

"Yup, that's the word on the street," Twerp said, fighting back a guilty grin. The teacher was beginning to lecture. Class was now in session. Everyone grew quiet. Martin wasn't going to wait to hear the story. This was too pressing. He'd be squirming for the next forty-five minutes. So, he leaned over a bit, and back just a tad, toward where Twerp was sitting, and whispered.

"Where did you hear that?" Martin asked, trying not to act too terrified.

Twerp whispered back, "From Sal Squizzero. He said he heard Rude talking about it in the cafeteria. He says you're a dead man walking."

And right at that moment, like magic—but the worst kind—Ricky Rude was standing outside their classroom, the door wide open. Ricky was at his locker, late for whatever class he was supposed to be in. Twerp nudged Martin and gestured to the hallway. Martin saw him. His stomach hurt.

Doesn't this kid ever go to class? Martin wondered, his face growing warm and droopy, like a heated marshmallow.

Their mutual friend Kenny had been listening the whole time. He sat right behind Martin in class and began chiming in, sharing impressive stats on Ricky Rude.

"He's already eighteen," Kenny whispered. "Soon to be nineteen. He got expelled last year—you know that, right?" Kenny continued. "He's been in fourteen verified fistfights and is fourteen and zero." He raised his eyebrows at Twerp and Martin, signaling how impressed he was.

"I'm gonna be sick," Martin said aloud, although he hadn't meant to verbalize it. He was so disoriented that his thoughts were spilling out without the consent of his brain.

"What did you do to him?" Kenny asked.

"*Nothing. I didn't do anything.*"

"I heard he dunked your head in a toilet," Twerp said, unable to hide his satisfaction. "Is that true?"

"Kind of," Martin replied.

"Everyone is talking about it," Twerp told him.

"This guy's no joke," Kenny said, pointing toward the hallway for impact.

"I know," Martin sighed, looking paler by the second as he watched Ricky Rude—this epic man-child—hang his brown leather jacket in his locker. He looked like someone's father punching in for a shift at a factory job. A *hard* factory job, where you needed to be strong and durable.

Kenny leaned closer to Martin and Twerp and continued with his scouting report.

"I heard he even beat up a teacher," Kenny said.

"Whoa," Twerp exclaimed in an animated whisper, nodding his approval.

"Yeah. True story," said Kenny.

"What are you gonna do, Martin?" Twerp asked like a reporter digging for details.

"I don't know," Martin whispered as he turned back to the front of the classroom where the teacher was speaking.

Kenny leaned forward again.

"I also heard he has his own apartment off-campus," he said. Martin glanced back and nodded.

"Jeez. He looks like a man," Twerp said as he admired Ricky through the door.

"I know, Twerp," Martin said, rubbing his own neck with growing impatience.

"He drives a motorcycle," Twerp added, a little more loudly.

"I know, Twerp," Martin shot back, his consternation evident as his shoulders slouched.

"He's got chest hair, for Christ's sake," Twerp whisper-yelled, pulling at Martin's arm to ensure he had his attention.

"I know, Twerp!" Martin snapped back, his voice too loud this time.

"Gentlemen—"

The boys turned to the front of the class, where their teacher, Mister Bonfiglioli, stood. "Is there something you'd like to share with us?"

The class looked at Martin and Twerp. Kenny played small, pretending to take notes.

Mister "Bonfig," as he was known, sported a Dutch-boy haircut styled to one side. It looked like a wig, but it wasn't, making it even more cringeworthy. He wore clothes that seemed to have been bought when he first started teaching years ago, always tainted with a smudge of white chalk on his pants—just like he had now.

"No, sir. Sorry," Martin said, mustering as much contrition as he could.

"And you, Mister Twerpinski?" the teacher asked.

"No, sir," Twerp replied in a meek voice.

"Twerp!" someone called from the back of the classroom, sparking a quick murmur of laughter from everyone, including Mister Bonfiglioli.

Twerp shook his head in exasperation, resigned to a lifetime with a nickname he would never escape.

"Then, if you don't mind, I'll continue with class," the teacher said, turning back to the whiteboard and resuming his lecture. The class fell silent, the lesson was dull, and Martin was left to wallow in an absolute ocean of dread.

Emily's mother arrived around mid-morning for a meeting with Misses Mansuetto, the school headmaster. Though she was a principal by all definitions, she insisted on the title "headmaster."

Emily waited outside the office while the two women met privately. After a short while, her mother emerged, took Emily by the hand, and they left the building together. She had officially been written up.

Two months into her freshman year, and her record already had ink on it. She felt like a rebel.

Her mother was not pleased, but she wasn't the type to scream either. She remained terse and cold—not too different from her usual demeanor. Emily could feel her mother's unhappiness; mom didn't have room in her schedule for a ride to school today. She didn't even need to say it.

Standing in the quad amidst the dorms, her mother bent slightly forward to be face-to-face with Emily.

"What's wrong with you?" her mother asked, as though she genuinely wanted an answer.

"Nothing," Emily replied.

"Then why am I here, *Emily*?" she said, placing particular stress on her name. Whenever she was annoyed, her mother would verbally emphasize *Emily*, as if the very word was some kind of pejorative.

Her mother continued, "I pay ten thousand dollars per semester just to get a phone call about you breaking bedtime protocol?" There was a slight tremor of anger in her voice, a sign she was truly upset.

"I lost track of time, that's all. We were playing a game. I'm sorry," Emily said, looking down at her feet.

"Who's the girl you were with? I don't want you hanging around her anymore. Misses Mansuetto said she's a bad influence."

"Gia. We're friends," Emily answered, looking up at her mother.

"Not anymore, you aren't," her mother said, stuffing her tiny planner into her purse.

Emily decided to explain. She thought that if her mother heard the truth about how hard it had been to make friends, how lonely she felt since arriving, and how meeting Gia and Betsy had given her the first glimpse of joy since school began, maybe her mother would understand that staying out a little late on a Friday night wasn't a big deal.

"I met Gia. She's fun and creative. We played with a Ouija board,"

Emily said, sounding like a defense attorney trying to make a case. It wasn't working.

"You have to be kidding me," her mother responded, putting her hands on her hips and tilting her head slightly. "A Ouija board? Are you ten?"

This is pointless, Emily thought as she sighed. She decided to get to the heart of it. She would open up to her mother right now.

"I felt something, Mom," she said, looking at her mother with pleading eyes. She needed to be heard.

"Felt what?"

"Do you remember the nursing home? When that man died?"

"Emily…" her mother said with exasperation.

"Listen to me! *Please*. We've never even talked about it," Emily pushed back, surprising herself with her boldness.

"There's nothing to talk about, honey. You were a little girl. You had a bad dream. Let it go," her mother said, offering the closest thing to compassion she could muster, yet still delivered too dismissively to be tender.

Emily was decisively shaking her head "no" as she replied, "It wasn't a dream, Mom. I watched someone murder that old man. I saw it happen! He wrapped a plastic bag over his head and—"

Her mother slapped her face, ending the conversation in an abrupt and truculent manner. Emily stood there, holding her cheek. Her mother hadn't struck her since she was a child. It hurt, too. The shock of it caused her throat to lump up and her eyes to water.

She wouldn't cry, though. Not today. She was still angry at herself for giving Miss Warburton the satisfaction of seeing her break down. No more of that.

"You stop it," her mother said, pointing in her face. "I don't want to hear one more word of that nonsense."

Emily didn't say another thing. In fact, she remained silent for the rest of the morning. Her mother walked her back to her dorm room, helped fold some clothes, and gave her fifteen dollars for snacks. They exchanged the most unfeeling hug in the history of mankind, and then her mother left.

Emily sat on her twin-sized bed, which felt like an army cot, and brooded. A part of her hated her mother, which made her feel guilty. Was their strained relationship her mother's fault, or did Emily simply blame her for it?

"If you never expect anything from anyone, you'll rarely be disappointed," she'd heard her mom say once. It stuck with her. Those were low expectations, but that seemed to be the point. It was a sour irony that it would come to define their own relationship.

She was gone now, though, which was a relief, even if part of her would miss her mom. Emily did love her mother, she even needed her, and sometimes wished they were closer.

The write up drama was over. If she got another one, she'd go on probation, so she had to be careful.

"I think I hate my mother," Emily told Gia that afternoon as they sat in Gia's room eating snacks Emily had bought at the commissary with the money her mother had given her.

"Why? Is she a bitch?" Gia asked, leaning forward, eager for gossip.

"I think so. But sometimes I wonder if I'm just being ungrateful," Emily replied with some uncertainty.

"I doubt that," Gia said. "If you think she's a bitch, she is."

Emily appreciated Gia always having her back. It felt good.

"What did Miss Warburton say to you?" Gia asked, referring to the woman who had written Emily up.

"Nothing, really. She just looked all happy that I was crying."

"She's just bitter because she can't fit through the door with those hips," Gia said, a guilty smirk flashing across her face for the cheap shot.

"Unless she turns sideways," Emily quipped, and the two girls laughed together. It wasn't like them to be mean, but Miss Warburton had it coming.

"Seriously, though, my mother tried to tell me I couldn't hang out with you anymore," Emily said, digging a spoon into a pint of ice cream.

"Oh," Gia said, her laughter fading. She looked surprised. "What did you say?"

"I didn't say anything. But I'm here, so—"

They both smiled.

"I'm glad," Gia said.

"Me too," Emily replied.

It was an affirmation of their friendship, something they both needed for their own reasons.

"That night, though," Gia said, her expression growing serious. "The Ouija … things got heavy at the end. I know you felt it."

Emily nodded. She felt almost grave, reflecting on how this all began.

Gia sat on a giant pillow on the floor, crossing her legs as she continued, "We conjured something real, Em. I saw your reaction. That was no game."

Emily nodded again, but didn't reply. She was hesitant to get too deep into it all again. She wasn't sure she ever would.

"Do you know I have my own YouTube channel?" Gia asked.

"No," Emily said, looking up at Gia, pleasantly surprised.

"Yup. I've got two thousand followers."

"Oh my God, Gia, that's awesome!"

"It started as a Ouija channel. I wasn't sure what I wanted to do with it initially. It sort of organically turned into videos about my experiences with Wicca and Voodoo, and then it became more storytelling—horror and ghost stories. I'm trying to make it more of a ghost-hunters channel, investigating haunted spots around town."

"That's a great idea. I would totally watch that," Emily encouraged.

"I want to make a video with you," Gia said.

"What kind?"

Gia leaned forward, her expression focused as she lowered her voice for effect.

Emily felt a pang of excitement.

"I know some girls who graduated from Ashley Hall a few years ago," Gia said. "They grew up in Bluffton, where I'm from. They're older, but I know them from being friends online. They practice Wicca and Voodoo, like me." Emily nodded as Gia continued, "Do you know the old building on the north end of campus? Kelly Hall?"

"Yeah. The abandoned one with the fence around it, right?"

"Right. Well, it's haunted," Gia said, falling silent to emphasize her statement.

"Isn't every condemned building supposedly haunted?" Emily replied with a grin and a roll of her eyes.

"This one really is," Gia insisted. "There used to be a tradition here at Ashley Hall School every Halloween. A small group of students—a maximum of five—would accept the dare to spend a full night in the abandoned dormitory. There's no power, no water, and no heat."

"Creepy."

"Did you know a girl committed suicide in there in 1984?"

"Really?" Emily's eyes widened.

"That's why they built that fence around it—to keep people away."

"Over that?"

"Well, after that incident, the building started having problems. The plumbing went bad, and the water came out reddish. They thought rust was the cause, but even after replacing the pipes, it continued. People suspect it might have been blood—the blood of the building itself," she said dramatically.

"Gross," Emily exclaimed, putting down her pint of ice cream and focusing on the story.

"Yup. Plus, the electricity was erratic, so the lights flickered all the time, even with new bulbs. The heat wouldn't work, then it would turn on and get so hot they had to open the windows in the middle of winter. People swore they saw apparitions and ghosts in the hallways." Gia waved her hands around as she spoke as if painting a picture for Emily.

"Translucent images of the girl who'd killed herself, hovering in the air, her eyes as black as eight balls, her skin pale and dusty. Eventually, the students refused to live there, and the school had no choice but to make a change."

"What did they do?" Emily asked, resting her chin on her knuckles.

Gia leaned in closer, as if trying to keep others from hearing.

"They didn't want to admit any of this was true, so they claimed they were turning it into offices and classrooms instead of a dorm. But rumor has it, the construction workers encountered something so terrifying that they refused to return and finish the job."

"What was it? What did they see, Gia?"

"Nobody knows. But after that, the school declared the building strictly off-limits," Gia explained with breathy excitement.

"Anyway, the building was locked up, but that didn't stop people from getting inside. At some point—no one knows exactly when—a challenge was laid down by a group of seniors: every year, around Halloween, one group of girls from the freshman class had to spend a full night in Kelly Hall from dusk until dawn. It was supposed to be fun—a tradition they thought would carry on for years. But nobody ever completed it.

"One year, a girl had such a severe allergy attack from the dust that she had to be med-flighted to the city hospital. Her face was blue! Another year, a girl got bitten by a rat and developed something called spirillary rat-bite fever."

"Nasty!" Emily shrieked, her face contorting in disapproval.

"Yeah. But then, one year…" Gia lowered her voice again, preparing to deliver the payoff, becoming more animated with her gestures. "These three girls made it all the way until five A.M. The sun was almost ready to rise when suddenly, for reasons unknown, all three of them came running out of the dorm, screaming that someone was inside. The police were called, and the girls were admitted to the psych ward."

"Holy crap!"

"Yeah. Nobody knows what happened to any of them. Two of them never returned to school. Their parents picked up their belongings super early one morning, and just like that," she snapped her fingers, "there was no trace of them ever having been here. The third girl returned, but she refused to talk about what happened, and a month later, she was diagnosed with tuberculosis and forced to drop out. She was French, but claimed to be British, by the way. But that's just a side note—it's not relevant to anything," she said with a casual shrug.

"Oh," said Emily.

"Yeah."

"Wait, so what are you asking?" Emily said, suddenly intrigued.

It was quiet for a few moments. Gia smirked at her.

"No," Emily said.

"Let's do it," Gia pleaded.

"That's just a bad idea, Gia."

"It'll be so fun! I'll wear a GoPro on my forehead so we can livestream it. It could go viral. We'll be famous!"

"The building is totally locked up. We won't be able to get inside. It has padlocks and stuff. I've seen them," Emily said.

"We'll scout it out in advance. It can't be that hard to break in. It's not a Taylor Swift concert."

"You want to spend a night in a haunted building?"

"Emily, I have a theory: Places aren't haunted … people are."

"How do you know that?"

"It's just a hypothesis, but one I've been developing over the last several years. Spirits don't reside in brick and mortar. They live in flesh. They exist within people's minds and souls. They need flowing blood to survive. It's *people* that are haunted, and many don't even realize it," Gia said, continuing.

"Everybody loves the idea of a haunted house or a haunted building— a haunted asylum of some kind. But the reality is far more terrifying. The notion that it's *ourselves* who get invaded by spirits is so much more terrifying. There's no distance far enough to escape. The monster is inside of you!" she finished, wiggling her ten fingers ghoulishly.

"Do you think it's safe?" Emily asked, hinting that she might be open to the idea, which thrilled Gia.

"I do, yes. But I'm not going to tell my viewers that," she said.

"It's probably gross in there," Emily remarked.

"For sure. If I can convince Betsy to go, will you come?" Gia asked, trying to seal the deal.

Emily played it up, making Gia wait for her answer. Then, she nodded. The two girls squealed with excitement, breaking into uncontrollable laughter.

She knew it was a bad idea—the night in Kelly Hall. The experience with the Ouija board had been far more traumatic than she had let on. Gia and Betsy both spoke about it with her, recalling the terrified look on her face and how disturbing it had been. Still, neither of them knew what Emily knew—or at least what she thought she knew. She couldn't be sure. She was already second-guessing herself, as she so often did. Chalk it up to her lack of self-confidence.

Had she maybe gotten a little too caught up in the game? Was it a coincidence, perhaps? She was an expert at doubting her instincts, a result of growing up with more criticism than was necessary or healthy.

Also, she didn't want the girls to know she was scared. She didn't want to ruin whatever fun might come from all of this. She knew how excited Gia was.

She had to be careful, though; she had already been written up once and would have preferred to lay low for a while. Breaking into an off-limits building was surely a major offense. She'd probably be expelled if caught.

This was what Emily was ruminating over as she dressed for the big night at Kelly Hall. It had arrived so fast. Unsure of what to bring, she packed lightly: some water, a bag of Cheetos, a protein bar, and a few napkins. Her phone had been confiscated by the school as punishment for her write up.

The early evening sky was gloomy as the trio made the short trek to the condemned building. They never did go on that scouting mission Gia had mentioned. That realization struck Emily as she approached the building surrounded by a high fence topped with barbed wire and a padlocked chain holding the gate closed.

Behind the fence loomed Kelly Hall, a cement colossus that looked like it might house Count Dracula. It had massive cracks in the gray concrete walls that were either beautiful or terrifying, depending on one's mood. The steeples at the top formed narrow, upside-down V shapes. Pipes and chimneys dotted the roof, poking up into the air—too many to count. The building lacked any color, making Emily feel as though she was watching a movie in black and white.

"You guys, that building looks scary," Betsy said without her signature giggle.

"You think? I think it's beautiful," Gia said, her gaze fixed on the structure.

Rain began to fall, and the tiny droplets felt hard as they pelted Emily's face in an irritating way.

The girls navigated around the perimeter of the fence until they found a small trench dug beneath it. It seemed to have been refilled with loose dirt, but they easily scraped it away using a plastic sandcastle shovel that

Gia had brought. They shimmied face-down under the fence and soon found themselves on the wrong side of the barricade.

"You *guys*…" Betsy said again.

"I hear you, Bets," Emily replied. There was something wrong with all of this. It didn't feel fun—not yet, anyway. More so threatening.

Gia was headstrong, leading the team like a sled dog, and before they knew it, they were inside the building. The doors were locked, but Gia had found an unsecured window at ground level. The rain and mud over the years had caused the wood around it to deteriorate, making it easy to break off some pieces and push the window open.

They climbed inside, landing in the basement. It was dank in the clearest example of what "dank" means.

There was no power, therefore no lights. The air smelled horribly stale and was stifling to the point of triggering periodic gag reflexes from the girls.

"I should have brought a mask," Emily said, covering her nose and mouth with the front of her shirt. The "ew-iness" factor was a ten, and as a person sensitive to smells, Emily knew this place would rent space in her nose for years to come.

"I really don't want to get in trouble, you guys," Betsy reiterated, elongating her trademark expression, "You guys…"

"Chill, Betsy. We won't," Gia told her, offering no evidence to support her claim. Gia was looking around like a cave dweller searching for bats, wielding a tiny handheld flashlight.

They cautiously roamed the building for several minutes, staying close to one another. They arrived at a classroom where writing still covered the chalkboard—science notes and excerpts from the periodic table. It was hard to see, but not pitch-black either. Gia's flashlight was already flickering, though, which didn't bode well for them.

The storm outside intensified, providing periodic flashes of lightning that weren't yet accompanied by thunder. Emily felt anxious, but they had each other, and there was comfort in that. As they sat on the floor on a blanket Gia had brought, they lit a small candle and decided to discuss their plans for the night—the syllabus, so to speak.

That's when she heard it: a familiar sound, soft and distant, that caused Emily's head to tilt sideways with concern. She leaned toward the open classroom door, hoping it might help clarify what she was hearing. She could feel Gia and Betsy watching her. *Could they hear it too?*

Emily certainly could—a squeal, not a squeak. Definitely not a mouse or a bat. No, this was a squeal, like a little wheel on a bucket that needed replacing or oiling.

"Shh," Emily said, raising her hand toward her friends even though they were already silent. They were busy studying her expression, waiting for cues. "Turn it off," she demanded of Gia, who clicked off her unreliable flashlight without hesitation.

It was happening again, like that night in Gia's room. Adrenaline surged through her body as she became fiercely alert. Her head still cocked, her eyes fixated on nothing—the kind of look you give when you're pouring all your energy into what you're hearing instead of seeing.

"Do you hear it?" Emily whispered as softly as she could, her hand still raised to caution them against responding.

She looked almost comically frozen.

"No," Betsy whispered.

They sat there, the three of them, listening.

"Feels warm in here," Gia said nervously.

Emily slowly made her way to one knee, paused, then carefully stood up without making a sound. She crept toward the open classroom door, her eyes wide open, trying to fight the uncomfortable darkness. She kept her hand up, signaling the girls to stay back. She could hear her own breathing.

Emerging from the classroom, she placed her hand on the wall for guidance and slowly walked down the hallway. There were no windows for the moon to illuminate the area. The darkness closed in around her like a cloak. At the end of the hallway, where the only option was to turn left, Emily cautiously peeked her head just past the wall, still holding onto it for whatever comfort it brought. She froze, not from what she saw, but from what she heard again—the gentle squeal of a wheel on a bucket, closer this time. Much closer.

The memory came rushing back to her with a ferocity she wasn't prepared for—the old folks' home. She could instantly smell it, even through the stagnant stench of dampness in Kelly Hall. Her spirit took her to that moment, that awful place. She was five years old again, peering through a tiny crack in the door. She could see their faces—the old people. They were staring at her in silence. Toothless. Bony. Frail. Close to death. Her bladder suddenly felt weak, and she panicked at the thought of peeing her pants and having to explain it to Gia and Betsy.

She began trembling uncontrollably, like a puppy in a cold storm, and she turned to look back at the girls. When she did, there was a huge problem—they weren't there. The jarring realization made her eyes instantly water.

As she turned back to look around the corner again, he grabbed her. He snatched her off her feet as if she were a toy, slamming her onto an old wooden chair. Within seconds, he'd duct-taped both her wrists to the arms of the seat. His strength was prodigious; she felt helpless and puny in every way.

Scream! she thought, but as she tried, a plastic bag was deftly wrapped around her head in an instant. He yanked it tight from behind and taped it around her neck. She couldn't breathe! She couldn't make any noise, no matter how hard she tried.

He illuminated his face from underneath with a small cigarette lighter and smiled at her—one tooth missing from his mangled, discolored fangs. The purplish-black circles under his sunken eyes. The jagged cleft lip that looked like it might rip right open. He was taunting her as she kicked and squirmed with all her might, flailing violently. Her limbs felt heavy from restraint. Just as she was about to lose consciousness, the custodian held a mirror in front of her face, and with the assistance of his lighter, she saw it: her reflection, contorted in pain with a hint of blue from the suffocation. She looked like a monster! She lost control of her bladder and felt the bothersome warmth of her urine soaking her crotch and inner thighs. She tried to scream again with all her might as her body jerked upright, yanking her bedsheet off as her legs kicked wildly. She gasped for air, panting and crying.

"Oh my God, are you all right?" Dahlia called out to her, distraught by Emily's blowup. It took Emily a moment to gather her wits, but she managed to pull herself together. She was sweating profusely, her chest heaving, her underwear soaked with urine and sweat, as were her sheets. "Emily?" Dahlia said, leaning over her bed now with real concern. She looked frightened. "Do you need me to call the nurse?"

"No," Emily finally said through her panting. "I'm fine. I'm sorry. I had a terrible dream."

Emily inhaled deeply in and out through her nose, trying to take air into her lungs without hyperventilating, attempting to calm herself down.

Dahlia handed her a cup of water. "You screamed. You were kicking your sheets and flailing around. You scared the crap out of me."

"I'm so sorry, Dahlia. I'm okay now," Emily said, trying to cover her soaked underwear with her shirt.

"You don't need to apologize. As long as you're okay," Dahlia told her, looking nearly as shaken as Emily.

"I am," Emily said as her breathing slowly regulated. She was realizing this was Friday morning, and tonight they would go live. There had been no scouting mission, they would be flying blind, just like in the dream.

She cleaned up her bed and made her way to the bathroom. As she stood in the warm shower, a single word kept popping into her head, fueling her fears further: Premonition.

"Maybe I should cancel," she mumbled through the water splashing on her face. "I should probably cancel."

In his unyielding pursuit of personal transformation, Twerp decided to play a sport. Not just any sport; it had to be a manly sport. He chose wrestling. He liked that it was a combat sport, yet still controlled—no striking involved.

There were weight classes, so he would only compete against people his own size, which greatly appealed to him. Twerp weighed ninety-five pounds and would have to compete in the 106-pound weight class, the lightest available. He figured he could 'bulk up' in the meantime. Wrestling didn't start for another month, giving him a little time.

The doctor responsible for giving physicals to athletes was on campus, so Twerp made an appointment. All athletes wishing to compete in winter sports needed a physical examination. It wasn't much—just a heart check and a hernia test. The latter was the rub; nobody liked it. As a boy, you had to pull down your pants so the doctor could place two fingers from each hand on either side of your testicles. Then he asked you to cough to feel for a protuberance. It was brief but awkward. Cold hands made it worse.

Twerp stood in line in the nurse's office with about twenty other boys. A small curtain separated the exam area, and after about thirty seconds, a student would emerge—all eyes on him—before the next victim stepped up, and the curtain would close again. He felt like a cow in the slaughter line, instinctively sensing that something wasn't right.

As fate would have it, just as Twerp reached the front of the line, the doctor stood up, checked his watch, and whispered something to the nurse. She nodded, and he walked off. Twerp stared at her as she took the seat where the doctor had been and waved him into the small area behind the curtain.

He wondered if he could just leave.

"Come on," she said impatiently. He shuffled forward in tiny steps, hoping the curtain would stay open, praying she would just listen to his heart and assume he didn't have a hernia. Those hopes were dashed when she yanked the curtain shut with an audible zip.

Nurse Rosenberg was her name, an older woman deep into her fifties. She had not aged well. One of her front teeth was half brown for some reason, and a long, curly hair dangled from her chin—impossible to miss and even harder to understand why she never plucked it.

Pluck that thing! Twerp thought. He wanted to do it himself.

"Take off your shirt," she told him. Twerp obliged, unveiling his epically scrawny physique. He looked like an immigrant from the 1920s arriving in America after a long boat ride with little food.

Nurse Rosenberg placed the cold stethoscope on his chest. He held his breath, hoping all was well. It seemed to be. Then she said it—those awful words:

"Lower your pants."

Twerp froze. *Was she serious?* She looked him in the eyes, and he felt dizzy. "Roger, drop your trousers," she said with a nod. He unbuttoned his pants, looking down in shame.

Twerp pulled his pants down to about mid-thigh, realizing for the first time that his genitals were exposed in front of a woman—at least since being a baby. The magnitude of the moment wasn't lost on him. Naked in front of a *woman*. Suddenly, Nurse Rosenberg didn't seem so unattractive after all. She had nice legs, smooth and tanned, enhanced by her pantyhose' alluring sheen.

Then it happened: Twerp got a boner. His wee wee inflated like one of those narrow birthday party balloons attached to a helium tank.

Twerp didn't have a big penis, but it certainly was commanding attention at that moment. He looked up at the ceiling, hoping it would all end soon. His wish was granted when Nurse Rosenberg matter-of-factly picked up a reflex hammer from the small table next to her and tapped the head of his penis with the rubber triangle.

"*Ow!*" he yelled as his hips retracted. His erection went instantly limp, falling like a curtain at a magic show during the grand reveal.

His eyes watered as the nurse placed her cold fingers next to his testicles.

"Turn your head and cough," she commanded. He complied. A moment later, it was over.

The plastic curtain opened with a loud zip, revealing Twerp's traumatized expression to the group of boys still in line. All eyes were on him now, begging the question: *What happened?*

Twerp walked gingerly out of the office, trying not to cry. His penis hurt, and he wondered if he'd ever be able to get an erection again—more from the emotional trauma than any physical damage. The saddest part was that he wasn't even sure he wanted to wrestle.

The news of Twerp's humiliation spread like wildfire. Kenny had pressed him for an explanation of why he yelped from behind the curtain, and Twerp finally caved, telling him the story and pleading that he not repeat it. Naturally, Kenny kept his word—mostly. He only told a few people, but that was all it took. The anecdote was too good not to share, and within one school day, everyone knew.

Martin heard the story too. Normally, he would have enjoyed it, laughing along with everyone else about Twerp's daily tribulations as he tried to morph into his version of Nietzsche's Übermensch—an acorn destined to become a great oak.

But not today, not for Martin. He didn't have time for happiness or joy or levity. He was in crisis mode. The stress was taking a toll on him. He felt tired and weaker than usual—all because of Ricky Rude.

"What kind of frickin' name is that, anyway?" Martin asked no one, though Twerp was within earshot and chose to respond.

"I think it's French. Are you going to fight him?" Twerp asked.

"Are you kidding?" Martin replied, incredulous at the very idea. The two of them had been walking around the track that encircled the football field for exercise and sun. Twerp came to a sudden halt, as though an important conversation was about to ensue.

"You have to," he said to Martin, who had also stopped walking.

Martin stood confounded. "Are you *crazy?* Why?"

"Because if you don't, everyone will think you're yellow."

"Are we in the wild west now, Twerp? Who says *yellow?*"

"I do. And stop deflecting, Martin. This is the kind of fight that could put us in the books as verified ruffians. Even if you put up a little bit of a battle, you'll be untouchable."

"Or it could put me in the hospital," Martin shot back.

"You wouldn't fight him, Twerp," said Kenny, who suddenly appeared from behind. The unexpected voice startled Martin, giving him a verified jump scare.

"I can't live like this," Martin said, clutching his chest.

"You're awful skittish these days," Kenny told him.

"Where did you come from?" Twerp asked Kenny.

"I saw you guys walking and jogged up to join you," Kenny said. "I heard you talking shit to Martin. I promise you wouldn't fight him yourself, though, Twerp."

"How do you know?" Twerp challenged.

"Cuz you're a wimp," Kenny replied.

"Say it to my face, Kenny," Twerp said back.

That had been Twerp's go-to line since he was a young boy, as far back as kindergarten. Anytime someone insulted him, he'd respond with, "*Say it to my face.*"

As a child, he had a lisp, making it sound like, "*Thay it to my faythe.*"

Of course, nobody was going to fight Twerp. He was too little. It would be mean. People heckled him all the time, almost to the point of harassment, but they left him alone physically. Beating him up wouldn't even qualify as low-hanging fruit—more like fruit that had already fallen and was rotting on the ground.

"Look," Martin said, "I don't want to be a verified ruffian because I'm *not* a ruffian, and if people think I am, someone will want to fight me to prove they're tough too. It's a bad plan, Twerp."

"It's an opportunity," Twerp insisted.

"Wrong. You know what it is, Twerp?" Martin said, grabbing Twerp by the shoulders as they all stopped walking again.

"What is it?" Twerp asked.

"It's another pull-my-pants-down-in-public moment in a long line of pull-my-pants-down-in-public moments masquerading as my life," Martin told him.

"That's a bit much," Kenny said.

"Is it, Kenny? I don't think so. In fact, I'm leaving."

"To where?" Kenny asked.

"Across the pond," Martin said, gesturing toward Ashley Hall School on the other side of the water.

"You still want to go?" Twerp asked.

"More than ever."

They both knew Kenny wouldn't join them. He never broke the rules. Kenny was an athlete and a straight-A student, scared shitless of his father, and would never risk getting in trouble, no matter how slight the possibility.

Normally, Martin would have bailed on the idea too. It sounded cool, but in practice, it would probably be a train wreck. His m.o. would be to make up an excuse about why they needed to push it out a few weeks, and eventually, it would join the pile of things they said they were going to do but never actually did.

But not today. Not with Ricky Rude running around, purportedly on the prowl to do more than just flush Martin's tiny face in a toilet. No, he wouldn't be bailing on these plans. Tonight, he would climb aboard that pedal boat and he … would … flee …

"Feels good, doesn't it?" Martin said to Twerp as they pedaled across the pond, a light breeze blowing the cool evening air into their faces.

"It does, yeah," Twerp admitted with a smile. "We're totally breaking the rules!"

"Yup," Martin said, glancing back at the shoreline one last time to ensure his own personal Bigfoot wasn't swimming behind them.

"How long do you think it will take us?" Twerp asked, already starting to breathe heavily.

"Twenty minutes at most. It's not as far as it looks," Martin replied.

Martin appreciated having Twerp with him. It was comforting. He needed a friend right now. Twerp might have enjoyed being the bearer of bad news, but he was always a reliable sidekick.

"Thanks for coming with me, Twerp," he said.

"No problem, bro," Twerp said as he nodded. Martin figured he was happy to leave Porter-Gaud behind for now, having heard enough laughter about his incident in the nurse's office that day.

The two boys pedaled on—eyes forward—able to see the comfortable glow of the campus in the distance. They hoped to meet some girls. They would, too. That, and a whole lot more.

5

Martin felt like a coward, and he hated it. Yes, he had planned to take the boat that night to Ashley Hall School. He could cling to that fact; it would have worked in a court of law to prove that he wasn't "running away" from anyone. But deep inside, where that scared little person in all of us lives—the one who knows our most embarrassing secrets—Martin knew he was afraid of getting beat up, and that was the most compelling reason for him to have gotten on the boat and crossed the pond to safety.

The feeling would stay with him. He was familiar with it, and it would bother him, maybe forever. Inside, he wished he were big and strong and tougher than leather, capable of cracking Ricky Rude across the jaw with a right hand that would make his teeth chatter and send him stumbling backward. But he wasn't big and strong and tough, and that reality gnawed at him during the silence of the trip, even with the gentle sound of the water undulating around their small boat.

He snapped back to reality when he saw how close they were to shore. He was getting his first good look at the school. Ashley Hall School had a majestic campus with ornate, historic buildings and meticulous landscaping. The soft lights glowed gently against the bluish nighttime sky.

The dormitory buildings resembled castles in the German countryside more than residence halls.

"Everything looks so European," Martin said to Twerp. "On the campus, I mean."

"I don't know. I've never been to Europe," Twerp replied.

"Neither have I," Martin said.

They pedaled the final stretch of the pond, and the boat softly crunched onto the sand.

"I can't believe we're here," Twerp exclaimed, as if they were seeing the lost city of Atlantis.

"Right?" said Martin, giving his friend a quick high-five.

"What now?" asked Twerp, as the pedal boat began floating in the shallowest water.

"I don't know," Martin said, shrugging.

They couldn't just roam the campus freely, or they'd be stopped by security or a staff member and reported to their own school's administration.

"Let's just scope it out for now," Martin suggested as they climbed off and pulled the boat onto land. The mission was vague enough that it sounded doable.

"Good idea," Twerp said, beaming with excitement. *We're breaking the rules!*

The two boys crept onto the lawn along the perimeter of the large campus and laid flat on their bellies. The dewy grass would leave an uncomfortable moistness on their clothes for the rest of the night. This would be their perch, shrouded and safe, from which they would stake out their prey. The trees provided excellent camouflage, and from their position, they could see students walking around without being spotted themselves. It felt exciting without being dangerous.

The campus buildings were all made of stone or brick, tall and narrow with pitched roofs and thin chimneys reaching high into the air. Their beauty would be even more magnificent if they weren't so spooky. Or perhaps they'd be spookier if they weren't so beautiful. Either way, they somehow encompassed both elements and the boys noticed.

The two of them laid there talking and laughing and commenting on anything and everything. They made fun of some people and admired others. They watched like spectators, critiquing the girls and pointing out the ones they liked best. But mostly, they all looked good.

"This is crazy," Twerp said excitedly. "They're all so hot!"

"I told ya'," Martin replied.

It would be a great story to tell the boys back at Porter-Gaud, no matter what happened that night. They'd embellish it as needed, naturally. That was standard practice.

They had broken protocol, stolen a boat, and pedaled across the pond to the all-girls school. These are the stories of legends.

An hour passed. Then another. Halfway through the third, it happened. Under a tall, bright streetlamp that stood high above a series of wooden benches, three girls congregated. It unfolded in slow motion in Martin's mind. They didn't walk; they flowed like supermodels strutting down the runway in expensive lingerie.

And the girls *were* pretty. All three of them.

"Whoa, check it out," Twerp said, elbowing Martin and gesturing at them. "Looks like the spider just caught a fly," he added, prompting Martin to muffle a laugh.

The girls were close to them, relatively speaking. In fact, this was the nearest anyone had come to them all night. They could have thrown a rock and hit them.

Martin and Twerp tightened up, pressing themselves to the ground, as if sensing some hidden threat. They were like a pair of outdoor cats watching strangers walking on their property—not quite ready to flee, but on high-alert.

"I feel like I'm playing soldier, like we did as kids. Remember?" Twerp whispered to Martin. A smile crept across Martin's face as he nodded in acknowledgement. He remembered those nights spent stalking their neighbors' houses, pretending to be special forces operatives under the cover of darkness, armed with cap guns and clad in camouflage.

The girls stood in a circle beneath the tall lamp, appearing to be deep in discussion. Martin squinted and then grabbed Twerp by the shoulder.

"It's *her*," he said in a whisper-shout.

"Who?"

"Emily Cox. Remember I told you..."

"Oh, yeah. Which one?"

"The tall one."

"They're all tall."

"The tallest one, Twerp. The one with the braid."

"Okay, yeah, gotcha. She *is* hot.

"Super hot," Martin confirmed.

Time passed, and the silence became thick enough for Twerp to finally ask, "Are you going to go talk to her?"

Martin didn't answer. Moments later, Twerp repeated, "*Martin?*"

"I heard you, Twerp," Martin replied, his tone tinged with annoyance.

"What's wrong, Martin?"

Martin rolled onto his back and sat up, gazing toward the pond. Twerp followed suit. Clearly, it was time for a sidebar.

"I don't think I can," Martin admitted.

"Can what?"

"Talk to her."

"Why? I thought you knew her?"

"I do. But I'm not sure if she knows me," he said, his expression a mix of embarrassment and shame.

"Well, just introduce yourself," Twerp suggested.

"I get all weird around girls I like. I can never think of anything to say. It's so awkward. If she was ugly, I could talk to her all night. But with each rung they climb on the ladder of attractiveness, I lose twenty points off my IQ."

"You don't have a lot of points to spare, either," Twerp said.

"Shut up, Twerp."

"Look, it's no big deal. Just walk up to her and strike up a conversation. I do it all the time," Twerp claimed, though Martin knew that was a crock.

"Twerp, you've never even said hello to a girl like her."

"What? Dude, I talk to girls like those three *all the time*," Twerp insisted, mustering as much confidence as he could.

"Oh really? Okay, let me see you do it then," Martin said.

"Fine, I will," Twerp replied, rising to the moment as he stood up and brushed some dirt off his shirt and the seat of his pants. He clearly meant business—or at least wanted to convey that impression. He was selling it, too, although as he walked toward them, he looked more like a guy about to get pranked.

Regardless, Martin had to give credit where it was due. Twerp approached the girls, who were so engrossed in their conversation that they didn't notice him. Even when he stood right next to them under the bright streetlamp, they remained oblivious to his presence. He was shorter than all of them by a few inches, standing there with his hands on his hips, looking up at them as they chatted away.

Gia was mid-sentence when he arrived and didn't miss a beat.

"We have to walk over there casually so security doesn't notice us— hiding in plain sight, kind of thing," she said to Emily and Betsy.

"Right," Betsy replied with a nod.

"Once we get inside the building, we can set up my phone on the tripod for a stationary shot, and I'll keep the GoPro attached to my hat for the live feed," Gia explained.

Emily and Betsy began to talk over one another, but Emily deferred.

"I'm just worried about my allergies, you guys," Betsy said.

"It'll be fine," Gia answered almost dismissively. "We're not going to move things around too much. Plus, I have surgical masks."

This seemed to assuage Betsy's concerns enough that she didn't press the issue further.

Emily, however, appeared anxious. The others could tell by her quick speech, her dialogue peppered with tics she normally didn't display. "What if we decide to leave? Like, what if something really scary happens that makes us just say—"

"Then we'll go," Gia interrupted. "If we want out of there, we'll just take off. We're not in lockdown," she said as nonchalantly as possible, hands out to her sides as if it were all so simple.

Meanwhile, Twerp was desperately trying to join the conversation, his eyes darting from one girl to the next as they spoke.

He wanted to scream at them: *Notice me!*

He tried smiling and nodding, even making small noises like "mmmhm" and "ah" as warm affirmations of their statements. None of it worked. He felt himself starting to blush, which he hated, and his heart began to race. He realized he was experiencing another humiliating episode in super slow motion. Worst of all, *Martin was watching.*

"Okay, look, I'll go if you both want to go," Emily said, her voice filled with trepidation. Her approval would tacitly bring Betsy along for the ride.

"*Yes!*" Gia exclaimed, pumping her fist. She looked like a jock when she did it, her muscular shoulders flexing with the movement. Betsy and Emily privately admired her physique.

On the periphery, Twerp mumbled something unintelligible. Even he didn't understand it; he just knew he was crashing and burning in real time.

"Great…" he said a bit louder now, trying to be heard as he made an awkward hand gesture. The girls didn't notice him. They were too busy plotting and fleshing out their plans.

Acknowledge me, damn it! he wanted to scream. He could feel Martin's eyes on him—judging with glee. His fighter jet was in a flat spin, and he needed to eject *now*.

Don't panic, he thought to himself. *Don't panic, Twerp!* And then— he panicked. Twerp turned around and sprinted toward the shoreline, heading in the direction of the pond. That's when the girls finally noticed him.

Betsy screeched at the quick flash of action, thinking it was a wild animal. A split second later, they realized it was a young boy running like a frightened deer into the wooded area on the edge of campus.

As he grew smaller in the distance, they saw him clip his toe on a root sticking up from the ground, causing him to fall violently onto the grass.

"Whoa," Gia exclaimed with a snort as they watched him faceplant.

"What the—?" Emily said, covering her mouth with her hand, wondering if he'd hurt himself.

The fall knocked the wind out of Twerp and would have put him out cold if not for the adrenaline coursing through him.

He scrambled back to his feet and continued running, his arms flailing as he tried to keep his balance after taking a shot to the head.

"Who was that?" Betsy asked, cackling at the absurdity.

"I have no clue," Emily replied as the three girls burst into laughter, watching the final image of Twerp disappear in the distance.

A moment later, the trio gathered their belongings and set off on their own adventure, periodically glancing back toward the pond.

When Twerp arrived at the patch of grass where Martin was still lying, he slid to the ground next to him like a baseball player stealing a base.

"What the hell was that?" Martin asked, pointing at the location of the scene he had just witnessed.

"What?" Twerp shot back defensively, his face now discolored with a mix of grass, dirt, and a bit of blood from his ignominious wipeout.

"You didn't even talk to them," Martin said.

"Yes, I did," Twerp declared defiantly. His ego was bruised; he felt smaller than usual and was willing to gaslight Martin as much as necessary to salvage whatever dignity he had left. Martin wasn't capitulating.

"I saw the whole thing, Twerp. They never even looked at you."

"Et tu, Marte?" Twerp replied, feigning betrayal.

"Don't give me that crap, Julius Caesar-salad. You choked!" Martin retorted.

"Hey, at least I tried," Twerp said, his pride stinging. "You just laid here like a coward," he added, momentarily silencing Martin. After a pause, Martin finally responded.

"You're right," Martin said. "It took a lot of guts to do that. Good for you, Twerp."

"Thanks," Twerp replied, starting to catch his breath from the sprint.

"Come on, let's follow them and see where they're going," Martin suggested, helping Twerp up off the ground.

"Cool," Twerp said, feeling reinvigorated.

The boys were back on track as they headed in the general direction the girls had gone.

In the distance, they could see the threesome, shrouded by the night, heading toward the northern part of campus to a condemned building surrounded by a fence. That area was poorly lit and less traveled, resembling the closest thing to a "bad neighborhood" that a posh school like this would ever have. To Martin, it looked … haunted.

Martin and Twerp were now following the girls without any shame.

They were both small boys, and from a distance, they could easily be mistaken for girls, especially on weekends when uniforms weren't required, and most everyone wore shorts or blue jeans. This allowed them to blend in amongst the female students milling about campus.

"What are we doing?" Twerp asked. "Do we have a plan?"

"I'm just trying to see where they're going. They seemed to be having an intense discussion back there—the one you weren't a part of. Remember?" Martin replied, glancing back at Twerp with a teasing smile. Twerp made a face in response. "Besides, it's too early to head back anyway."

"You're just afraid to go back because you think Ricky Rude is going to beat you up," Twerp shot back.

"Shut up," Martin said.

They fell silent and walked on, listening to the crunch of the earth under their shoes. Martin focused on the girls, moving a bit closer to them. He noticed they had arrived at the fence surrounding the gloomy, dilapidated building. They looked around as if they were about to break some sort of rule.

"Come on," Martin urged, waving his hand to encourage Twerp to hurry. "I want to see what they're up to." Twerp followed, and the two boys knelt behind a hill. Martin pulled a pair of small binoculars from his backpack and looked through them to get a better view of the facility.

"You have binoculars?" Twerp asked, surprised.

"Yeah, I always carry binoculars—binoculars and a slingshot with one marble," Martin replied, pulling the slingshot from his backpack to show Twerp.

"That thing's *sweet!*" Twerp exclaimed, admiring the slingshot.

"Thanks."

"Why do you carry the marble?"

"In case I can't find a rock to use with it. For emergencies," Martin explained.

"Good thinking. Why do you have them with you all the time?"

"I don't know. They just fit. I like having a backpack, but I don't have much to put in it, so I carry those items. Sometimes crackers, too."

Martin spotted the girls again. They were now lying on the ground, wriggling their way underneath the fence one-by-one at a spot where the land dipped.

"I think they're breaking into that building," Martin said excitedly as he stared through his binoculars.

"*Wow*, nothing hotter than rebel chicks," Twerp said, genuine admiration in his voice.

"Come on," Martin said, stuffing his binoculars into his backpack as he jogged toward Kelly Hall. A dense fog had rolled in, providing them with cover to complement the darkness.

The boys reached the same spot in the fence in about a minute, slipping under more easily than the girls had, which added a bit more dirt and moisture to their already damp clothes.

"Where are they?" Twerp asked.

"I think they must have gone inside the building," Martin replied.

"We're going to get in trouble here, Martin," Twerp cautioned.

"Come on, Twerp. This is what we came for, right? Let's check it out," Martin urged as he gave his friend a little tap to the chest.

Twerp nodded, and the two of them scampered toward the building, ducking their heads as if it would help.

The girls found a window with a broken pane of glass that someone had unlocked, probably long ago, and they sneaked into the building.

Inside Kelly Hall, Emily, Gia, and Betsy were simultaneously making the same '*this is gross*' face without even realizing it. Their noses were scrunched up, mouths pursed, and eyes half shut.

The building wasn't necessarily *scary* on the inside, much to Gia's dismay, who was recording with a GoPro tethered to the front of her baseball cap with a rubber band that wrapped around her head. It even had a little light on it.

No, the building wasn't spooky at all; instead, it had more of an "I don't want to touch anything because of the inch of dust on it" vibe. There were still desks for studying and bunk beds in the dorm rooms, which could have passed for prison cells—suffocatingly narrow with cement walls and floors.

None of the lights worked. The windows were closed and painted shut, as if permanently sealed. It stank the further in they went. The air surely hadn't moved in years, and that was easy to believe when it hit their faces.

"I'm gonna have a massive allergy attack," Betsy whispered behind Emily, who was positioned behind Gia. The two girls in the rear had both hands on the shoulders of the girl in front of them, like a three-person choo-choo train.

"You don't have to whisper, Betsy," Gia said. "No one can hear us in here."

"It feels like the right thing to do," Betsy replied.

"I agree," Emily whispered back. "I can't get caught in here. I just got written up."

The adorable little light on Gia's GoPro camera provided just enough illumination for them to see a few feet ahead. Any further than that faded into shades of gray and black, depending on whether there was a window nearby for the moon to shine through, which wasn't much help tonight.

Emily could see that Gia had come prepared. This was her night. She'd packed a small power source to keep her phone and camera charged if needed. She wasn't going to let a technical glitch ruin the moment if something compelling were to happen.

"Are you filming live right now?" Emily asked her.

"No," Gia said. "I haven't mastered the live thing yet. I'm just recording, and I'll edit and post it later. Hopefully, we'll see something shocking that will—"

She *screamed* as she turned the corner at the end of the hallway, interrupting her own sentence, which prompted Emily and Betsy to scream too. They all saw it: two figures standing in the darkness. Their instinct to run faltered when they realized the figures were two boys, smaller than themselves, now illuminated by the GoPro light.

"You look like a coal miner," one of them said, pointing at Gia's forehead.

"Shut up, geek," she shot back, shoving Twerp enough to make him stumble backward two steps. She was recovering from the sudden scare they'd given her. "You scared the crap out of us. Who are you? What are you doing here?"

"Wait, is that Martin Grabarz?" Emily asked, studying the boys more closely.

"Hi, Emily," Martin said, raising his right hand to wave but not moving it, making it look more like a pledge. The gesture made him appear even younger than he already did.

"What are you doing in here?" Emily asked, bewildered by his presence.

"*That's* the kid who ran from us," Betsy exclaimed, pointing at Twerp. Gia shone her light in Twerp's face like a cop, prompting him to squint against the brightness.

"Oh my God, it is!" Gia said with a muffled laugh.

"Are you following us?" Emily asked.

"*No*," Martin said emphatically, then added, "Well, yes, actually. We were just seeing what you girls were up to, that's all," he said with a shrug, stuffing his hands in his pockets as if all of this were normal.

"Who are you?" Gia asked.

"I'm Martin. I grew up in the same town as Emily. I go to Porter-Gaud. We took a boat across the pond."

"Wait, you two are in *high* school?" Betsy asked, unable to hide her disbelief.

"Yeah," Martin said, nodding as he looked down at the floor, feeling some shame that she perceived him as more of a little boy than he was.

He tried to think of something to say to save face, but nothing came to mind. After all, the girls were taller than both him and Twerp. They weighed more, were certainly stronger, and might even have had more body hair. What could he say in response? *Wait until we hit puberty. Then you'll rue the day you mocked our smooth, un-muscled, pre-pubescent bodies.*

It just didn't sound like the clever retort he longed for. Silence hung in the air for a moment until Twerp spoke.

"And my name is Rocky," he announced, seemingly eager to try out his new nickname, though the crack in his voice betrayed his nerves.

"*Rocky?*" all three girls echoed in synchronized disbelief.

"His name is Twerp," Martin interjected after an awkward pause. The girls nodded, a sign of understanding. That made more sense. Twerp slouched at the loss.

Gia had had enough.

"You're going to screw this up for us," she scolded the boys.

"Let's just keep going, Gia. It's fine," Emily replied.

Gia capitulated. Emily was the one truly in charge, even if she didn't realize it. Gia and Betsy took their cues from her.

So, the three girls continued their adventure through the dark halls of the dormitory, while Martin and Twerp trailed behind, maintaining a safe six feet of distance to avoid becoming targets.

"She knows my name," Martin whispered to Twerp, giving him an enthusiastic thumbs-up. Twerp's response was muted. No matter; it was a victory in Martin's book, which had painfully few triumphs in the chapter on love, sex, and related topics.

Emily *was* beautiful—there was no doubt about that. Martin had grown up near her, but they'd never spoken. Until tonight, he wasn't sure if she actually knew who he was.

Knowing that she *recognized* him felt good. He felt lighter on his feet now, even tingly. For the first time in days, he forgot about Ricky Rude. He couldn't stop smiling, "like a mule eating briars" as his grandmother would say. He was glad he'd made the trip tonight, no matter the reason.

The girls popped in and out of a few rooms, poking around but not finding anything particularly interesting. Martin and Twerp stayed out of their way. The girls acted as though the boys weren't even there, which was fine; it was better than being sent away, a possibility that loomed large.

Unbeknownst to him, Martin would irrevocably change the course of the night with one simple question: "What's that in the vent?"

By this point, his eyes had adjusted to the dimness, and he was seeing things better. He and Twerp had been silent for quite some time, so it felt like he'd earned the right to participate, provided it was something relevant. He hit a home run with this one.

"I don't know," Gia replied, her curiosity piqued as she looked into the rectangular heating vent near the floor. She could see it too when she flashed her light inside. The object was pushed back a bit, but Martin had a good viewing angle from where he stood.

Gia wasn't quite ready to give him too much credit just yet.

"It looks like a book," Emily whispered.

"Unscrew the vent," Twerp interjected, pulling out a small jackknife he often carried but rarely had cause to use. He was so excited for it to finally come into play that he fumbled the knife while trying to open the Phillips head screwdriver. The knife made a cacophonous noise as it landed and bounced on the tile floor, tainting his moment of glory.

Gia picked up the knife and began the methodical process of turning each of the twelve screws, removing one at a time. She was filming and narrating, reminiscent of Geraldo Rivera opening Al Capone's vault—hopefully with better results.

Peering inside, Gia was flanked by Emily right behind her and Betsy right behind Emily. The boys remained in the bleacher seats.

"What is it?" Emily whispered, the first hint of excitement all night. Something was finally happening.

"It's a video cassette," Gia announced as she pulled it out and displayed it to everyone. The box for the tape was covered in dust. Martin and Twerp moved in closer to get a better look alongside Emily and Betsy.

"Shit just got real," Twerp said dramatically, prompting Martin to cringe at the corniness of the remark.

"Would you shut up?" Gia snapped at him, causing Twerp to visibly shrink.

"Who puts anything on a video cassette anymore?" Emily remarked.

"It's got to be old," Gia deduced. "Come on, let's see if there's a VCR in one of these rooms."

Outside, a rumble of thunder groaned as tiny droplets of rain began to fall. Emily peeked out the window and saw that fog had settled around the campus, making it hard to see more than a few feet ahead. Things were getting a bit spookier than she'd hoped for.

The dormitory contained an unexpectedly large amount of "stuff" left behind for a building that was supposed to be condemned. There were TVs, microwaves, textbooks, desks, coffee makers, towels, linens, DVDs,

CDs, clothes, and just about everything else you could think of—most of it haphazardly strewn about, stored in odd places as if moved without any rhyme or reason.

The property still belonged to the school, and maintenance would periodically move old equipment there—things they didn't quite know what to do with. It was like a massive junk drawer.

After some further digging, the group of five—now officially all together on this—found a storage closet filled with anachronistic electronic devices crammed together. In that closet was a television sitting on a stand with a VCR on a tray below it.

"Hello, beautiful," Gia said upon seeing it.

She immediately began the process of extracting it from the cramped closet into the hall. The stand had wheels, but there were items that needed to be moved to clear a path. Everyone helped, and within a minute or two, they had the TV and VCR in the hallway.

Gia went to work plugging them into the power source she had in her backpack.

"Will it work?" Emily asked.

"Let's find out," Gia replied as she turned on the shoebox-sized power station she'd bought from Walmart for ninety-eight bucks. As sure as the rain intensified, that little power source fired up the TV and VCR, both of which warmed up in no time.

"They really did make things better back then; our parents weren't lying," Gia said. It took her a couple of minutes to tune it to the right channel and settings, but it wasn't rocket science.

"You ready?" she asked with an enthusiastic grin.

"This is getting fun," Betsy replied, tensing up with enthusiasm and squeezing her hands into little fists like an excited baby.

The video began to play. They watched intently as a teenage boy sat alone in front of the camera. He was a good-looking kid, in his early teens, wearing glasses and a Dungeons & Dragons T-shirt. The lights were off, but he held a single candle. He looked excited about something. He checked his watch, then removed his glasses and laid them on a table. He began to speak.

"It's 8:45 PM on October 4th, 1985, and we are here in the basement of Kelly Hall—a dormitory at Ashley Hall School—where tonight we will be creating a haunting live on camera. You will be witnesses. We are documenting this for posterity."

Back in the hallway, Emily asked in a whisper, "What's today's date?"

"October 4th," Betsy replied.

"Exact same date," Emily said, still watching the television screen.

On the screen, the boy continued, "You can see we have our usual suspects for our monthly 'horror club' meeting: the eight of us," he said as the camera panned the dim room. There were no other people to be seen.

"What is he talking about? There's no one there," Gia said.

"I don't know," Emily replied. All eyes remained on the television as the boy continued.

"From this night forward—if all goes according to plan—Ashley Hall School will be a haunted institution. Haven't you ever wondered how places get haunted? How does it *happen?* Well, the eight of us decided to try to create one, to see if it's possible," he said with an enthusiastic clap of his hands. He then looked around as if others were speaking. There was silence. He then said something that sounded like he was replying to another person.

"That's true. We just may do that," he said, pointing at no one. He looked back into the camera and continued with his narration.

"Two months ago, we all read the book *Frankenstein*," the boy said. "Sometimes we read books, sometimes we watch movies—always horror. Then we get together and talk about them. That's the 'horror club'.

"Anyway, *Frankenstein* is the greatest tragedy ever written. There is nothing better than a well-crafted tragic tale. Just ask Nietzsche. He says the best stories are *all* tragedies."

The boy spoke as though he were lecturing to a class. "You see, in the story, Victor Frankenstein didn't set out to create a monster like the ones you see in the cartoons and movies. That's not what the creature was supposed to be. Victor wanted to create a superhuman. He stole body parts from the morgue, but only from the most exceptional people in town who had passed away.

"He took the joints and limbs of the best athletes. He used the muscles of a strongman, the brain of a brilliant scientist, the eyes of a marksman, and the hands of a masterful surgeon. He stitched them together to form a human that would be superior in every way. It worked, too! The creature was brought to life and was able to learn languages fluently in a matter of months. He was physically powerful beyond measure—fast, athletic, brilliant, and innocent, brimming with the potential to become a great person," the boy declared loudly, smiling broadly and gesturing enthusiastically into the camera.

The five friends remained glued to the TV, riveted by the recording. The boy on the tape continued.

"But he was ugly—the creature was. That was his one shortcoming. Not just a little ugly, either. He was hideous, stitched together like a baseball glove. His face was terrifying to look at. He was huge, intimidating, and socially undeveloped.

"Society turned against him, not because he did anything wrong, but because they were afraid of him. He was scorned by the people of the village because he was grotesque. Children ran from him. Eventually, the adults cornered him, carrying torches and spears, terrifying the innocent creature. He had to fight for his life."

The boy on the tape took a quick break from his diatribe to pour himself a drink. He swallowed from a shot glass and winced.

"Nice," he said, adjusting the camera slightly to change the angle as he sat on a tall stool and continued.

"Victor was his father—his creator. He abandoned him, afraid he would be held accountable for this supposed monster. It was only then that the creature became enraged and vengeful. He swore retribution and directed his anger at the townspeople. He became the monster they had made him out to be.

"The story is masterful—a tragedy of unfulfilled potential and the shallow ignorance of mankind. Right, guys?" he said, looking around and nodding. "Who needs a shot?"

"Who does he keep talking to?" Betsy asked, raising her hands in confusion.

"I have no clue. There's no one there," Emily replied, shaking her head.

"We'll use this book to help," the boy on the tape said, holding up a small book for the camera.

"This book is one of only 13 in existence. The author is a rebel-philosopher who claims we can create our own version of hell by impregnating the devil, which is what we will be attempting tonight."

He stood up from the stool and began pumping his hips as if engaging in sexual activity, laughing loudly as he did. After about ten seconds of this nonsense, he stopped and sat back down on his stool.

"You heard that right. The devil is a *woman*," he said. Then he leaned close to the camera, cupping the back of his hand to the side of his mouth as if sharing a secret, and whispered, "And I'll bet she's a bitch."

He laughed at his joke, then looked around the room and asked, "Are we ready or what?"

"Wow, this is so creepy," Gia said in a giddy whisper. "He made this tape forty years ago *to the day*. Isn't that nuts?" She turned to the group, breaking her fixation on the TV screen for a moment.

"*Sshhh!*" Emily insisted, holding up a hand to Gia. "Turn it off," she said. Martin pressed stop. The video shut off and automatically ejected. They all fell silent, watching Emily. Her eyes were focused on nothing, once again. She was listening *hard*.

"What is it?" Betsy asked in the gentlest of voices, beginning to breathe heavily. Emily shook her head *no*, but that was it. She remained frozen. Everyone kept silent.

Then she heard it—a tiny squeal. It was soft and muffled but growing louder ever so slowly. This wasn't a dream; she was wide awake and knew it, if for no other reason than the burst of acidic adrenaline that coursed unpleasantly through her body, instantly warming her up.

"*Run!*" she screamed with all her might.

She didn't wait for a reaction from anyone; Emily was *gone*, breaking into a full sprint as fast as she could run. It was the kind of reaction nobody would question, and they all followed suit, charging down the dark hallways, turning corners, and plowing through doors as if their lives depended on it.

Emily jumped through the window they'd slid open, breaking off pieces of old wood around the frame and shattering some of the remaining glass. She raced across the lawn toward the deep divot in the fence they'd climbed under, never once looking back to see who was behind her. Even through the dense fog, she never slowed down, not for a second.

She arrived at the fence and scurried along the bottom until she found the opening. Forcefully, she crawled under it and scrambled to her feet, continuing to sprint with every ounce of energy she could muster straight back to Gia's dormitory.

Emily burst into the dorm through the front entrance, the other four right on her tail. They ran past the girl at the front desk, who was signing in guests and checking school IDs. Emily raced up the stairs two at a time to the second floor and headed directly to Gia's room, which was always unlocked. She opened the door, and once again, the rest of the group was right there with her.

Once inside, they closed and locked the door. All that could be heard was their heavy panting. Their mouths were dry. Emily's hands were bleeding, and dirt smeared her face. Martin and Betsy were in similar condition, and everyone's clothes were wet and grimy.

Emily grabbed a towel and quickly soaked it in the sink. She pressed it to her face. It took a good sixty seconds before anyone spoke; they were just gasping for air. This wasn't a prank, and they all knew it. She hadn't done this for fun; it was too visceral.

"What..." she paused to catch her breath and continued, "the fuck..." Gia said.

"What happened?" Twerp asked, looking more frazzled than anyone.

"I'm sorry," Emily repeated over and over.

"What was it?" Betsy asked her. "Was it the video?"

"No," Emily replied, wiping blood and dirt from her face and hands.

"What then?" Gia pressed, eager for answers.

"I just got spooked," Emily said, shaking her head and trying to downplay it.

"Bullshit," Gia retorted, opening her army trunk and pulling out her Ouija board. "Something definitely triggered you, Emily. The spirits are strong. I can smell them on our clothes," she said, sniffing her own shirt. "We are going to Ouija—right fucking meow," she continued as she turned to Twerp and *hissed* in his face like a cat.

"Down girl," Twerp said.

"Maybe we shouldn't," Betsy said, her voice sounding like a plea. "That was a lot."

Gia was already setting up the board. The others looked to Emily for answers, but she had none. *What could she say? Had she overreacted?*

Maybe she'd heard a mouse or a bat. Perhaps it was a squeak and not a squeal. Was she really going to do this to herself again? Was she going to doubt her own ears and instincts? She felt embarrassed now; she had made a fool of herself. Nobody chased them. They never saw anyone. Betsy took Emily's hands in hers and stood face-to-face.

"Are you all right, Emily?" she asked, her concern genuine. Emily's eyes glossed over as she nodded, covering her mouth before speaking.

"I think so," she finally said. Betsy hugged her.

Emily didn't want to Ouija, as Gia would put it, but she also didn't want to be alone. The boys stood quietly, half shaken up and half excited to be hanging out in a dorm room filled with high school girls. This was going to be a legendary story for the guys at Porter-Gaud.

"Ouija boards are for kids," Twerp said, trying—and failing—to sound cool.

"How old are you?" Gia asked him, her tone serious.

"Fourteen?" Twerp replied, his voice rising at the end as if it were a question.

"You look ten," she said back.

"Say it to my face," he challenged weakly, almost under his breath.

Gia turned from arranging the board and stood right in front of Twerp, towering over him, and repeated clearly, "You look *ten*." Twerp froze. After a very pregnant pause, Gia continued, "I'd send both of you dorks home if I had my druthers, but the more human souls at the table, the stronger our presence will be in the spiritual universe. Come on," she instructed as they all sat around the table on the floor, taking their positions at the Ouija board.

Gia reached out to her sides, and everyone took hands around the table. Martin felt excited to be holding Emily's hand on one side, but he had Twerp on the other.

Twerp's hand was clammy, best described as 'overly moist'—more so than wet. It was small, too, and felt like it hadn't been washed. He wanted to let go but instead focused on Emily's hand, which was dry and soft, the cleanest hand he'd ever held.

Gia took a deep breath, closed her eyes, and began her ancient Voodoo incantation: "Hounkou Bolokou Djavohoun Bohoun."

She repeated it again, and again after that. Eventually, she opened her eyes and let go of the hands she was holding. She gestured at the table and the planchette, and everyone placed their index finger onto the "floaty thing."

"Who is with us? Is there a demon in this room?" Gia asked, getting right to it. No time for small talk. "Are there spirits of the witches of Salem who can hear me? Are you with us tonight?"

Gia ran through question after question. She called on the spirit of the fallen angel Lucifer, the spirit of Judas, and the spirits of all the greatest sinners known to man, along with the demonic beasts that keep their souls eternally incarcerated.

The planchette moved occasionally, but mostly it just hovered over letters that didn't spell anything or slid off the board. They tried for half an hour, maybe longer.

"Let someone else speak," Martin offered. It was the first thing he'd said since they began. Gia looked a tad miffed, but she acquiesced, considering how little had materialized after so much promise.

"That's a good idea," she said with slightly pursed lips. "You ask something, Emily," she suggested, looking at her.

"Like what?"

"Whatever comes to mind. Whatever you feel or think of," Gia replied.

They sat for a moment in the dim room, candles flickering, while storm clouds loomed outside the partially cracked window. The fog was even denser than it had been earlier. Emily appeared to think of something. She closed her eyes and asked out loud a very simple question: "Was that you?"

The group exchanged glances, mostly just moving their eyes. Nobody was sure whom she was addressing. A moment later, the planchette began to move—it floated slowly, deliberately, to the word "yes." It landed there, stopping on a dime.

They all witnessed it. A palpable sensation filled the air; something was happening. Emily was clearly the focus of the spirits tonight. If she was acting, she was destined for an Oscar. She paused, then continued.

"Who are you?" she asked, her voice quivering with nerves.

A moment later, it moved again, as if on its own, gliding quickly from letter to letter. There was no doubt among the group; nobody was moving it with their fingers. It floated to the letter 'H,' then to the letter 'I,' and finally to the letter 'M.'

"Him," Gia whispered. She made eye contact with Emily and immediately knew something was very wrong. Emily looked like she was about to cry.

"*What?*" Gia asked softly. She was sympathetic but also nervous.

Emily took her hand off the board. Everyone's eyes were on her, waiting to hear what she would say.

"I've never shared this with anyone before," Emily said, pausing. The group collectively held their breath. This was going to be heavy; you could have heard an ant burp.

"When I was five, my mother took me to a nursing home to visit my great-grandmother, whom I'd never met. I woke up in the middle of the night while we were there. I heard something, so I opened the door and peeked out just enough to see," she continued, struggling to clear her throat to stop her voice from trembling.

"What did you see?" Betsy asked with trepidation, placing her hand on Emily's for support.

"I saw a man get murdered."

The group gasped, riveted. "I saw this giant person wrap a plastic bag around another man's head and suffocate him."

"Oh my God," Gia said, her eyes wide.

"And right before he died—right as he was about to go lifeless—the man held a mirror in front of his face, forcing him to watch his own death. His final vision was his reflection—struggling, terrified, and alone," Emily explained.

"That is horrible," Betsy said, nearly in tears.

Emily was trying to catch her breath, not from physical exertion but from the anxiety of reliving and articulating the trauma.

"It was the most awful memory, and it haunts me."

"That would haunt anyone," Martin said supportively.

"The worst part was, nobody believed me," Emily whispered, almost to herself, yet she glanced at the group one by one, pleading as if she were still trying to convince someone that it had happened. "I heard it again tonight—the tiny squeal of the wheel on his metal bucket. I heard it in

Kelly Hall. That's why I ran."

Emily picked up a shirt from the floor, the closest thing she could find, and covered her face with it, as if she just wanted to hide for a moment, like an ostrich burying its head in the sand. She then wiped her eyes to dry them, and when she looked up, she saw an expression on Gia's face that made her feel sick.

"*What?*" Emily said, her voice so timid it practically echoed with fear. Gia's eyes grew watery. "Gia, what's wrong?" Emily insisted, her angst spilling over like kerosene.

Gia responded in a hushed voice, looking shaken—something that took a lot.

"Did he have a blue jumpsuit on?" she asked. Emily froze, covering her mouth in shock. Her eyes glossed over, which caused Betsy's eyes to gloss over, too.

Emily nodded at Gia, who continued speaking.

"I forgot about it until just now. But I had a dream last night—a bad dream. I have them all the time, so I didn't think much of it. I watch a lot of horror films. But I dreamed I was alone in my dorm room, and I heard this squealing sound, like from the wheel of a bucket. So, I got up and opened the door, and there was a man standing there. He was big and fat and ugly, with dark circles under his eyes, pasty skin, and lots of scars. He was bald and wearing a blue, zip-up jumpsuit, like a janitor's uniform," she said, looking directly at Emily as she asked, "Is that what he looked like?"

Emily nodded, unable to speak. Her face contorted awkwardly as she fought off the resurfacing tears.

"So, I asked him who he was looking for," Gia said. "And he said your name," she added, tears streaming down her face. Emily began to cry as well. They leaned toward each other and hugged, both kneeling on the floor.

"This can't be real, you guys," Betsy said, looking overwhelmed and struggling to process everything. "This isn't fun anymore. I want to stop," she stated.

The boys sat helplessly, unsure of what they had gotten themselves into. It was late, and they needed to leave soon. There was nothing more to be done that night, but the game was definitely over.

The whole group walked Emily back to her dorm room, where Dahlia was thankfully waiting. Afterward, the boys escorted the girls to their dorm, just to the front door, before making their way to the pond to tackle the more challenging journey back to the other side. For some reason, the trip felt longer going home.

Betsy headed to her room on the third floor, while Gia returned to her room on the second floor. Gia lived alone; her roommate had dropped out of school before the year even began, granting her the enviable privilege of living alone.

Once inside, she almost wished she had a roommate—at least for that night. Regardless, she pulled out her belongings from her backpack: the power source she had brought, her cameras, and the VHS tape she had retrieved from the vent. Yes, she had grabbed it just as they ran.

Her VCR was set up. Gia was a fan of old horror films and owned many on VHS: *Rosemary's Baby*, *Amityville Horror*, *The Shining*, *The Exorcist*, *Friday the 13th*, *The Omen*, *Burnt Offerings*, and countless others she'd found at flea markets.

Tonight, however, she would be watching something different. Something real.

She inserted the tape into her VCR and pressed rewind. It hummed for a minute or so before stopping. She closed her eyes for a moment and took a deep breath, and then she pressed play.

rofessor Joe was what everyone called him. He taught philosophy
and was undeniably smart. While some teachers could convey the
material from that day's lesson, they often lacked the intellectual
depth that Professor Joe possessed.

Emily enjoyed his class, although some students complained that the
material was too esoteric for high school freshmen. The class was simply
titled "Philosophy," which was pretty straightforward.

Gia did not share Emily's enthusiasm. Though she also had Professor
Joe for philosophy, she found the class boring. In fact, she found *him*
boring.

"All he does is talk," she lamented to Emily. "I can barely stay awake."

"I think it's interesting," Emily replied.

"Are you kidding? Ambien listens to Professor Joe lecture when it
can't sleep at night," Gia joked, eliciting a giggle from Emily.

"You don't like him?" Emily asked.

"He's fine. The class sucks," Gia said.

Emily was recalling that humorous exchange with her friend as she
watched her from across the classroom, Gia's head bobbing forward
periodically as she fought to stay awake during the lecture. Gia was seated

in the second row, while Emily sat a few rows back. She was smiling to herself, trying not to laugh every time she'd see the tell-tale head bob.

"The impediment to action advances action. What stands in the way becomes the way," Professor Joe read aloud from a text he held in one hand. He looked up at the classroom of students. "That's classic Marcus Aurelius," he said.

He placed the textbook on his desk and began to stroll around the room in a peripatetic manner, reminiscent of ancient philosophers wandering the desert or wherever they went to share their rhetoric. He enjoyed lecturing this way. Emily could tell he considered himself not just a teacher of philosophy, but an actual philosopher. She admired that; he immersed himself in it, and it was clear he loved it.

He looked the part, too. Joe often wore a tweed jacket over an untucked button-down shirt. His pants were baggy, and his shoes looked old. He wore glasses and rarely took them off. He was one of those people who seemed destined to don spectacles. He may have been born with them on.

"So, how can the impediment to action advance action?" he asked rhetorically, knowing that no one was likely to answer the question except for himself.

"I'll tell you why," he said. "Because when something stops you from reaching your goal, it forces you to take action and find another way to get there, doesn't it? It compels a change in direction, attitude, or game plan. It requires you to alter your course in some way.

"It's like a housefly trying to get through a pane of glass, bouncing off it repeatedly. They never stop because they aren't smart enough to realize they need to find another path. Humans, however, have the ability to make adjustments."

He made eye contact with Emily, and she nodded at him. She would do this often in class to make him feel some reciprocation from the gaze of fifteen frozen faces. Everyone seemed hesitant to participate, afraid of giving wrong answers or sounding foolish by asking questions. Professor Joe continued as he walked over to one of the massive windows in the classroom and looked out at the campus.

"So, when he says 'what stands in the way becomes the way,' he means that the very obstacle that seems to prevent you from achieving your goal *is* the actual path to achieving it, because you learn what *doesn't* work," he said, tapping on the window with his knuckle.

"You are the fly, but you're smart enough to understand that no matter how many times you bounce off that clear pane of glass, you aren't going to get through it. That obstacle, which seems to be our nemesis, is actually the path," he said, gesturing passionately with his hand, lifting it into the air as if making a grand declaration. "Does that make sense?"

That was his trademark closing line for every lecture: "Does that make sense?"

Emily gave him another nod. She figured he appreciated it, and it might make the difference between a B+ and an A-.

Across the pond at Porter-Gaud School for Boys, Martin and Twerp had settled back into their daily routine. They'd hidden the boat in the shrubbery at the edge of the pond. It seemed as though they'd gotten away with their caper.

They were in the school gym for physical education class, which mostly involved putting on shorts and shooting baskets. This suited Martin just fine; he wasn't much of an athlete and preferred the relaxed approach of the P.E. teacher, who spent most of the time sitting in the bleachers eating a sandwich.

"What's it like over there?" Kenny asked as he bounced the basketball and took a jump shot.

"Dude, chicks *everywhere*," Twerp replied, exaggerating as much as he could.

"Nice," was all Kenny could say as he nodded in approval at Twerp.

Martin took a more reserved approach, keeping his bragging to a minimum for fear of being told on. He was also preoccupied with the fluffy sensation of puppy love. He couldn't stop thinking about her. She knew his name! She recognized his face. And now, they'd hung out together for an entire night—not just any night, but a memorable one. He wanted to text her, email her, or call her, but none of those options were available since he didn't have any of her contact information. He'd been too nervous to ask for it, scared that she would say no and be put off by the idea of him pursuing her.

Yet, she didn't own his thoughts and dreams; those were his alone. In his mind, she was his future girlfriend in a wonderful world. He envisioned them living together, kissing, holding hands. He pictured her face—those eyes, that adorable little freckle on her upper lip.

He didn't tell anyone about her. It wasn't like that with Emily. He genuinely cared about her. It might have sounded funny to other people, but he was in love with her.

He could still smell her— that hint of vanilla mixed with baby powder: intoxicating.

And then, Kenny ruined the moment with one annoying question: "Did you hear what happened?"

Record scratch. Martin was jarred back to reality. He sensed that something "not good" was forthcoming, as the instinctive spike in his cortisol gave him a burn in his chest.

"No, what?" Twerp asked, immediately stopping his dribbling as if he needed to hear better.

"Ricky Rude…"

He said it! The two most unwelcomed words in Martin's vocabulary. The rest of the story didn't even matter. *Damn you, Kenny!*

Even so, Martin had to listen. He had to know. Kenny continued.

"…beat the ever-living crap out of Chris Kazemekis."

"Seriously?" Twerp said with a level of excitement Martin had never seen Twerp display.

"Yup. Kaz just got his license and accidentally backed his mother's Volvo into Rude's motorcycle. Rude waited for him after class and knocked him out cold with one punch."

"Wow!" Twerp exclaimed, his eyes as wide as a child's at a carnival ride.

"Oh yeah. Kazemekis pissed his pants while lying unconscious on the cement right in front of everyone. You could hear the whizzing sound as the crotch of his tan khakis darkened with a big stain. Totally epic," Kenny said, taking another jump shot.

"I can't believe we missed it," Twerp yelled.

"It's all over TikTok. He finally came to and started crying. A school administrator had to walk him to the nurse's office while he bawled like a baby with a wet diaper," Kenny chuckled. "No offense to Kaz; he's a good guy," he added with a solemn nod.

"Oh, yeah, he's totally cool," Twerp said, making it even more odd that he took such joy in the boy's humiliation.

A moment later, Kenny and Twerp turned their attention to Martin, staring at him in silence.

"What are you guys looking at me for?" Martin asked, bouncing his basketball to appear casual. They didn't answer. They didn't have to.

Martin had had enough. He wasn't going to go through life afraid of being pummeled to the point of urinating in his pants by some Neanderthal. *This ends now*, he decided. He was going to handle it the way real men do. He was going to tell on him.

The school principal was new to the job. He had been the athletic director for nine years at Porter-Gaud and coached the football team as well. He was the only applicant for the vacant principal position, so he was hired with five yeses and two noes from the school committee, plus one abstention. The irony was not lost on the kids—the only candidate, and he still didn't receive all the votes.

Mister Urban was a husky fellow—strong, with thick, hairy forearms and a giant Buddha belly. He had been wearing the same pair of shorts and white socks with two blue stripes—pulled up over his massive calves—for so long that the staff joked he might show up to his new job in the same outfit: whistle and all.

However, Mister Urban was not wearing that outfit on the day Martin tapped on his open door. Instead, he sported pants and a short-sleeve button-down shirt with a brown tie that looked as if he had bought it at Sears.

"Come in," he said to Martin, who had emailed him to request an appointment.

Mister Urban sat up in his creaky chair, folded his hands, and said, "What can I do for you, Martha?"

Martin was stunned. Had he heard correctly? *Martha?* Was it a Freudian slip? Or worse, was it intentional?

"Son?" Mister Urban said, breaking Martin's train of thought. At least he knew he was male.

"It's Ricky Rude, sir," Martin replied. "He's been telling people he's going to beat me up."

"Well, what would you like me to do?" Mister Urban asked, his hands open in a gesture that indicated he wasn't inclined to help.

"Talk to him? Maybe threaten to suspend him?" Martin suggested.

"I can't suspend a student for something he *might* do," Mister Urban said, snorting a laugh. "Besides, this is all hearsay."

Mister Urban stood up from his chair and walked around the desk, gesturing for Martin to stand. He obliged. "How old are you, son?"

"Fourteen," Martin answered.

"Take your shirt off," Mister Urban instructed.

"Seriously?"

"Yes."

Martin hesitated for several seconds, contemplating the unusual request. *What could he do?*

He removed his shirt and shifted to an apologetic posture as he stood topless in front of the man. Mister Urban scrutinized him as if he were reviewing a bad report card.

"Have you considered lifting weights?" he asked.

"No, sir."

Mister Urban raised his eyebrows and looked away as he said, "You should. We've got a respectable weight room here." He then waved his fingers at Martin's torso without looking and added, "You can put your shirt back on; you're killing me."

Martin didn't appreciate the dig. This meeting was not going well, and he had hoped to find a sympathetic figure in the principal.

Martin re-robed, realizing he was not one of the kids Mister Urban favored. Urban liked strong, athletic kids—especially football players. In fact, Ricky Rude was one of the players on his team.

"Your testosterone levels should be starting to rise soon. That's a good time to take up weight training. You'll find you'll have fewer issues with being so easily intimidated once you put some muscle on your frame. You look like a coat hanger. Do you wake up with an erection in the morning?" he asked. "You know what an erection is, right?"

"Yes," Martin replied, staring at the floor. He felt the urgent need to leave the room; things were getting weird.

"Good. And I hope it's girls you think about when you have one," Mister Urban said with a wink. He then delivered a mock one-two punch combination to Martin's belly, followed by a condescending tussle of his hair.

Next, he opened a mini fridge, took out a Tupperware container, and placed two hot dogs onto a paper plate before putting it into his small microwave oven and turning it on.

"I am starving," he said, watching the hot dogs spin in circles. He popped off his tie—apparently a clip-on—and tossed it onto his desk.

That was it. He didn't say anything else. The only sound in the room was the hum of the microwave.

Martin waited fifteen seconds to see if anything else would happen. It didn't. A moment later, he stood up, nodded a thank you at the back of Mister Urban's head in an unreciprocated gesture, and walked out of the office.

A couple of weeks had passed since the girls had their adventure in Kelly Hall. There hadn't been much in-person contact among them. School was in full swing, with tests to study for and papers to write. There was also a three-day weekend tucked in there somewhere, during which most of the boarders had gone home to be with their families.

Everyone was gearing up for the big push—the second half of the semester leading to a long Christmas break.

By the time Emily was able to spend any real time with Gia again, it felt like a month had passed since the night in the condemned building. Emily's cell phone had been confiscated by the administration as part of her write up, which was standard practice. She would have it back soon. The two girls were walking along the exercise trail that ran around the perimeter of the campus, with workout stations positioned every hundred yards or so.

"I watched the tape," Gia said flatly.

The bombshell statement made Emily stop in her tracks.

"Wait, you have it?" she asked, grasping Gia by the arm.

"Yes. I grabbed it before we ran out of the dorm that night."

"And you watched it?" Emily pressed.

"Yes."

Emily was aware of Gia's penchant for giving less information than the other person would want, a result of her flair for the dramatic, especially regarding anything juicy. So it was no surprise that Gia stood there, practically making Emily beg for more.

"*And?*" Emily prompted earnestly.

Gia looked around to ensure no one was within earshot and then said in a hushed voice, "It was blank."

"The tape?"

"Yes."

"How could it be blank? There was stuff on there."

"I know."

"Did you mess up when you were—"

"No," Gia interrupted before Emily could finish. "I know how to use a VCR. I played it all the way through a couple of times."

"Are you sure you grabbed the same tape?"

"Yes."

Emily shook her head in confusion. "I don't get it."

Gia's expression suggested she wanted something as she stared at her friend.

"Why do you have that look?" Emily asked.

"I want you to watch it," Gia said as she pulled the tape from her backpack and handed it to Emily. They both looked around this time as if they were involved in a drug deal.

"Why do you want me to watch it?" Emily asked.

"Because I think maybe it won't be blank for you."

"Why wouldn't it be blank for me if it was blank for you?" Emily replied, still confused.

Gia stood in silence for a long moment. She tried to be gentle. "Places aren't haunted, Emily; people are," she said, her voice tinged with sadness.

"You think you're haunted, so the tape won't play for you?" Emily questioned.

Gia didn't respond. Emily read her reaction, a lump formed in her throat. "Oh God, it's me. You think *I'm* haunted, don't you?" she said, her voice cracking.

The realization struck Emily hard, and she felt very alone in that moment. A tidal wave of consternation washed over her. She felt isolated, just as she often did as a child. Her emotions spiraled into a dark place. *Maybe I am haunted*, she thought.

Perhaps that's why her father left the house and never returned. Or why Baghead appeared in front of her at such a young age. Maybe all her problems stemmed from being a haunted girl, and she was only now realizing it.

"Don't be afraid," Gia told her, placing her hands on Emily's shoulders in a gesture of camaraderie.

"There's no worse feeling in the world than being alone when you're scared. That's when the devil shows up," Gia said. "He comes when you feel the most vulnerable. He preys on your weakness. He sits right next to you, and he talks to you softly, right into your ear. He tells you you're right, and that there's nobody coming to help. He presses your spiritual bruises, so you remember they're there. He delights in your prickly isolation," Gia said in a rant that left Emily's mouth hanging open.

Emily knew these things already because she lived with them her entire life. She had just never heard anyone articulate them so lucidly.

And then Gia said, "But you're not alone, Emily." Then she hugged her. Emily hugged her back, needing the comfort, desperate for it. She didn't want to let go; she felt so small.

They finally broke the embrace.

"You can use my room," Gia offered. "I'll find something to do. The VCR is hooked up."

"No, I can't," Emily replied without hesitation. "I'm too scared."

Gia nodded. "Okay. Do it whenever you're ready. I never lock my door," she told her, giving her another quick hug. A school bell rang from one of the classroom buildings, resonating across the landscape.

"I've got to get going," Emily said, stuffing the cassette tape in her backpack before walking away.

Sitting inside Professor Joe's office—unsurprisingly—was Professor Joe himself. He was there often, keeping more office hours than required by the school. He was grading papers, as he always seemed to be. If he didn't assign so many, he wouldn't have so many to grade, but that was a discussion for another day.

He wanted his students to learn to think critically. If they took nothing else from his class, they should take that.

Emily enjoyed his class most of the time. They studied Marcus Aurelius, as well as Franz Kafka, Socrates, Nietzsche, and Kierkegaard. Although the material was dense for his students' age, he focused on the most accessible aspects of their philosophies, doing his best to present it in an engaging way, making it relatable for teenagers.

She knocked on his open door.

"Emily, come in," he said, gesturing to a small wooden chair next to his desk. He seemed pleased to have a distraction from his mundane chore. Emily sat down and smiled at him.

"What's going on?" Professor Joe asked.

"I have the paper I finished. I just wanted to drop it off," she said, laying the document on his desk. He preferred assignments to be printed at the school's writing lab so he could mark them in red ink.

"Thank you," he replied.

"Can I ask you something?" she asked.

"Fire away."

"Have you ever been inside Kelly Hall?"

The question caught him off guard. There was a noticeable shift in his demeanor, a distinct pause in his usual flow of conversation. He was typically unflappable, so Emily noticed the hesitation.

"The condemned building? Yeah, I've been in there. They'd already shut it down by the time I started teaching here, but it hadn't been fenced off yet. People used it for department meetings and administrative purposes. The school board eventually put an end to that. I guess they felt it was a safety issue. Why do you ask?"

"My friend told me it's haunted," Emily said.

"Oh, yeah?" he replied, forcing a smirk.

"Yeah," she said. She paused, then added, "We went inside."

His smirk faded. "You did?" he asked, sounding almost nervous.

"Yes," she replied, observing his expressions, always able to read people. She knew Professor Joe wouldn't write her up for going inside the dorm. He wasn't that kind of authority figure. He was an academic who didn't have time for, nor care about, frivolous rules and the associated write ups. If someone were going to get caught with beer in their dorm room or smoking a joint under the moon in the middle of the soccer field, he was the guy you'd want to get caught by.

"Did you see any ghosts?" he asked, his forced smile now even more awkward.

"Goats? I didn't know animals were allowed," Emily replied with a smile of her own, trying to ease the tension. "Anyway, I just wanted to drop that off," she said as she stood to leave.

"Thank you," he said. As she was about to exit, he spoke up. "Emily…" She looked back at him. "Close the door, please," he said.

"You mean, on my way out?" she asked.

"No. I mean, close it and stay here," he said.

She felt a tingle—a chill creeping across her skin. Closing the door, she sat back down, hoping he was simply going to warn her about violating school rules, that Kelly Hall was off-limits for safety reasons, and that even though he wouldn't write her up, she needed to understand that rules exist for a reason—and then—

"I've seen him, too," he said.

And just like that, everything changed.

She took a moment to study his face, to gauge his expression. She needed to be sure they were on the same page—no room for a humorous misunderstanding. He nodded at her, and in that instant, she knew they were. There was an immediate comfort in it; she wasn't alone anymore. Professor Joe was an adult—strong and smart.

"What is he?" she asked.

"He's a monster," he replied. Then, after a long pause—as if he were struggling to hold himself together emotionally—he opened his desk drawer and took out a pack of cigarettes. He lit one, his hand shaking slightly. Taking a long drag, he slouched his shoulders in exasperation. "He's also my son," he added.

He had a gaunt look on his face, and his voice sounded strange when he made the admission, as if he were fighting back emotions. Joe was stoic through and through, so feelings didn't come easily to him.

She sat there, slack-jawed with shock. "You *smoke?*" she said, furrowing her brow.

Professor Joe couldn't help but give one quick snort of a laugh before growing serious again.

"I really want to laugh at that well-timed joke, but I can't right now," he said. "You're a smart girl, Emily. Beyond your years."

"Thanks," she said.

He snuffed out the cigarette after just one puff.

"I created him, so in that respect, he is my son. But he's a monster first and foremost. That was me in the video. You found it, didn't you?" he said, looking at her. The expression on her face must have revealed everything, because Joe didn't wait for an answer before he continued.

"I knew someone had. I dreamt it. He appears in my dreams as vividly as you are to me right now. They're dreams I can't wake up from, no matter how hard I try," he said softly, rubbing his eyes beneath his glasses. "I went to high school here. Ashley Hall was co-ed back then. The school was smaller, and they hadn't procured the land for Porter-Gaud yet. There were far fewer students.

"A group of us started a "horror club" run by this older guy in his 50's. He was a part-time professor—adjunct, they call it. He taught a class on filmmaking and managed the media department for the school, overseeing the TVs and educational tapes. Easy gig," he explained.

Joe lit another cigarette and took a drag.

"Anyway, he was a total film junkie who loved anything dark and spooky. We thought he was weird for wanting to hang out with high school kids. I don't think he had many friends. But he'd buy us beer, so we let him come around for the horror club meetings. Turns out he was a pretty good guy after all. Just a loner.

"I had read the novel *Frankenstein* around that time, and I became obsessed with the idea of bringing to life a monster that would haunt the school forever. It excited me—the idea of manufacturing a real-life haunting."

Professor Joe stood up from his chair as though he needed to move from distress. He turned to the window, looking out at the campus parking lot, and put his hands on the wall as if he were being arrested, hanging his head in anguish.

"Things were never the same after that night. The group I was with—we all had horrible nightmares. *Horrible*," he said, glancing back at her for emphasis. "Some of us got chronically sick with no medical explanation. One by one, members of the club began to die. Every time one of us passed away, they were eliminated from the video we'd made—it's like the cassette was alive, keeping score of the kills and taunting us. There were eight of us that night. Now there's just me," he said, making a fatalistic gesture with his hands, as though accepting his penance.

"I didn't recognize you in the video. You haven't aged well," Emily remarked, more candidly than necessary.

"Thank you," Professor Joe said, injecting as much sarcasm as he could muster.

"I'm sorry. I didn't mean to be rude. I just meant—you were a handsome young man. You look like someone who's been carrying a burden for a long time," she explained.

He nodded in agreement. When he pulled off his eyeglasses, his face looked instantly different. It always took Emily several minutes to adjust whenever he removed them. No wonder it worked so well for Clark Kent.

There were two deep grooves on the bridge of Professor Joe's nose where the glasses had rested. They looked uncomfortable, as if they would never pop back out. He massaged them with his fingers as he said, "I wanted so badly to feel the power of creation." After taking another drag of his cigarette, he continued, "I probably should have just had children the old-fashioned way."

He sat on the corner of his desk, close to Emily, his voice hushed as he continued, "Anyway, I went on to get a degree in philosophy and took a teaching job here. I needed to be close. I felt..." he paused, "I *feel* responsible. I hid the tape in the vent, hoping maybe he would go there and stay, where he sprang from. I thought maybe the city would condemn the building and demolish it. It was a long shot, but it was all I could think to do. I didn't want that cassette anywhere near me.

"He killed the last of the others about ten years ago—the older guy, the teacher. Since then, I've been the only one on the tape. I've been waiting, every day, for him to visit me. It's been torture."

"Why hasn't he killed you yet?" she asked.

He sat back down in his chair and covered his face with his hands, speaking through them.

"To punish me, I suppose. I'm on death row, and I don't know my execution date. What could be crueler? He hates me," he said, then looked directly at Emily. "Don't we all hate our parents? Especially when they deserve it?"

The comment resonated with Emily.

"He died at a nursing home. I saw him kill the man you're talking about," Emily told him. "I was five."

"The monster—he must have sensed your presence that night. He must have been searching for you for years. He willed you here. The law of attraction works," Joe said.

"How did you do the haunting?" she asked.

"I wanted to create a demon that captured the souls of people who had lived as frauds. I used a book by a rebel philosopher named Volkan Krauthhammer. He was a nobody in the world of philosophy, but I liked him because his book was banned. I owned one of only thirteen copies. I thought it would be worth a fortune one day.

"So, we had a séance, prayed to the devil, and I read excerpts from the book. We drank, smoked, and called upon the anti-Christ. Like Victor Frankenstein, I cobbled him together, not from body parts, but from theory, metaphysics, and spirituality. The whole experience was very transcendental."

He paused, looking at Emily with absolute contrition and said, "I didn't think it would really work."

His voice was barely above a whisper, his eyes glossed-over, looking shrink wrapped with regret.

"But how? I mean, how did it happen? There had to be a final ingredient," Emily pressed.

Joe stood up, grabbed his tweed jacket from the back of his chair, and asked, "Do you drink coffee?"

Emily shrugged. "Tea."

"Come on. I'll buy," he replied.

Professor Joe and Emily walked across campus in silence, a refreshing break from their heavy conversation. They were headed to a café on the school grounds, which had an outdoor seating area where Emily settled as Joe went inside to buy their drinks.

The warm sunshine felt good on her face as she leaned back with her eyes closed, until Professor Joe emerged with their beverages. He sat down and began tending to his coffee.

Emily waited for him to speak. They weren't there just for tea, and she could see he was struggling to start. So, she remained patient.

"This is embarrassing," he finally said. "And it's not really appropriate for someone your age." He looked at her as if seeking permission. She nodded.

"It's okay," she assured him.

"You asked about the final piece of the equation—the thing that made it really *happen* that night," he said, stirring his coffee with a wooden spoon. "I was about your age at that time," he added, lighting a cigarette and taking a drag. He then rested it on the edge of the table, letting the hot ash dangle over the cement.

"That night in Kelly Hall—the night from the video—things got so confusing. I don't remember most of what happened; I can only see it in flashes.

"I know we had literature on how to conjure the devil herself." He looked directly at Emily and said, "That was the final piece of the puzzle. According to the philosophy of that book I mentioned, we had to impregnate her in order to open a new gate to hell—our very own V.I.P. room with a monster as the doorman," he said, sipping his coffee and glancing around to ensure no one was close enough to hear.

"The séance got weird. At some point, I felt like I was watching a movie, as if I weren't even there."

"I know that feeling," Emily replied with a small nod.

Joe paused for a moment, then leaned closer to her and whispered nervously, "I impregnated her that night."

Emily asked, "Who?"

"The devil," he told her, as if it weren't completely ridiculous. He looked at Emily like he halfway expected her to call for help.

"What are you talking about?" she pressed, seeking clarification. Joe picked up his cigarette, tapped the long ash onto the ground, and took another drag.

"I don't know if I should be talking to you like this," he said. "It's inappropriate."

"I need to know," Emily said, leaning forward and fixing her gaze on him. "This affects me, too."

He could see the desperation in her eyes, and he knew this was all his fault, so he nodded and continued.

"She showed up. I can't remember exactly when, but I felt her presence. I saw her, too, but I can't recall what she looked like. I remember seeing her, but I can't—" he paused, struggling. "I cannot remember her appearance no matter how hard I try," he said, his tone heavy with frustration.

"It's okay," Emily reassured him.

"When she arrived, it felt overwhelming. I had no control over myself—my thoughts, my actions. It's hard to articulate, but I knew she was there—the devil herself. We all did. She had a feeling to her, it was like invisible, icy water pouring over my body, freezing cold and painful. The others lay there watching; they couldn't leave, couldn't move.

"I was alone with her, even with people watching. I was in a trance. Paralyzed."

He took a sip of his coffee and cleared his throat.

"What happened then?" Emily prodded, desperate for details.

He continued, "Every erotic thought I'd ever had, plus hundreds more I'd never imagined, all wrapped up into one event. My whole body became a sexual organ," he said, looking away, embarrassed to be discussing this with someone so young. "I'm sorry," he added.

"Stop apologizing," Emily said with audible frustration. Joe nodded and continued.

"I felt like she'd spun a silk wrapping around me, like a spider. I couldn't even twitch, not an inch.

"Then, she entered me. By that, I mean she melded into my body. It was erotic, beyond my ability to describe. The experience was so otherworldly that I couldn't handle it. I remember yelling from the intensity of it. I couldn't stop. It lasted for hours."

Joe paused, short of breath and flushed in the face from the recollection.

Emily noticed his hand shaking as he lifted his coffee for another sip. A minute later, he was able to continue once again.

"There was no intimacy to it, though. No love. On the contrary, I was scared. I felt violated. She raped me," he whispered. Emily could see his expression; he looked ashamed and humiliated.

"I'm sorry," she said softly. "Do you want to stop?"

He shook his head. "I need to tell you everything. It's just so degrading," he said. Emily felt bad for him and wanted to help him feel more comfortable. Before she knew it, she blurted out,

"I have a bed-wetting problem."

At that moment, two students walked past the table carrying drinks. They both looked at Emily, and her face turned pink as they made eye contact.

"Crap," she whispered in embarrassment after they were gone.

Joe glanced at her, surprised by her odd comment.

"Come again?" he asked.

She lowered her voice and looked around to ensure no one *else* was about to walk near them.

"Yes. I've had it since I was a little kid. It started after I saw him that night—the monster. I think it's from the trauma," she told Joe with total candor. "It's the most embarrassing secret I have, and nobody knows about it but you. Well, you and those two random girls who just walked by. So, whatever you're ashamed of telling me, maybe that will make it a little easier," she added.

They sat in silence for another minute, watching the students walking around campus. Joe lit another cigarette, took a drag, and placed it at the edge of the table with the tip hanging off. He took a big sip of his coffee as it began to cool.

"You'd have to read the book—the one I told you about—but that's one philosophy about how hell can be created. That's how we haunted the school."

"What happened to you after?" she asked.

He paused, turning his face away from her to hide his expression as he admitted, "I was rendered impotent."

Emily sat quietly, taking a sip of her tea to quell the awkwardness. Professor Joe continued, still unable to look at her.

"Do you know what that means?" he asked her.

"Kinda," she said with a shrug.

"I was never able to achieve an erection again. I never had another orgasm, either. All those processes in my body became blunted. That part of my mind was so damaged."

"I'm sorry," Emily said, seeing how emasculated he felt. "Have you tried—"

"Yes," he interrupted. "I've tried everything: drugs, therapy, girlfriends, hookers. There's nothing there. As a teenager, I thought not being able to have sex was the end of the world. But as I grew older, I realized all of that was nothing compared to what I had unleashed on others."

He looked at Emily and said, "This is all my fault. I'm so sorry."

A tear rolled out of the corner of his eye and trickled down his cheek. Emily was digesting the fact that all of this was true. There would be no looking back with amusement at the misunderstandings. Baghead was a living monster, and he was out to kill her.

It felt as if the ground dropped out from under her chair, sending her plummeting twenty flights on a runaway elevator, her stomach lodged in her chest. She wanted to cry, or puke, or scream.

"Maybe he won't kill you," she said, trying to offer him some hope— and herself, too.

"He will. He's just playing with his food," he replied, his eyes fixed on the table. She had never seen anyone so defeated.

"So, what do we do now?" she asked, hoping he had a plan to resolve this.

"I don't know," he told her, wiping his face with the consternation of a doomed man. "I really have no idea."

Emily sat in her dorm room with her roommate, Dahlia. They weren't talking. They often shared silence, not because they were so close that they could comfortably sit together without words, but because they simply didn't have much to say. They had both accepted that, in its own way, an understanding had formed. You sit over there, and I'll sit over here. We'll concede to being different from each other and won't try to force a friendship that feels unnatural and disingenuous.

Emily reflected on the paper she had submitted to Professor Joe. It was about his most recent lecture on Marcus Aurelius and the quote: "The impediment to action advances action. What stands in the way becomes the way."

What was her impediment? she wondered. What was holding her back from confronting Baghead? Fear. Paralyzing fear was her impediment, she realized. So fear *must* drive action, if Marcus Aurelius was correct.

"Fuck Baghead," she mumbled to herself.

"Who's a fuckbag?" Dahlia asked.

"No one. Sorry. I'm just mumbling nonsense over here," Emily replied. She felt crazy for officially using his name: Baghead.

She had made up her mind. She grabbed her things and left the room. Walking to Gia's dorm, she signed in as a guest and headed to Gia's room. She knocked and then pushed open the door. The room was empty. A pit formed in her stomach, as if she needed to poop. She was praying Gia would be there and tell her this wasn't a good time, maybe she had the flu or something—*anything.*

Nope. Gia was gone. Emily shut the door behind her, and it felt like a jail cell right away. She became short of breath. There it was—the VCR. The table was set, so to speak.

In that moment, Emily had never felt so alone, and for a girl who had grown up feeling very isolated, that was saying a lot. Even so, it almost felt like she was walking through a practice session of some kind. She felt detached from herself, as if experiencing an out-of-body moment. It wasn't out-of-body *enough*, though. She would have preferred to be a million miles away, but this had to be done.

The sun was still up, and she found some comfort in that. She worried a dorm monitor might walk in on her. If she were caught in someone else's room without them there, she could get written up.

She closed the curtains. Gia, of course, had blackout blinds that kept the room dark when pulled tight.

She turned on the TV and reached for the cassette tape, but paused, staring at it, remembering what Professor Joe had said. Was it really *alive*, documenting murders like some kind of sports ticker running digital scores across the screen?

She picked it up with some degree of caution and inserted the cassette into the VCR. It sucked it in, and the television displayed a blue screen. Her heart rate sped up. Her palms grew moist.

She sat directly in front of the screen, put on a set of headphones, and plugged them in.

The "play" button on Gia's VCR was missing, so she would press play with the tip of a knife she kept resting on the television. Emily picked it up, took a deep breath, aimed the knife at the spot she needed to hit, and pressed it.

The tape began to hum. After a moment, the same image appeared on the screen that had played in Kelly Hall the night they had broken in together.

The teenage version of Professor Joe appeared on the TV, and he began to speak. Now, she could see the resemblance, which made her want to chuckle. There was something in his face that she recognized but hadn't noticed before.

Even his mannerisms reminded her of his lectures. She wondered how she had overlooked them.

Time passed, and she reached the part of the recording where they had all run out of Kelly Hall. She was witnessing unseen footage.

"What is that sound?" she heard Joe ask.

The camera began to wander down the hallway, but there was no noise. Emily turned the volume all the way up on her headphones, yet all she could hear was a gentle hiss, the sound of nothingness.

The camera crept along, passing door after door in the dormitory. It looked like any other dorm at Ashley Hall School. If she hadn't known better, she might have thought it was an active residence with everything but the students.

Then the camera focused on one particular closed door. A man's hand reached out from behind the camera, turned the doorknob, and pushed it open. The room was dark, but Emily could make out some objects: a bed, a desk, clothing. It looked lived-in. Emily leaned her face closer to the screen, squinting at the TV.

On the left side of the screen, she saw a figure—a girl wearing headphones and staring at a television. It dawned on her: she was seeing herself! She gasped just a bit as she covered her mouth.

The camera zoomed in closer, and now she felt something behind her—the warmth of human flesh.

Her eyes watered as she whimpered, "Oh, fuck."

On the TV screen, she could see the camera operator standing right behind the girl, the images repeating over and over hundreds of times.

She began trembling, making small weeping sounds as she slowly turned around to find him—Baghead—towering above her, inches away. He was more massive than she remembered.

He smelled like hot garbage rotting in the summer sun. She looked up at him, and he smiled. She recognized his corpulent baby face and bald, scarred skull. She knew those deranged eyes with purplish circles beneath them. His gigantic blue onesie was zipped up to his neck.

This was the first time she'd seen him in the flesh since that night in the old folks' home, and he looked exactly the same, but twice as ugly.

She could see his teeth, brownish and slick with saliva, all at various stages of decay. He had a slanted eye and a cleft palate. From her seated position, he appeared seven feet tall.

He was every bit the monstrosity she remembered. When she whimpered, she inadvertently swallowed his repulsive stench, triggering an involuntary gag reflex. He giggled at her, as if all of this were amusing.

Emily could have sat there, frozen in fear. She could have let him kill her without resistance, feeling it would be pointless. But she was too shocked—so shocked that she screamed with all the power she could muster, though it still felt insufficient.

From her seated position, she jammed her hand into his stomach, unsure if she was still holding the knife she'd used to press the play button on the VCR or if she had put it down. She got her answer when she felt the warm liquid flow onto her fingers.

The monster howled in pain. He grabbed her by the hair and flung her tiny body across the room. She'd never been thrown like that. She bounced off a wooden closet, knocking the wind out of her and causing her to nearly lose consciousness.

He turned to her with fury and took a giant step forward. That's when Emily saw the door handle jiggle, and then it opened.

"What in God's name?" yelled Miss Warburton, barely able to utter the phrase before gasping at the horrifying sight of the obese, bleeding man in front of her.

"Who are you?" she demanded with terrified eyes, but it took him only a second to grab her by the neck, kick the door closed with his foot, and slam her down into a wooden seat. He pulled out duct tape from his side pocket and bound her wrists to the arms of the chair.

It happened so fast. He tucked the roll of tape back into his pocket and retrieved a clear plastic bag, which he wrapped over her head and pulled taut.

There wasn't much of a fight. Miss Warburton struggled, but she was overmatched and overwhelmed. She lacked the strength and began to wither. Emily lay on the floor in a state of half-consciousness, unable to move, yet still aware of what was happening as she watched Miss Warburton suffocate through the bag—her face displaying anguish and terror. Miss Warburton's mouth was open but silent, *desperate* for air, trying to scream. The scene was disturbing, like the book cover of a horror story.

Her eyes bulged, and yet it was quiet, save for the sound of her bucking legs banging against the furniture—a disturbing dance that was more instinctive than deliberate.

Her body went stiff for a moment, then limp. The muscles in her face gave out, and she seemed to relax in the worst way, her eyes fading from wide open to nearly shut, her mouth drooping as if she were terribly sad.

In that moment, with his free hand, Baghead took out a small hand-held mirror from his side pocket and showed her the reflection of her face.

For one cruel moment, her eyes *widened* with panic, a reaction to the nightmarish image.

A second later, her eyes drooped again, fully closing this time as she wilted to her death.

7

There was a funeral and memorial service for Miss Warburton held in the chapel at Ashley Hall School. She had been an employee in various capacities for over thirty years and lived on campus in her own dorm room. Known as a punctilious disciplinarian by the students, she seemed to evoke indifference from the administration and faculty.

Miss Warburton had little to no family. Most attendees at the memorial were employees and students, and attendance was mandatory.

Authorities determined she died of natural causes, being an overweight woman in her late sixties who never exercised and smoked cigarettes. The girls didn't know the specifics of "natural causes," but it didn't sound like murder.

Emily had been knocked out, suffering a mild concussion from her head striking a closet. When she awakened, an EMT was checking her. They suspected she had fallen and cracked her head.

At the funeral mass, Emily had gauze wrapped around her head to protect a wound on her skull. Gia sat next to her in a church pew and leaned over.

"You look like a text message emoji with that bandage," Gia whispered, prompting a snort and chuckle from Emily that drew looks from others.

"You guys…" Betsy whispered at them.

It felt good to laugh; Emily couldn't remember the last time she had.

After a viewing of the coffin, the pallbearers moved the casket from the chapel to a car outside, which would take her body to a cemetery on campus, just a short drive away. The grounds were reserved for staff or employees who wished to be buried there, and they would receive a discounted plot.

As they turned the coffin around and began wheeling it down the aisle toward the door, gentle organ music played. Gia gave Emily a little nudge.

"Are you doing okay?" she mouthed, and Emily nodded in response.

Outside the chapel, the girls stood in a circle chatting. A loud murmur filled the air as the students began to release some pent-up energy.

"I feel like I should tell someone," Emily said, watching them load the coffin into the back of the hearse.

"Tell them what? That a monster is chasing you and that he murdered Miss Warburton? They'll call your mother, and she'll come here to have you committed to an asylum, Emily," Gia said.

"I can't handle this," Betsy replied. "We need to get help. We have to tell the police, a teacher, or someone in authority."

"It's not a person, Betsy. He's a spirit," Gia insisted. "I can feel him."

"How can you feel spirits? I don't get it," Emily asked.

"I've always been able to. I never realized it until I got a little older. I just assumed everyone could do it. I thought it was normal. But I can contact the spiritual universe, wherever that is. That's how you and I were brought together—through divine intervention. A sign, not a coincidence, remember? Look for the signs," Gia explained.

Emily wasn't sure if Gia truly connected to the spiritual world, but she believed in it at that moment. She also felt she needed her friends *badly*. She felt close to both Betsy and Gia and was grateful they were there with her.

In Professor Joe's philosophy class, the mood was best described as morose. Miss Warburton's passing had an impact, as death does—the disconcerting permanence of it. She had suffered a massive asthma attack, or so said whoever disseminates that kind of information.

Though the students hadn't loved her, her death was still a shock.

Professor Joe was as unflappable as ever. He handed out literature that the school administration had instructed him to distribute, containing information about grief counselors and available resources for students and staff. After that, he began his lecture.

He had shifted to a new philosopher: Franz Kafka. The class would be discussing his famous novel *The Trial*. Although they weren't assigned to read the book in its entirety, he provided them with excerpts to peruse and interpret, along with an overview of the novel itself and Kafka's contributions to the field of philosophy.

The Trial is about a man known simply as Joseph K, who spends the entire story trying to learn what crime he has been accused of. This is where the term 'Kafkaesque' originates. It reflects Kafka's ability to place his characters in situations that are beyond their control or understanding. They become pawns in a massive machine that governs us all. We live in a gigantic, manufactured society that we have built ourselves, becoming our own jailers in a way," Joe said.

"You may have heard someone say, 'I feel like I'm stuck in a Kafka novel.' It means the same thing as saying 'Kafkaesque.'"

For the first time in class all year, Gia raised her hand. In fact, she rarely raised her hand in any of her classes. She was bashful and had a fear of public speaking, often trying to fly under the radar since she was already someone people saw as an outsider. Although she was perceived as very shy, Emily knew a different side of her; once you got to know her, she was anything but.

"Gia?" Professor Joe said, pointing to her. He looked a bit surprised at her participation.

"When that Marcus Aurelius guy said, 'the obstacle becomes the way' or whatever, how would that play out in real life?" she asked.

"Well, we've moved on from that particular segment, and we're discussing Kafka now, but I'd be happy to give you some examples before we return to today's lesson," he replied, not wanting to discourage her participation despite its timing.

"I suppose a real-life example might be a writer who focuses on novels but struggles to find success. She can't get one published despite her efforts and talent. So, she decides to adjust her path and try writing a television script—a series pilot. She presents it to some agents and ends up selling it," he explained. "If it weren't for the obstacle of failing as a novelist—at least financially—she wouldn't have discovered her niche as a television writer. That's just an example off the top of my head," he added. "Does that make sense?"

"What if the obstacle is a demon?" Gia asked, prompting a few giggles from the class. Emily noticed Kristen McClain glance back at Gia from the front, rolling her eyes dramatically. Kristen was a notorious "mean girl," and other girls feared getting on her bad side.

"Well, it depends on what kind of demon you're talking about," Professor Joe replied, carefully addressing the term Gia had used. "If someone's demon is something like alcoholism, an abusive relationship, or something similar, then counseling would be the appropriate way to heal."

"What if your demon is a monster?" Gia asked, eliciting more snickers and an even more disapproving reaction from Kristen. The class seemed eager to judge, as teenagers often do.

"A real monster?" Professor Joe asked, looking somewhat amused, but perhaps a little uneasy, too.

"Yes," Gia replied. "An evil spirit that manifests in the flesh and terrorizes people. What if that's what stands in your way?"

"I'm not sure Marcus Aurelius ever addressed that," Professor Joe stated diplomatically, just as Kristen McClain jumped into the conversation.

"Or how about the fact that monsters don't exist?" she said to Gia with a condescending smirk. The class laughed. "I think you've spent too many nights alone watching horror movies. Find some friends," she added.

Gia's face flushed into a blotchy red. She looked down at her desk while the class continued to titter for several seconds after the exchange.

Emily could see how belittled Gia felt, and it made her angry. She had never liked Kristen McClain—her arrogance, her privilege, her condescension. In an unexpected move, Emily decided to speak up.

"Fuck you," she said.

Silence fell over the room as she glared at Kristen, whose face turned ghost-white. "Don't talk to my friend like that," Emily told her firmly.

No one made a sound for what felt like a minute until Professor Joe finally spoke.

"Emily, that's not okay," he said in a disciplinary tone.

"That's fine," Kristen McClain retorted with a forced, phony laugh. "They can be outcasts together."

Emily was too furious to back down.

"Do you know you have a stupid laugh?" she shot back.

"*Emily…*" Professor Joe admonished.

"It's true," Emily continued despite his warning. "She has a big, toothy laugh that makes her face look ridiculous."

Kristen must have known it was true, as the remark seemed to sting her. She turned her vitriol right back at Emily.

"At least I'm not weird," she fired back.

"No, you're not weird," Emily said. "You're not unusual or unique or even interesting. You're Plain Jane, trying to feel better by insulting people who are far more gifted than you are."

"That's enough," Professor Joe asserted. He hadn't yelled, but it was as close as he would come to it. His strong voice silenced everyone.

"Emily, outside now," he commanded, pointing to the door. She got up, and they walked out together into the corridor.

In the hallway, he paused to let her calm down. He could see she was upset.

"No matter what you're going through, you cannot speak to people in my class like that," he said. She didn't reply.

"I'm not going to write you up for this because I understand you have a lot going on. I want you to go back to your dorm room and calm down," he continued.

Emily walked away without saying another word. She wasn't angry or even upset; she felt okay with it. She was proud of what she'd done. It was very much *unlike* her to speak up in any confrontation.

As she walked back to her room, she felt a sense of strength. She had a lot to think about. It felt like she was becoming a different person than she was just a few months ago, which made her realize she could be *very* different if she wanted to. She liked that.

Across the pond at Porter-Gaud School for Boys, Martin and Twerp were on a field trip of sorts. The boarders were taken out on a bus every two weeks to downtown for shopping—clothes, toiletries, food items, and such. They always had fun.

The two of them were in a clothing store browsing around. Twerp noticed Martin kept wandering close to the women's section.

"What are you doing?" he finally asked.

"I was thinking of buying Emily a gift," Martin said with an insecure shrug, glancing at Twerp to gauge his reaction.

"Don't," Twerp replied.

"Why not?"

"She'll think you're a stalker. You don't even have her phone number."

An attractive young woman in her twenties approached; she was a store employee, and the boys noticed her immediately.

"Can I help you gentlemen with anything?" she asked with a kind smile, exuding girl-next-door charm.

"No, thank you, ma'am," Martin replied in his best "aw-shucks" voice, the one he used to show how polite he was.

"Well, let me know if you need help with anything," she said before walking away. They watched her leave, all eyes on her rear end. Twerp leaned toward Martin and suggested, "She can help me with my virginity…"

The two boys laughed at the joke.

"Good one," Martin said, nodding sincerely.

"You can see her panty lines," Twerp pointed out.

"Yeah," Martin replied without much enthusiasm.

"I like that," Twerp said.

"Why?"

"It's hot. I try to imagine what color they are and what they're made of. I try to picture them wearing the panties. It exercises the mind, almost like playing chess or doing crossword puzzles," Twerp explained.

"You have issues," Martin said.

"Oh, come on! You've never liked visible panty lines?" Twerp pressed.

"I've never really thought about it," Martin admitted, then pivoted the conversation. "Speaking of which, do you want to go back to Ashley Hall this Friday?"

Twerp looked away, as if to ignore the question.

"What's wrong?" Martin asked.

"I don't think it's a good idea," Twerp said in a deflated voice.

"Are you kidding? "*Why?*" Martin asked incredulously. He thought Twerp would be on board.

"We could get in trouble," Twerp replied.

"Twerp, we met three cute girls. Let's go see if they want to hang out again."

When Twerp didn't respond, Martin asked pointedly, "You're not afraid, are you? Of that boogeyman stuff that happened?"

He may have been half-joking, but Twerp didn't smile or laugh. Instead, he looked at Martin and said, "Yeah, I am."

Martin's expression went blank; he could see Twerp was serious.

"Oh, come on, man…" he said, lacking conviction.

"That stuff that happened over there was not normal, Martin. I was raised in a religious home and never really believed in demons and devils. But something wasn't right that night—the things that went on. I don't want anything to do with it," he told him.

Martin was surprised. It wasn't like Twerp to take a stand on anything. Twerp was a natural-born follower, doing whatever Martin asked without question. It forced Martin to confront a reality he hadn't wanted to acknowledge: he was spooked by it too.

"Well, I'm going back," Martin said quietly, trying to convince Twerp he wasn't nervous. He wasn't sure he'd actually go alone, but this was the card he had to play.

"You can't pedal that boat over there by yourself," Twerp said.

"Yes, I can."

Twerp shrugged and said, "Well, I'm not going."

Friday night was football night at Porter-Gaud. The team was traditionally strong, and they even had cheerleaders—female cheerleaders—who came by bus from Ashley Hall School to perform on the sidelines and during halftime.

The game was the place to be, which is why Martin, Twerp, and Kenny were there. They weren't particularly big sports fans, and in his mind, Martin found himself rooting against his school's team. He had seen most of the players around campus and didn't like them very much—none more so than you-know-who.

"Martin," Twerp said, tapping him on the arm. Martin looked in the direction Twerp was pointing. There he was—Ricky Rude. He'd been suspended from participating in all after-school activities, including football, for his urination-inducing beatdown of Chris Kazemekis. As a result, he was in the stands in street clothes, watching the game rather than playing in it. He looked angrier than King Lear.

And wouldn't you know it? Just as Martin spotted him, Ricky noticed him back. Out of all the people at the game, what were the odds they'd make eye contact at that exact moment? About 100%. All set up by Twerp's knack for screwing things up.

Martin's stomach sank. He saw Rude's face, the complete lack of humanity in it. He looked like the shark from *Jaws* when it was eating Quint.

Martin couldn't hide his diminishing physical posture as their eyes locked. He dwindled like ice cream in a running microwave.

He had once read a book about prison that described death-row inmates needing to be dragged to the execution chamber because they would lose control of their legs from fear and wouldn't be able to walk. The guards would lug them down the corridor by the arms while the convicts cried uncontrollably. Martin understood that phenomenon better now.

"He looks pissed," Twerp said with a twinkle in his eye.

Ricky didn't pause as he began the short trek toward Martin. When he arrived, the crowd made room for him. A tight circle formed around the two boys. People listened and watched as Ricky pointed in Martin's face and uttered two horrifying words: "Cemetery. Halftime." Then he walked away.

The witnesses to the exchange sprang into action like journalists with a hot scoop, spreading the word. The executioner had spoken. *There will be blood.*

The cemetery he referenced was on campus, in a peripheral area that staff didn't bother to monitor. The school had inherited the patch of land through a will. Random headstones were scattered about, barely legible from the passing of time. There was a church next door, so it may have been their burial grounds originally.

Students sometimes met there to smoke pot or to fight.

"Meet me at the cemetery" was a common refrain at Porter-Gaud. It was where boys went to be boys.

The big digital game clock took on new meaning now. It was a metaphor for the countdown to Martin's departure from life.

People were staring at him, whispering. A crowd began to gather around him, encircling him as if to keep an eye on the sacrificial lamb. He felt ill.

Nothing at Porter-Gaud School for Boys drew a crowd like a Ricky Rude fight. He was the Mike Tyson of white prep schools.

The game clock was not Martin's friend that night. It ticked down like it had been snorting meth, and before he could compose himself, halftime had arrived.

The people surrounding Martin escorted him to the cemetery. For some reason, he complied. At that moment, he thought of the poem by Emily Dickinson that read: "Because I could not stop for death—he kindly stopped for me." It was like she was posthumously rubbing it in his face.

The trek to the cemetery was brief, and the group stayed with him every step of the way, though he didn't feel they were there for support.

By the time he arrived at said location, Martin could feel the crowd of students coursing with testosterone. He could almost smell it. They came to witness a massacre. Violence is a drug. Tonight, Martin, you die.

This is bullying, Martin thought. *Bullying! In this day and age. Has Lady Gaga taught us nothing?*

Martin doubted Ricky Rude listened to Lady Gaga, and that notion was confirmed when Ricky rolled up to the cemetery in grand fashion on his black motorcycle, adorned with skulls. He had Guns N' Roses blaring on the radio, the lyrics strikingly apropos to the moment: *"You're in the jungle, baby! You're gonna die!"*

Ricky shut down his bike and climbed off, sliding out of his leather jacket and pulling on black gloves. He looked like a doctor prepping for surgery—methodical and deliberate.

Martin felt so weak he thought his knees might buckle under him, causing him to collapse before a punch was even thrown.

And in truth, he *was* weak, which further exacerbated that feeling. It was like putting weakness on steroids, except the steroids made you weaker, not stronger—like anti-steroids.

Martin had heard about the "fight or flight response" that all animals possess. It's nothing more than a massive adrenaline dump coursing through the body, forcing a reaction of some kind. And before he could analyze it, he was running.

He couldn't believe it himself, as if he was watching someone else from a few feet away. His legs and arms pumped like four pistons in perfect synchronicity. He could really fly, too. That was one beneficial side effect of being both skinny and scared shitless: speed.

He didn't look back; he didn't want to know if anyone was chasing him. He was too far gone, racing across the campus of Porter-Gaud, trying to distance himself from the cemetery and the football field as much as possible. He would deal with the fallout later, figuring out what to say and how to justify his actions. He'd concoct whatever excuse he needed. If necessary, he'd live as a social pariah, cast out for his act of cowardice. Nothing mattered now except escape, and the farther he ran, the better he felt.

He reached the pond before he slowed down to look back. When he did, there was no one in sight.

He hunched over, hands on his knees, gasping for air for a few minutes. He kept glancing up, watching and listening for people. Nobody came. He grimaced as he felt a stitch in his side from the exertion. *I need to get into shape*, he thought.

Then, an overwhelming sense of shame washed over him. He felt like a coward, and a wimp. His high school career was over, and he would be publicly vilified.

He walked into the trees where they stored the boat, climbed onto it, and sat down to rest. He felt small and humiliated, recognizing he didn't even have the courage to fight. Chris Kazemekis may have lost, but he didn't run away.

It all made him think of home and how much he missed being there. He hadn't wanted to go away to boarding school; his feelings were hurt when his parents encouraged him to consider it, as if they no longer wanted him at home. He felt so sad about it. So lonely. He missed his mother and father, and his cat. And then he began to cry.

He covered his mouth with the front of his shirt to muffle the noise in case anyone was nearby, but it was mostly a way of not having to hear it himself. He sat there and cried hard for a few minutes. He cried about all of it, and a few other things, too.

When he was finished, he climbed off the boat, grabbed it by the front, and dragged it with all his might toward the pond. It felt much heavier without Twerp, which surprised him; he hadn't thought Twerp added much horsepower. He was still fighting against the occasional spasms of a post-crying episode—those quick bursts of inhalations and little sobs, along with watery discharge from his nose.

He managed to get the boat into the water and he climbed aboard. He wasn't sure if he could pedal it all the way across the pond by himself, but he knew he didn't want to go back to campus. He wanted to disappear from Porter-Gaud and get as far away as possible.

Martin was only about a hundred feet from shore when he heard a voice call out.

"Martin!"

He looked back and saw Twerp waving him in. Martin turned the boat around and picked him up at the beach. Twerp climbed aboard.

"You're coming?" Martin asked.

"Yeah. Last time was weird, but I still had fun. Let's go back," Twerp said as the two boys began pedaling the boat together. They remained quiet for a minute before Martin brought it up.

"I ran," he said, needing to put it out there without excuses.

"I know," Twerp responded.

"I feel stupid," Martin admitted.

"What choice did you have? I would have run too," Twerp said with a supportive chuckle. "Besides, you made Rude look silly, standing there all by himself, too slow to catch you."

They both laughed at Ricky's expense, though it was a small consolation. Still, Martin appreciated Twerp having his back; he needed that. He then shifted the conversation.

"Hey, name a celebrity you had a crush on growing up," he said to Twerp, who thought about it for a moment.

"Serena Williams," he said.

"Really?" Martin asked.

"Oh, yeah."

"Why her?"

"I don't know. She's so *alpha*. Don't tell anyone this, but I've always fantasized about having a girlfriend who could kick my ass," Twerp confided.

"Huh. That's weird."

"I used to imagine Serena wearing a one-piece Wonder Woman bathing suit, scooping me up like a professional wrestler and body-slamming me through a glass coffee table," Twerp said in a moment of total honesty. He nodded enthusiastically at Martin for some affirmation. None was forthcoming.

"Damn, Twerp," was all Martin could say.

The two boys pedaled in silence for about fifteen minutes as they made their way back to Ashley Hall School, where a different monster awaited—one much scarier than Ricky Rude.

artin and Twerp sat on the loveseat across from Gia, who was silently staring at them. In fact, they were all silent. The boys had arrived at Gia's dorm after making landfall, unaware of where Emily lived.

"This is awkward," Twerp whispered, wiping his damp palms on the thighs of his pants.

Gia dialed her cell phone. The boys could hear the ringing and then Emily's voice as she answered.

"Hey," Emily said.

"You got your phone back?" Gia asked.

"Just today."

"Dork and Dorker are here," Gia said.

"Who?" they heard Emily ask.

"*Dork* and *Dorker*," Gia repeated, louder this time, ensuring she made eye contact with the boys in a ninth-graders version of a power move. Martin and Twerp looked away, not wanting to pull the tail of a lioness.

"Oh, those two guys are back?" Emily said.

Martin and Twerp exchanged glances.

"At least she remembers us," Martin whispered to Twerp with an optimistic shrug.

"I texted Betsy, too. Come by," Gia said into the phone. She hung up, and silence fell again.

Though Gia didn't explicitly say she was happy they were there, Martin could tell by the way she broke out the Ouija board and began setting it up that she was glad for the extra bodies.

Two minutes later, Betsy tapped on the open door and walked in. She hugged Gia and sat down without acknowledging the boys. Shortly thereafter, Emily arrived.

"Good timing," Betsy said to her with a smile. Emily smiled back.

"Hi," Martin said to Emily, raising his hand in a goofy wave, as if he were in class rather than greeting someone.

"Hi," Emily replied. No one else exchanged pleasantries.

Martin felt good. The night was off to a solid start; Emily had said hello to him, which he considered a win.

Gia shut the door, turned to the group, and said, "Let's Ouija, bitches."

Despite Gia's enthusiasm, the mood among the group could best be described as worried. Martin was still riding high on the endorphins from Emily's greeting, having already forgotten the worries that plagued him just an hour before. Twerp, however, looked concerned, haunted by flashbacks from the last Ouija session. Betsy appeared uneasy as well.

Emily was in a perpetual state of jitters since her face-to-face encounter with Baghead, and it was evident to everyone by the way she overreacted to every little noise or sudden movement.

"Do they know?" Emily asked Gia.

"I didn't tell them," Gia replied, as Martin and Twerp exchanged curious glances, wondering what new information was about to emerge.

"What happened?" Martin asked. It took Emily a moment to collect herself before she answered.

"He showed up. I saw him," she said, her expression grave. "He killed Miss Warburton—one of the dorm monitors."

"Holy crap," Martin exclaimed.

He could see how shaken Emily was as she spoke. He glanced at Betsy; she was a wreck. Gia, however, seemed composed, ready to cut through the chatter and get down to the business of "seancing". Martin turned to Twerp, who wore an unconvinced look on his face, as if he thought this whole ordeal was a prank.

But to Martin, this was major news. *Murder?* What had he stepped into? Was it real?

"Why don't you just shoot him?" Twerp suggested, his tone glib, as if mocking the seriousness of the situation. Gia didn't appreciate his flippancy.

"Because we don't have a gun," she said, glaring at him. "Do *you* have a gun, Twit?" she added, leaning forward toward him.

"It's Twerp, not Twit. And no, I don't have a gun," he replied, looking away from her truculent stare.

"Well, there goes that idea," she said with derision.

"You could buy one," Twerp offered, perhaps trying to save face or provoke her further. She lost patience with his game.

"Ya know, Twerp, if brains were dynamite, you couldn't blow your nose," she said to him.

She then turned her attention back to the Ouija board, but Twerp managed to squeak out one more half-hearted remark.

"Say it to my face," he challenged.

She was ready for him. Leaning forward again, she fixed her gaze on him and said quite clearly, "If brains were dynamite, you couldn't blow your nose."

The others watched the exchange in silence, ever-so-slightly amused. Twerp noticed Martin looking at him, and despite his usual feebleness, he remained defiant.

"Say it to my face," he repeated, turning toward Martin as if he was hoping she would let it go and allow him to declare victory. It did not work out that way.

When Gia stood up and walked around the table to confront Twerp, Martin thought for a moment she was going to punch him. Instead, she leaned down, put her face right in his, squeezed his cheeks together with one hand, and said, "If brains were dynamite, *Twerp*, you couldn't blow your fucking nose."

They held that pose for several seconds before Twerp, with scrunched cheeks, chirped, "Say it to my face."

"She *is* saying it to your face!" Martin yelled as Betsy and Emily moaned their discontent. Gia shook her head, walked back around the table, and took her seat.

"You guys…" Betsy whispered, not finishing her sentence. They all watched Gia finish setting up the board.

Emily took Betsy by the hand, worried about her. She was also concerned about herself and her own mental state. She felt as though she was clinging to her sanity. She knew now that none of this was a hoax or a product of her overactive imagination. Gia was right; she was haunted.

Emily had known the truth all along. Her mother had managed to instill the tiniest bit of doubt over the years, making her wonder if maybe it *had* all been misconstrued by the inexperienced eyes of a young child. She realized now that she hadn't, after seeing Baghead again—in the flesh—some ten years later. She touched him. She could still feel his big, soft belly pushing in like a plastic garbage bag full of Jell-O as she plunged that knife into his gut, the uncomfortable warmth of squirting blood coating her fingers.

The recollection made her subconsciously rub her hand, as if trying to clean it for the millionth time since the stabbing.

She remembered the dried blood becoming sticky. It took repeated scrubbings to get it all off. Some of it burrowed under her fingernails, forcing her to clip them so short that they hurt for days whenever she touched something.

She would only eat with her left hand—the untainted one—and wasn't sure that would ever change. She brushed her teeth lefty, too, not wanting her right hand to come anywhere near her mouth with even the slightest possibility that there could be remnants of his DNA lingering. The thought alone made her examine every inch of her palm, fingers, and nails once again.

"What's our goal here?" Emily asked, still looking at her hand, trying to distract herself from thinking about the blood stains.

"We have to reach out to him. We have to engage and find out what he wants from…us. Or, you, maybe," Gia said. "Remember that whole impediment to action advances action—or however it goes," she added as she finalized the setup.

"This is a really cool board," Martin said, inspecting the Ouija more closely. "I didn't notice all the details the first time we used it."

"Thank you," Gia replied, not looking at him. Still, she seemed flattered. Twerp noticed and tried to cash in as well.

"Yeah, I was about to say the same thing. *Really* nice," he said to Gia, waiting for her acknowledgment, which didn't come.

"Now, follow my lead," she instructed, once again reciting the incantations to launch the séance.

The group held hands in a circle, their eyes darting around at one another. Emily felt a cold breeze waft through the room, as if the air conditioning had come on.

"Did anyone feel that?" she asked while Gia continued chanting.

"Feel what?" Betsy whispered.

"That chill?" Emily said, noticing Gia had stopped chanting, her eyes still closed.

"No," Betsy replied, "but it seems like it got darker all of a sudden."

"I noticed that, too," Martin said to Betsy, looking concerned.

"I've had enough already. I don't want to do this," Betsy said. It sounded like she was pleading for mercy—the awkwardness of her delivery. Emily could tell she was struggling.

"It's okay, Betsy. We don't have to if you don't want," she said supportively. She would have been fine leaving it alone tonight as well.

"We need to," Gia insisted. "And we need everyone to participate. You can't leave," she told Betsy.

Emily thought she was being forward, even insensitive, but there was no further discussion. Gia immediately resumed her focus on the séance. Betsy stayed, either out of loyalty to her friends or perhaps fear of being alone if she left.

So, they began—all five of them placing a finger on the planchette. Gia started with a series of softer, almost perfunctory questions about whether any spirits were present and whether they were good or evil. It didn't take long for her to pull out the heavy artillery, though. She relished it, that was clear. She was the Barbara Walters of mediums, facilitating the séance with confidence.

The board was active, so much so that it had all five kids on high alert. The planchette moved too quickly for anyone to be intentionally maneuvering it, zipping around the board with perfect dexterity and no hesitation. Emily felt they could have removed their fingers from the planchette, and it still would have floated. She was afraid to suggest the idea for fear it might actually happen.

Emily believed there were spirits in the room. For the first time, she could feel their presence, and she could see that Gia felt them too.

The breezy air suddenly smelled like unwashed human flesh, and the temperature fluctuated noticeably. Sometimes it became difficult to breathe; other times, Emily felt as if she couldn't speak, or believed she wouldn't be able to stand if she tried. She was in a trance of sorts and wondered if the others were experiencing the same.

Gia remained Steady-Freddy, manning the helm like a mad sea captain, valiantly spinning the wooden steering wheel of her ship as they were tossed about by a violent storm, their vessel rocking in wild undulations.

"Is Baghead here?" Gia finally asked. The question jarred Emily. The mention of his name made her tremble and shrink.

The planchette moved decisively to the letters: W, E, A, R, E.

"What does he mean, *we are?*" Martin asked.

"Him and the spirits he's captured, maybe?" Emily replied, her voice shaking so much it sounded like she was about to cry.

Martin looked at her with heartfelt compassion as he placed his hand on her back and said, "It's going to be okay, Emily."

She nodded at him once and managed an appreciative smile. She tried to say "thanks," but the words simply vanished.

"Who are you hunting?" Gia demanded of the spirit.

There was a pause as all ten eyeballs were laser-focused on the board. Emily believed she could hear the collective heartbeats in the room as they waited for an answer. A slight sense of relief washed over her when the planchette moved to the letter V, then to I, C, T, O, and R.

"Who's Victor?" Gia asked.

Emily's eyes widened as she realized what it meant.

"Professor Joe," she said in a panicky whisper. They all turned to her. "That's his Victor Frankenstein," she added.

She pulled her hand off the board, and everyone else followed suit, as if being freed from something.

"We need to contact him," Emily said as she grabbed her cell phone and dialed his number. She had it saved along with her other teachers, which was standard protocol at the school. It rang several times before going to an electronic voicemail message.

She hung up and texted him. They waited. There was no response.

"Maybe we should call the police," Betsy suggested.

"And say what?" Gia asked. "That a Ouija Board told us he might be in trouble?"

"We need to go to his house," Emily insisted.

"I'm sure he's fine," Martin said dismissively.

"How do you know?" Emily shot back. He didn't respond.

Twerp looked uncomfortable. He sensed another misadventure on the horizon, and he wasn't okay with it.

"We need to go back," Twerp said to Martin, trying to nip it in the bud. "We can't go looking for a missing teacher. We have to get back to campus, Martin."

"Then go," Gia said without looking at him. She was already searching for Professor Joe's address on her laptop and found it quickly. "He lives on Ogier Street. It's close," she said, turning the computer toward Emily. "We can ride our bikes there or take an Uber."

Martin and Twerp exchanged glances, looking to each other for help.

"We need to head back, Martin," Twerp said again. It made sense, and Martin nodded in agreement. The five of them stood up and quickly split ways. The girls were on a mission to find Professor Joe, while the boys would make their way back across the pond. Nobody seemed to feel good about any of it.

Martin and Twerp were pedaling across the pond, heading back to Porter-Gaud School for Boys.

"How about that Gia, huh?" Twerp asked, raising his eyebrows.

"What about her?" Martin replied.

"She's a real firecracker," Twerp said.

"You like her?" Martin asked. Twerp kept looking straight ahead, a small grin on his face.

"The way she got up in my face—so dismissive and rude. It's irresistible," he said, his voice trailing off as if he were talking more to himself than to Martin.

"Don't let Serena Williams find out," Martin joked.

The boys pedaled for several more minutes, listening to the soft splashing of the water around them. Martin fell deep into thought. Something was bothering him, and he spoke up.

"We should have stayed with the girls," he told Twerp. "We shouldn't have left them."

"We didn't have a choice. We have to get back to campus," Twerp replied.

"No," Martin said, shaking his head. "What if they're not okay? What if something happens to them?"

Twerp didn't respond. Martin gave him a soft backhanded slap on the shoulder, as if to emphasize that what he was about to say was gospel.

"I'm not doing that anymore. You hear me, Twerp? Never again. I'm not leaving or running away scared. I'm done being afraid."

"The girls are going to be fine," Twerp said, trying to reassure his friend.

"Even so. I'm not doing it anymore," Martin emphasized. The two boys pedaled on; there wasn't much farther to go.

Professor Joe rented the house he lived in. He'd been teaching at Ashley Hall School for many years. He found a place he liked, moved in, and never left. The rent was affordable, and the location was great, so he never bothered to buy a home of his own. This still seemed strange to his colleagues, some of whom would rib him about it—his fear of commitment. It kept him single. It kept him renting. It kept him tattoo-free. Nothing permanent.

Joe would joke, "My trust issues stem from the girl at the drive-thru window telling me there was a straw in the bag, only to find out a mile down the road there wasn't."

He had a dry sense of humor, but it was endearing.

After the séance, Emily, Gia, and Betsy rode their bikes to his house. It had grown dark outside, and the girls were off-campus past the allowable hours. They were violating every rule and would surely be written up if they got caught.

Fortunately, his house was only a few minutes away. The cool air felt good on Emily's face and helped calm her nerves.

When they arrived, they leaned their bikes against some trees and walked around the front and side, looking for signs of life.

"Maybe we should knock," Betsy suggested.

"You do it," Gia replied.

"No, you do it," Betsy countered.

"I'm not doing it," Gia insisted.

"I'll do it," Emily said, flanked by her two friends. She tapped a few times and waited. When no one came, she knocked again, harder. There was still no response.

"Maybe he's just out of town or something," Betsy said.

"We're breaking in," Emily declared as she scanned for witnesses.

"Are you serious?" Gia asked, her excitement barely contained.

"Yup," Emily affirmed.

Gia smiled and said, "I like your style, bro."

Emily led them to the back of the house, away from the street and out of view of the neighbors. She found a plastic milk crate and set it up to help them reach the windows.

"You *guys…*" Betsy warned from the back of the pack.

Professor Joe must not have been too worried about crime because, as it turned out, all of his windows were unlocked. Emily discovered this when the first one she tried slid right up.

She jumped up and shimmied her hips through the small opening. Gia assisted by placing her hands on Emily's buttocks and giving her a push, even adding a playful squeeze.

"You could have bought me dinner first," Emily quipped from inside the open window.

Gia jumped up next, adrenaline coursing through her veins. This was a *crime,* and Emily knew she was loving it. Within seconds, Gia had wiggled her way inside Professor Joe's house.

"We shouldn't be doing this," Betsy said, standing on the milk crate and talking to the girls through the opening. She sounded uneasy.

"Get your ass in here before someone sees you," Gia told her, prompting Betsy to hop into the space. With the assistance of her two friends, she was in the house, too.

"That hurt my boobs," Betsy said, massaging them for a moment.

"At least you have boobs," Gia replied, prompting a quick giggle from all three of them.

"Sshh," Emily said softly as she scanned the dark room.

"What are we gonna do?" Gia whispered.

"We're going to look around for him," Emily responded.

"What if he has a gun and thinks we're intruders?" Gia asked.

"We *are* intruders," Betsy added. "And you know what else? What if we're in the wrong house?"

These were valid points, Emily thought.

"Well, damn the torpedoes," Emily said as she forged ahead like Angela Lansbury.

"What does that even mean?" Gia asked.

"It means just follow behind me. Stay close. If I scream and run, *you* scream and run. Got it?" Emily instructed. Gia gave a hand salute while Betsy nodded.

Emily led the way as they crept further into the house, each hunched over, eyes wide open trying to fight against the darkness.

"Hello? Professor Joe?" Emily called, her voice sounding weak.

They moved from one room to the next, peering around each corner, skittish and jumpy. Betsy *gasped,* causing the other two to do the same.

"What?" Gia asked.

"Nothing. I thought I saw something," Betsy said. Emily sighed, and they kept moving forward.

"Professor Joe? Are you here?" Emily called again, this time with more force.

Gia was right on her tail, content to let Emily remain at the front. She pointed over Emily's shoulder at a closed door down the hall. They could see through the crack that a light was on in the room.

They made their way to the door, and Emily grasped the knob, slowly turning it, which made the faintest of sounds. She pushed the door open, and all three of them *gasped* at what they saw.

Professor Joe was sitting dead in a chair, his body stiff in a most awkward and uncomfortable pose, resembling a person with polio. His eyes were stuck open, and his mouth was agape as if he were trying to scream but couldn't. On the floor next to him lay a clear plastic bag with a spatter of blood on the inside.

Betsy turned and fled immediately. Gia tugged on Emily's shirt and said, "Let's get out of here!"

Emily didn't leave. Instead, she approached him, all the way up to his lifeless body, and placed two fingers on his neck to check for a pulse. She had seen it done in movies but had never tried it herself.

"He's cold," she said to Gia, her voice trembling.

"Let's go," Gia said pleadingly, pointing back toward the entrance. She looked terrified, on the brink of tears. For all the ghosts and goblins in her life, it turned out that seeing a dead body wasn't so fun.

Emily couldn't stop staring at his face. It was frozen with fear, like a Halloween mask. He barely resembled the man she knew; he looked more like a wax figure. This was in stark contrast to the calm, cerebral person he had been.

Tears streamed down her cheeks. He had finally met his son—his monster. She felt a wave of sorrow for him, sitting there all alone. It never should have happened.

She reached out and placed her open hand over his eyes, closing them. That was the first time she had touched a dead person.

She then pushed his mouth shut, which proved more difficult. His jaw was locked open, stiff and tight. It resisted her attempts to close it, which was deeply disturbing. With a final push, it popped shut, causing his teeth to clack together. After that, he just looked dead, and no longer tormented.

"Rest in peace," she whispered. She meant it. She looked back at Gia, who was halfway into the hallway.

"Emily, let's go!" Gia insisted, pointing toward the door.

A moment later, they left.

At the police station, the three girls were interviewed separately. The school and their parents were contacted.

The girls explained to the authorities that they were worried about Professor Joe—that they'd called and texted him with questions about an assignment but had not received a response. They decided to check on him.

The story checked out. The police did not suspect the girls of involvement in anything. Three fourteen-year-old females would have struggled to kill a grown man in his own home. Detectives examined the scene and determined it was a natural death; he had suffered a heart attack. That much was true.

Only Gia told the whole truth. She was deeply shaken after seeing his dead body, especially in the condition they found it. It would give her nightmares. So, she shared everything. She told them about Baghead, their séances, Miss Warburton, and the night at Kelly Hall, as well as the cassette tape they had discovered. The detectives thought she was crying out for attention, which made her angry and desperate. She tried to convince them otherwise.

"What about the plastic bag on the floor?" she asked, as if she were the one conducting the interrogation.

"We believe he was shake-and-baking some chicken, Gia. There was a packet of wings thawing in the kitchen," the detective replied.

"There was blood in the bag," Gia insisted, trying to persuade them to investigate further.

"He probably cut his finger while cooking," the other detective said. Then he added, "What's this really about for you?"

"What do you mean?" she asked.

"The way you dress, the macabre jewelry, the doom-and-gloom imagery you project. Is this story you're telling us more about getting clicks on your social media? We found your YouTube channel."

In that moment, she realized this was a waste of time.

Emily didn't bother trying; she knew better. Betsy mostly cried as the detectives led her down the path they wanted to hear. She complied. When her father came to sit with her, she felt an overwhelming sense of relief.

The school administration imposed no reprimands on the girls. The death of their professor, following closely on the heels of Miss Warburton's passing, dealt a "one-two" punch to the entire campus. The administration was reluctant to appear insensitive by punishing the students who had discovered his corpse.

Emily's mother spoke to her over the phone about the situation, and so did Gia's parents. The girls reassured them that it wasn't a big deal and that they were okay. They lied. Gia felt there was no point in telling her parents the truth after the police had not believed her.

A couple of days later, Emily sent a text message to Martin, informing him of what had happened. She thought he and Twerp should know; they were now part of this situation. She had something else to tell them, too—something to *show* them. She asked them to come to Ashley Hall as soon as they could, emphasizing that it was important.

Martin and Twerp made the easy decision to show support for their future wives—and Betsy—by taking an Uber to Ashley Hall School at Emily's request. This time, they did it properly. They requested and received permission to visit the school, and the girls had listed them as guests.

"We've been beckoned," Twerp said in the car.

"Why do you keep saying that?" Martin asked, annoyed.

"Because it's true. We were *beckoned* by the ladies."

"You sound like you're in 18th-century London when you talk like that," Martin replied.

"What are you talking about?"

"We've been *beckoned*," Martin mimicked in his best/worst Twerp voice.

Twerp leaned toward Martin and nodded as if he were explaining something to an imbecile. "It's a word, Martin. It's an English word. I'm sorry if you're not polished enough to know when to use it."

"You want a top hat and a pocket watch to wear?" Martin asked.

"You make no sense," Twerp said, staring back out the window. It had become easier for Martin to convince Twerp to come along since he'd fallen for Gia and her alpha ways.

"I wonder what Gia will be wearing," Twerp mused aloud.

"Oh, brother," Martin muttered to himself.

"Don't act like you're not excited. You'd ride a skateboard barefoot to the West Coast for a sniff of Emily's socks."

"Settle down, Twerp."

Twerp shifted to a more conciliatory tone.

"Maybe we should have a double wedding. How cool would that be?" he said, giving Martin an elbow to the ribs.

Martin fell silent, contemplating. The idea had merit. *Any* scenario where he'd be married to Emily would earn a stiff thumbs-up from him. He could hardly hear her name without his heart fluttering. If he focused hard enough, he could close his eyes and smell her body lotion.

The two of them squirmed in their underpants the whole ride over, stealing glances at the pond, which looked smaller than it had when they pedaled across it.

They arrived at the campus quickly and met the girls in Gia's room once again. As they entered, Martin stepped toward Emily and gave her an unexpected hug—unexpected for her. She recoiled slightly but managed to pat him on the shoulder, offering a feeble consolation. The exchange was awkward, and the others noticed.

Twerp changed the subject like a good friend.

"What happened to the teacher?" he asked.

"Baghead got him," Gia replied.

"How is that possible? He's not even real," Twerp said.

"He is real," Emily asserted, raising her voice an octave. She didn't appreciate the implication that she was lying or delusional. "He's a spirit, but he manifests in the flesh."

"How?" Twerp asked, still unconvinced.

"I don't know, exactly. But I washed his dried blood off my hand," she said, shaking her hands as if they were still wet.

"If he can bleed, he can die," Gia added.

Emily nodded with hope. "Maybe," she said.

"What did you want us to come over here for?" Martin asked, his voice tinged with meekness as he still processed his fumbled greeting with Emily.

Emily closed the dorm room door and dropped her backpack. She unzipped it and retrieved the VHS tape.

"I watched this today on another VCR after Professor Joe was killed. The tape should be blank, according to him. He said that each time someone was murdered, they would disappear from the recording. It's like a living scorecard, or a bill of some kind," she said.

"From who?" Martin asked.

"From whatever demon they made a deal with that night," Emily told him, prompting spooked glares from the others. She continued.

"He was the last one alive," she said as she turned on Gia's TV and inserted the tape into the VCR.

All five of them sat down in front of the screen. The room felt cold, and a nervous silence filled the air. They all sensed that something ominous was approaching—a bad moon rising.

She pressed the "play" button with the tip of a knife, and the machine began to hum. The blue screen changed colors as the recorded material started. It was a close-up of a housefly buzzing against a pane of glass. The sound was irritating in its persistence, as the fly repeatedly struck the glass, trying to escape to the other side. The camera focused on the insect, and the noise it made was insufferable.

"What are we watching?" Martin asked.

"It's a housefly on a pane of glass," Emily said. "Professor Joe talked about it in class one day—the fly's inability to understand that it can't get through the glass."

"Is this the whole video?" Twerp asked.

"No," Emily replied. "Just watch."

They continued watching for a couple more minutes until the camera pulled back from the insect. The room on the TV was dim, but they could make out shadows and hear something: voices.

The cameraman moved through a doorway into the hall. The camera floated along as the voices grew louder and closer. People were talking, creating a murmur, but it was impossible to discern what was being said.

Then the wandering camera turned into a dorm room—the door wide open. Inside, five teenagers were peering down at a heating vent in the wall, oblivious to being filmed.

Martin recognized it immediately. They were watching *themselves* in Kelly Hall. He could hear their own voices speaking the exact words they had exchanged that first night, all recorded on tape.

"What's that in the vent?" they heard Martin ask on the video.

"Holy shit. It's *us*," Gia exclaimed as she recognized the people on the screen. Then she heard her own voice on the recording.

"I don't know," Gia responded to Martin as she knelt down to get a better look into the vent.

"It looks like a book," Emily whispered on the recording.

The five friends in Gia's room sat there, stunned and speechless, watching themselves on video. They were in shock, trying to comprehend what it all meant.

"Unscrew the vent," Twerp urged on the video, pulling out his jackknife. He fumbled it as he attempted to open the screwdriver gadget.

Gia picked it up from the floor and began the slow process of turning each of the twelve screws, removing them one at a time. She was filming with her GoPro and narrating, too.

"What is it?" they heard Emily ask on the tape.

"It's a video cassette," Gia said as she reached into the dark space and retrieved it from the vent. She held it up for everyone to see.

"Shit just got real," Twerp said.

"Would you shut up?" Gia shot back.

"Who puts anything on a video cassette anymore?" Emily remarked.

"It's got to be old," Gia declared. "Come on, let's see if there's a VCR in one of these rooms."

They watched themselves exit the room, unaware of being filmed.

Inside Gia's room—set in the present—Betsy had seen enough.

"Shut it off!" she yelled, jarring the group back to reality. She repeated it, louder. "Shut it off, Emily!"

Emily pressed "stop." She could see that Betsy had started crying. "Why are we on that tape?" Betsy asked through her sobs.

"He's going to kill us all," Gia whispered, looking mortified.

"Don't say that," Emily replied.

"I'm not okay with this. I'm really not," Betsy said, her voice cracking.

"It's going to be all right," Martin said, trying to calm the girls. "We'll help you. We'll help each other."

"How?" Gia snapped. "We don't even know if we can."

"Professor Joe created him. There's got to be a way he can be destroyed," Emily said, attempting to follow Martin's lead. "We just have to find out how before…" Her voice trailed off. She didn't finish her sentence; she didn't need to.

On the Uber ride home, Twerp and Martin sat in the backseat, watching the pond pass by on the opposite side this time. Night had fallen.

"You got the Heisman Trophy back there," Twerp said.

"What?" Martin asked, confused by the statement.

"When you went in for that hug at the beginning of the night. Re-fucking-jected, *boy!*" Twerp said with genuine schadenfreude.

"Okay, Twerp. First off, the expression is "getting the Heisman," not "getting the Heisman *trophy*." That would mean I'd actually won the Heisman Trophy. "Getting the Heisman" just means you got rejected—which I did not," Martin replied.

"I know what it means. And you do, too, now. You got dismissed like a student when the bell rings to end seventh period, bro-ski," Twerp said, giving him a taunting poke.

"Get your hands off me," Martin said as they began poking each other in the ribs with their first two fingers.

"Cut the crap," Martin said, slapping Twerp's hand. They stopped tussling, both remembering they were in a stranger's car.

"Besides, I didn't see you making any progress with Gia," Martin added.

"No, but I definitely saw her panty lines through those tight pants. Did you notice that?" Twerp said with a smile.

"Well, good luck. Maybe someday you can marry a pair of her underwear," Martin replied.

"It wouldn't be the worst day of my life," Twerp whispered to himself as he went back to gazing out the car window.

The two boys sat quietly for several minutes, listening to the hum of the road. Twerp slipped into deep thought, his expression growing serious. He wasn't smiling anymore. He turned to Martin and asked, "You really think he's gonna kill us?"

The comment prompted the Uber driver to glance at them in her rearview mirror.

Martin was taken aback by the bluntness of the question. He hadn't even had time to consider it. He could see that it was bothering Twerp.

"I hope not," Martin said. The two boys remained silent for the rest of the ride.

The book was titled *The Philosophy of Voodoo, Satanism, Wicca, and Other Non-Traditional Religions* by Volkan Krauthhammer.

The title itself seemed unnecessarily wordy, taking up most of the front cover, but it left no room for confusion about the content. The author's name was in smaller print at the bottom of the cover. Emily thought it sounded cool; there was something very no-nonsense about it. This guy would have never ended up mowing lawns for a living with a name like that.

She remembered Joe telling her he'd used it to conjure the haunting, so she pored over his extensive collection of books, looking at each author, hoping to find it. She did.

The physical presentation of the book was simple: small and thin. It had a hardcover, and it was *hard*. You could put a dent in someone's head with one of the corners. The binding was wrapped in faded red velvet that felt nice to the touch.

The lettering on the front was gold and slightly raised from the scrunched velvet wrapping, giving it a satiny texture. The text on the pages was small and not easy on the eyes. This was philosophy; it was meant to be dense.

Emily felt as if she were holding something important as she slid it out of its spot in the bookcase and examined it for the first time. She wasn't sure if this feeling had emerged organically or if it was influenced by what Professor Joe had told her about the book.

She had done some research of her own. The book was banned, that much was true. Not banned in the way people claim that books with pornographic references are "banned" in elementary schools. This book was forbidden by the government of Romania and all its allies with whom it shared extradition treaties—prohibited from being read, printed, sold, or loaned out from a library. The penalty for possession was one day in jail or a $50 fine, which diminished the weight of the threat.

Still, the book was banned.

You couldn't find a copy of it in print anywhere. The author himself—a self-described "rebel" philosopher—had been killed by a radical cleric offended by the content of this very book. Joe's copy was one of only thirteen in existence.

So, she wondered to herself, was it the story behind the book that made her feel this way? Or was there something more—her instincts at play?

Her neck ached from holding her head sideways while perusing the titles in the bookcase. Initially, she thought he might have stored it in a safer, more protected location—perhaps locked up. However, her research revealed that there wasn't much demand or respect for the author's work. Volkan Krauthhammer was considered a dilettante by the academic community at large.

Joe kept it in his small office at the school, among a collection of other books in a simple bookcase. His office door didn't even have a lock. Maybe he didn't want the book at home for some reason. Perhaps the content made him uncomfortable, sleeping with it nearby. Or maybe Emily was overthinking it, as she was prone to do.

That's what bothered her—she wasn't thinking at all; she was feeling, which is very different. The human mind can play tricks on us, but our emotions don't know how to lie. One's feelings and instincts will always be their truest guide in life if they allow it.

Emily understood this, even at her young age. Yet, it was hard not to let her mind take control. She was smart, and she knew it. Smart almost to a fault. Intelligent people often believe they can reason their way through things that aren't connected to logic.

She took the book from his office, returned to her dorm room, and settled into a chair with her roommate Dahlia just ten feet away. For hours, she read, jotting down notes along the way. She and Dahlia exchanged only a few words, more out of the need for a break than a genuine desire to converse.

The writing wasn't as heavy as some of the philosophy Professor Joe assigned. He often cherry-picked lighter excerpts from philosophers to avoid overwhelming the young students. They read passages, but not entire books. He aimed to introduce them to philosophy and ignite their enthusiasm without making it boring or obscure.

Emily enjoyed reading philosophy. She knew Gia would be excited to learn about the book's tainted history. However, Gia hated reading and would likely grow bored with much of the content. Emily planned to break it down for her.

There was something unique in the writing. She connected with it and began to understand why Professor Joe had chosen this exact book to help shape the DNA of the monster he'd created.

"I didn't think it would work," she could still hear him saying, his voice heavy with regret. His words haunted her.

But it *had* worked—perhaps by way of serendipity, but the bad kind. *Was there a word for that?* The act of accidentally creating something horrible through a stroke of luck? She had to look it up and found "zemblanity," defined as "unpleasant events occurring by design." Close enough.

She felt a pit in her stomach as she read. She had grown accustomed to that feeling by now. It was as if she always needed to use the bathroom, but never could. She was so jumpy that she gasped a little whenever the fan turned on in the dormitory to circulate fresh air. Dahlia noticed.

"Are you okay?" Dahlia asked, her concern sincere.

"There's been a lot going on," Emily said to her. They fell into a brief silence before Emily added, "I just want you to know, Dahlia, that I think you're a good roommate, and I'm glad we live together."

Dahlia wasn't sure why Emily felt the need to share that, but she appreciated it. A smile crossed her face, and she felt a rush of emotion.

"Thanks," she replied. "I really appreciate you saying that, and I'm glad we live together, too."

That one kind remark made her feel closer to Emily.

"Are you hungry?" Emily asked.

"Yeah," Dahlia answered.

For the first time that semester, the two girls went to dinner together. They ate in the cafeteria, mostly in silence. Afterward, they walked back to their dorm room. Emily sat down to read, while Dahlia worked on homework at her desk a few feet away. They didn't speak anymore that night; they had said enough.

10

"He's capturing their souls in the mirror," Emily said as she walked through the door of Gia's room. Gia looked riveted right away, waiting for more.

"This philosopher that Professor Joe was so enamored with wrote his own theory about heaven and hell. He claimed there isn't one single hell, but hundreds, maybe thousands, all created by man. New ones can be spawned at any time, either accidentally or intentionally.

"He described it as impregnating the devil, so she gives birth to a new child. Evil needs to proliferate just like good does; it's no different from the physical world, but it takes place transcendentally.

"It's an immaculate conception of its own—the flip side of the coin to Mary and Jesus. That's why he got banned. He angered the church, and they insisted the Romanian government denounce the author and forbid future publication of his book," Emily said, pausing for a quick breath as she tossed her backpack onto Gia's loveseat.

"Professor Joe created a monster to stand at the helm of his own private inferno for people who have lived as frauds. Baghead captures them. That's what he does. He's a collector," she said.

"How does he capture them?" Gia asked.

"The author writes about the human spirit leaving the body at death, moving from the physical world to the transcendental world. According to his theory, the energy that *is life* leaves us when we die, floating unprotected between the two worlds for just one-trillionth of a second. That's when he imprisons them—just as they are passing between. He intercepts their souls and forces them to acknowledge their failures. He traps their spirits into a state of perpetuity—forever forged in a final, horrific reflection of themselves, dying without ever having truly lived," Emily explained.

Gia was fascinated. Emily kept glancing down at her notebook, which was complete with highlighted sections for her to touch on.

"I'm just checking my notes here," Emily said.

"Why did he kill Miss Warburton?" Gia asked.

"Collateral damage. She was in the wrong place at the wrong time. The whole 'horror club' group was collateral damage if you think about it. Baghead must have been enraged when Professor Joe abandoned him, just like the monster in *Frankenstein*. He took his revenge on them all. It's life imitating art in the cruelest way.

"That is some heavy stuff," Gia said, wide-eyed with enthusiasm. "You're wicked smart, Emily."

"Thanks," Emily replied with a smile. She then handed Gia the book, and Gia looked it over with deferential reverence.

"This is the banned book?" she asked, not taking her eyes off it, holding it as if it were a chalice.

"Yes," Emily said.

"Can I keep it?" Gia asked, looking at Emily with longing eyes.

"No," Emily replied, taking the book back.

"I knew this stuff was real," Gia said, a sense of vindication in her voice. "Voodoo, Wicca, and the transcendental world … people made fun of me for it, but it's real."

Emily took Gia by the shoulders and stood face-to-face with her.

"He's after us, Gia. Maybe it's because he saw me in the nursing home ten years ago, I don't know. We may just be collateral damage, too," Emily said.

Gia shook her head; she had other ideas.

"No. It's because we called him. He was dormant—hibernating like a bear, or a vampire," Gia said, walking around her room, looking at the floor as she thought aloud. "He was content to leave Professor Joe alone, to suffer for his sins by living in constant fear and regret."

She then turned to Emily and said, "We woke him that night. I'm sure of it now. The Ouija board—the séance. It's how he was born forty years ago, and we reopened that door. That's why he can manifest in the flesh for us. We did this to ourselves," Gia said.

"We have to fight," Emily replied to her. "We can't just wait for him to kill us. This is my fault. I got you involved, and now everyone's life is in danger. I'm so sorry!"

Emily began to cry tears of remorse as she hugged Gia tightly.

"It's okay, Em, don't cry," Gia said, returning the embrace.

"We can do this," Gia said, leaning back to look Emily in the eye. Emily nodded in agreement. It would be a tall order. It would be dangerous. But they didn't have a choice.

Emily texted Martin about what she had read and how she interpreted it. Her message was lengthy. Martin may have been a skinny little geek, but he was intelligent—she knew that about him. He was someone she wanted on her side for whatever lay ahead. He was thrilled to hear from her, even if the message didn't exactly qualify as pillow talk.

She instructed him to update Twerp with as much or as little information as necessary.

Emily and Gia climbed the flight of stairs to Betsy's floor to give her the cliff notes as well. They rarely spent time up there. The floor plan was identical to Gia's, but the faces were different. It felt like an alternate universe.

As they approached Betsy's room, they noticed her door was open and there was some kind of activity in the hallway. It looked serious. A school administrator was peering into Betsy's room, her expression solemn.

The girls froze in their tracks. A chill ran over Emily's skin, and the hairs on her arms stood on end.

A sudden squeak startled her, prompting her to spin around and gasp. She saw a school custodian pushing a bucket with a mop. He was an older man, short and skinny. She had seen him before, and he looked surprised by her abrupt reaction.

"Hello, young lady," he said with a warm smile. "I didn't mean to sneak up on you like that."

"It's okay," Emily replied, smiling back as best she could.

Her heart raced as she glanced at Gia and then down the hall toward Betsy's room. They were hesitant to get closer, afraid of what they might see. Holding each other's hands, they stood together.

"Tell me she's okay," Emily whispered.

A moment later, Betsy poked her head out of the doorway and looked down the hall. Emily sighed heavily, and Gia wrapped her arm around her.

Betsy was alive, but something was off. They could see she had been crying; her eyes were puffy and pink.

They approached her.

"What's wrong?" Emily asked softly as she reached her room, finally able to see inside. Betsy's parents were there.

"I'm quitting," Betsy announced, her voice cracking as she delivered the news.

"What? Why?" Emily inquired.

Betsy pulled Emily and Gia aside for some privacy.

"I'm scared. I don't want to be here anymore. I'm going home," she said, her tone heavy with regret, as if she felt she was betraying them.

"Betsy, we *need* you," Gia insisted.

"No, you don't. I'm the weak link here. I need to feel safe," Betsy replied. She then turned to Emily and said, "Emily, I love you. But if you're haunted, I don't want to be around you."

Emily was taken aback by the honesty of the statement. She couldn't blame her, either. If there was a way out for her, she'd take it too.

They both hugged Betsy tightly and promised to stay in touch. Betsy gathered some bags from her room, and she and her parents carried them down the stairs.

Emily and Gia watched from the window as Betsy climbed into her parents' vehicle.

"She was the sweetest girl I met here. I ruined everything for her," Emily said.

"I think it was all just too much for her," Gia replied.

"I don't blame her," Emily agreed.

They watched as Betsy's father loaded the bags into the back. He climbed into the driver's seat, and a minute later, they drove away.

Emily felt sick. She had become a tumor, consuming the healthy people around her. She stared out the window as the black SUV grew smaller and smaller until it disappeared down the road.

In that moment, she knew she'd never see Betsy again, one way or another.

The foursome decided to gather for a pow-wow. It felt odd without Betsy. If she had just been sick, or had to study for a test, it wouldn't have felt so strange. But she was *gone*. Not just because she wanted to leave school, or missed home, or hated her roommate—she left because she was terrified of being killed. She was gone because the monster haunting their group had scared her so badly that she ran from them. She was gone because she'd made the mistake of becoming friends with Emily.

The thought of that made Emily nervous. *Will they all run from me? Would she have run from one of them if the circumstances were reversed? Self-preservation is standard in all living creatures.*

Before the boys arrived, she had already asked Gia about it.

"Do you want me to stay away from you, too, Gia?"

Emily's throat tightened as she waited for Gia to respond.

"We're in this together," Gia said, nodding affirmatively.

"No matter what?" Emily asked.

"No matter what."

It felt good to hear. They then waited for the boys to arrive, both annoyed at how long it was taking, as if they could drive themselves over. When they finally showed up, Emily's message to them was less heartfelt.

"Betsy's gone, and if you two don't want to be here, you don't have to be," Emily said flatly.

"You made us come all the way over here to tell us that?" Twerp said, prompting Martin to punch his shoulder.

"Shut up, Twerp," Martin replied.

Gia ping-ponged her gaze between their faces, assessing their mindsets.

"There's no guarantee he won't kill you, even if you wimp out and leave," Gia noted. She was smart enough to know there was strength in numbers, and they were already down one person.

The boys weren't thrilled to be dragged into the horror story unfolding at Ashley Hall School. However, being teenage boys, they still enjoyed being around teenage girls.

Martin held onto a glimmer of hope that there was a reasonable explanation for everything: a school prank gone too far? Overactive imaginations? A series of coincidences? *Were they really in danger?*

Neither he nor Twerp had seen Baghead, and they had no idea what caused the deaths of Professor Joe or Miss Warburton. Wouldn't the police be involved if they had been murdered? Did two fourteen-year-old girls know more than a trained medical examiner?

Only Emily had actually seen the monster, aside from Gia's supposed dream about him. As much as Martin liked Emily, he didn't know her very well. She wouldn't be the first teenage girl to fabricate fantastical tales of drama.

He'd listened to Gia talk about her ability to connect with transcendental forces, and her pitch was compelling. She described feeling the monster's rage—an intoxicating mix of resentment, hatred, and vindictiveness. He was a tortured soul, intent on spreading torment to others. But if he had to be honest, Martin didn't believe her. People could convince themselves of anything if they wanted to believe it badly enough.

Even so, Martin preferred to be in a dorm room across the pond with two attractive girls rather than in his own room at Porter-Gaud. His reputation was tarnished after fleeing like a Frenchman from Ricky Rude. He was also anxious that next time he might not escape, and Ricky could knock him into a cryogenically frozen state with one punch to the skull. And so, he said:

"We'll stay," nodding at Emily and Gia.

The girls took the news well, smiling ever so slightly. Truth be told, they were scared and needed help.

"I want to thank all three of you for standing by my side through this. I am terrified," Emily said, showing genuine vulnerability. It made

Martin want to protect her.

"Where do I start?" she continued, wiping her sweaty palms against her pant legs. "The reason I just told y'all that is because I think it makes him weaker—Baghead. He's a collector of souls drenched in regret. I don't mean small regrets like, 'I should have seen Sicily.' No, it's big regrets, like 'I was a terrible father' or 'I could have been a great artist, but I never had the guts to risk failing.'

"That's what Professor Joe talked about in that video before he was erased from it," she said. "The regret of a person lying on their deathbed, knowing they took a safe path instead of exploring the talents and strengths God sewed into their fabric like his own little doll."

She paused for a moment, trying to gauge their reactions. *Do I sound ridiculous right now?* she wondered. It didn't matter.

"I don't want to hide anything anymore," she said. "Whether I live or die, I am going to write my own story with no apologies and zero regrets. So, I'm telling you I'm scared because it's true, and I'm telling you I feel close to you because I do," she said, her voice quaking at the very end.

Gia rubbed Emily's back for support as Emily continued.

"My father left us on my eighth birthday. Can you believe that? I had a cardboard party hat on with the elastic band under my chin while I watched him through the window as he climbed into his car. He never came back," she said, tears streaking down her cheeks.

"I always blamed myself," she said. "I think he left because of me. My mother never told me otherwise. I've carried that guilt my whole life. I ruined my family, and now I've ruined all of your lives, too, and I'm so sorry," she said, covering her mouth to hold back her sobs.

Gia reached out to her and held her hand.

"It's okay, Emily. Guilt is such a heavy burden. But you're a wonderful person. You can't blame yourself for what your father did," Gia said.

"That's right," Martin added.

"I've always felt like such an outsider, like nobody understands me," Gia said to Emily. "But you were open to me right away, and I'm so glad we became friends. I have so few of them, and I look up to you so much for how strong you are."

Emily looked surprised, even laughing for a moment through her tears.

"Wait, *you* look up to *me?*" Emily said, raising her eyebrows. "Why?"

"Because you're cool," Gia replied. "You're so cool that you don't even realize you're cool. That's how cool you are," she added. "But me? I'm just a weirdo."

"Yeah, you are," Emily said with a small smile. "The geniuses always are. You're the kind of weirdo who becomes a big, bright shining star, Gia. Haven't you figured that out yet?"

"Thanks," Gia said, looking down at the floor, blushing from the compliment. She paused for a moment before continuing. "I know people think it doesn't bother me when I get made fun of for how I dress or my makeup, but it hurts my feelings sometimes."

"You don't show it. You walk right through it," Emily said.

"I guess I'm a good actress," Gia replied.

The girls smiled at each other.

"I love you," Emily said.

"I love you, too," Gia responded.

The two girls glowed with emotion, feeling as if they had been cleansed. Being females, they were ready to experience more *sharing-of-feelings* as they looked at the boys.

Martin felt his face flush. He hated being the center of attention, even in such an intimate setting. He didn't like sharing his feelings either; it seemed girly.

"Talk to us, Martin. The monster is empowered by regret and dishonesty to oneself," Emily encouraged, trying to prompt him to be emotionally vulnerable in order to weaken Baghead in some way.

"How do you know that?" Martin asked, his voice weak with defiance.

"It said so in the video," Gia interjected, glaring at him with demanding eyes. "Now, talk to us," she urged, sounding more like an Army sergeant than a therapist.

Martin glanced at Twerp for help, but he just stood there silently, seemingly worried he'd be next.

Martin considered excusing himself to use the bathroom and just leaving. It was a tempting thought, but it reminded him of running from Ricky Rude. He wasn't that same person anymore; he wouldn't live like that.

"I'm not sure what to say," he told them, clearing his throat to buy some time. He found himself staring into three sets of eyes. Nobody spoke, so he felt compelled to continue. He began to share a story from his past.

"When I was a kid—about eight years old—I had long hair and was really small. Smaller than I am now. I think it bothered my father for some reason. I didn't care that I wasn't big; I was a happy kid. But I could tell he felt ashamed of me for being little.

"Anyway, one day we were at a high school baseball game, and I was really excited. I loved baseball. I had to use the bathroom, and when I came out, my father was talking to another man he knew—a friend he'd bumped into. I just waited for them to finish their conversation. Afterward, my father said to me, 'My friend asked if you were my daughter. I had to tell him you were my son.'

"I remember the embarrassment I felt. He didn't have to tell me that. He wanted me to cut my hair shorter, gain weight, and act more masculine, so he shared what the man had said just to humiliate me. It ruined my whole day."

Martin looked down at the floor, as if the memory itself still brought him shame. He couldn't meet the others' eyes even as he continued.

"It probably wouldn't have been a big deal to some people, but I always felt like my dad was ashamed of me. He was never proud of anything I did, or even things I couldn't control, like being more rugged. He wanted a son who was a good athlete—someone big and strong.

"I didn't want to come to boarding school. My parents talked me into it. The only reason I agreed was that I thought if they wanted to get rid of me that badly, then maybe I should go," he said, his voice catching for a moment at the end. It surprised him, and he had to stay quiet for a few moments to collect himself. He didn't want to cry in front of them.

"Now I've got this kid who wants to beat me up. Twerp knows about it," he said. He paused and then told the girls, "I ran from him. I actually ran away because I was so scared. When I was alone afterward by the pond, I sat in the boat and cried."

Twerp interjected, "I didn't know that part, Martin," he said, surprising them with a hint of compassion.

The girls looked at Martin with caring eyes, as if they wanted to hug him.

"And while I'm being so open here," Martin continued, turning to look at his friend Twerp. "Twerp, I like visible panty lines, too."

The remark caused a quick shift in demeanor from the girls, who exchanged glances.

"I knew it!" Twerp exclaimed, pointing at Martin. Then he added, "Thank you for your honesty, Martin," in a playful tone as he placed his hand on Martin's shoulder like a talk show host.

"What in the *hell* do visible panty lines have to do with anything?" Gia asked, her tone a bit aggressive. Then she followed up with, "You know what? Never mind. That was a touching story up until that point."

She then turned to Twerp and said, "You're up, Twerpie."

Twerp had a look that suggested he'd been preparing for this moment. He was ready.

"Well, okay, I'm going to tell you guys something that nobody knows about me," he said. The group waited quietly as he took a deep breath.

"I've never kissed a girl," he said.

The room fell silent for ten seconds before Gia cracked a smile at Emily, prompting Emily to laugh. Martin couldn't help himself and began laughing as well—hard.

"What?" Twerp said, hands outstretched as the trio shared a rowdy guffaw together.

"No shit, Twerp!" Gia blurted out, laughing even harder now. "I don't think you're breaking any news stories with that one," she said as she and Emily high-fived.

"Oh, really? Is that right?" Twerp replied.

"Twerp, if you didn't kiss a girl for a year, you'd be on a hot streak," Martin said.

"Say it to my face, Martin. Say it to my face," Twerp challenged, holding a fist up at Martin.

After a minute or so, their chortling wound down, and Emily said, "God, I needed that."

"Seriously," Gia added, still giggling.

"Anyway, thank you for being honest, Twerp," Emily said. "I think everything we talked about might have helped, and even if it didn't, it made me feel better."

"So, what are we going to do about him?" Martin asked. "We can't just sit around waiting to see how this unfolds."

"No," Gia said. "We can't. We have to be proactive. We have to eliminate the threat," she said. And after a pause she finished with a shocking declaration, "We have to kill him."

The gravity of her statement silenced them all. None of them were killers, and they all knew it. Martin asked the obligatory question:

"How?"

"At Fall Fest. We'll do it at Fall Fest," Gia said with a resolute nod.

Fall Fest it would be, Emily thought. It would give them a little time to plan.

For now, she'd head back to her room. She was exhausted and needed a nap. She was always so tired, it seemed. Stress was taking a toll on her. But before she went to bed, she had a phone call to make.

Emily was alone in her dorm room. She held her cell phone in her hand for a good fifteen minutes, trying to conjure the courage to make the call. Twice she pulled up the contact, and twice she put the phone back down. The third time, she pressed dial.

"Screw it," she whispered, her heart beating faster now, although it seemed silly that it would. It rang several times.

"Hi," her mother said with tempered enthusiasm.

"Hi," Emily replied.

"Is everything okay?" her mother asked, impatience creeping into her voice.

"Yes. I just thought I'd call. Is that all right?"

"Of course it's all right. Don't be fresh. But I'm working, and I'm busy right now."

Silence hung between them. Her mother blinked first.

"Did you hear me?" she asked.

"You need to be nicer to me, mom," Emily said. She had planned a lengthy diatribe, but her mind drew a blank, so she gave the extremely truncated version.

"What?" her mother asked, as if she hadn't heard her.

"You need to be nicer to me."

"What's gotten into you lately?" her mother replied.

"Do you love me?" Emily asked.

"Of course I do," her mother said, lacking tenderness.

"Then act like it," Emily told her. Silence fell again. She could sense her mother's surprise through the phone without a word being spoken. "And don't you ever slap me again," Emily added, using a firmness she had never displayed before.

"I won't," her mother said, her tone softer. "I'm sorry for that."

It seemed to Emily that maybe her mom had wanted to tell her those words but couldn't bring herself to do it until now. It might have even felt good to say it, even if her daughter had forced the issue.

Emily nodded but didn't respond verbally. She appreciated the apology but felt no need to express it. Her mother's slap had hurt her feelings. She was too old for that, and even if she were a child, it still wouldn't have been acceptable.

What bothered her even more was her mother's inability to believe her story about the trauma unfolding in her life.

"Goodbye, mom," she said.

"Goodbye, honey," her mother replied before hanging up.

That went well, Emily thought. Why couldn't she tell her that she loved her? Why couldn't her mother say it? They used to exchange those words all the time when she was a little girl, but over time, they were said less and less often, until it became awkward.

She was glad they had spoken. She had asserted herself, and it felt good. Emily was enjoying her newfound strength, which was important. She was going to need it.

Fall Fest was a long-standing tradition and the primary fundraiser for extracurricular activities at both Ashley Hall School and Porter-Gaud School for Boys. This was the first year that "for girls" had been removed from "Ashley Hall School."

Despite the institution being all-female, the school committee members deliberated for weeks about removing the "for girls" designation after a parent complained that it might be insensitive to anyone who could be offended by such little things. After a series of votes and intense debate, the school's name was officially changed, prompting many unforeseen expenses. Signs needed to be repainted, sports uniforms had to be replaced or altered, and print ads had to be resubmitted with the correction.

The entire ballyhoo around it was covered like a gladiator fight in local newspapers and blogs, prompting many parents and community members to question whether the school committee had their priorities properly aligned.

Porter-Gaud School for Boys had its own school committee, even though the schools were considered "sibling schools." That committee did not change its name.

Fall Fest was a major annual event for both schools and the entire town. The festival lasted five days and was open to the public. It took place on the sprawling campus of Ashley Hall School, on land that had been donated years earlier. The large swath of mostly unused property attracted students who would lie on blankets to sunbathe, play frisbee, and listen to music. It would be transformed into a full-blown county fair.

Students from both schools worked at the fair. The boarders were "volun-told" to work, while the commuters were merely encouraged. Classes were suspended for the week of the event, and a group of carnys would roll into town with their mobile village and begin setting up for the Wednesday-through-Sunday festival.

The townspeople looked forward to it, as evidenced by the massive turnout, which raised much-needed money.

There were rides and fair food, go-carts, games with prizes, a demolition derby, a petting zoo, live music, and bright, blinking neon lights that could be seen from miles away. And, of course, lots of people.

Emily herself had been to the fair many times while growing up. This would be her first year working there. Her job was simple: take tickets at the front gate and attach the appropriately colored wristbands—green for those who paid for unlimited rides and red for those who would have to buy extra tickets on a per-ride basis.

She would have been excited about working there, too, if things were different. What wasn't to like? No classes, lots of friends from town to talk to, and soft-serve ice cream just steps away, with a fifty-percent employee discount, too.

All fair workers were allowed to enjoy the fair for free during their off time as well. It would have been quite nice had it not been for Baghead and the supposed "plan" they were concocting to eliminate him. There hadn't been a single suggestion as to *how* to go about it. Never mind that none of them were capable of murder, even directed at a monster. It felt unrealistic.

"It's the mirror," Gia suggested in a late-night text to Emily. "Maybe if we shatter it, that will kill him."

"But what about the spirits trapped inside?" Emily replied. That was as far as any of them had gotten in crafting an assassination plan.

Emily was watching the carnys, wondering if any of them were hired killers. *Was she a bad person for judging them?* she wondered.

The carnys were an unusual group of folks. They were hobos who moved from town to town for short periods, working crazy hours and sleeping in their cars. Most of them owned vans or old SUVs with mattresses in the back.

They would pick up everything, load the trucks, and drive their mobile village a few hundred miles to the next stop, where they'd unload it, set it up, and do it all again. They had an impressive operation, and despite predictable hiccups, it worked like a well-oiled machine.

Emily was somewhat enjoying her first day of work collecting money and attaching wristbands. She even gave a few green ones to her friends without them having to pay extra, which made her feel like a bit of a big shot. The repetitive nature of the job relaxed her, providing a nice break from the continual stress she had been experiencing for some time.

Gia was tasked with overseeing a game—the "guess-your-pitch-speed" contest. The rules were straightforward: patrons paid five dollars for three baseballs and had to guess their speed correctly before throwing a ball at a thick curtain with a radar gun next to it. It also gave Gia a good opportunity to meet boys, as the game seemed to be more popular with males.

She discovered she had a damn good arm, tipping the radar at 60 mph by her first lunch break, which was faster than most guys her own age could throw. She was accurate too, hitting the center circle every time.

Twerp was assigned to the fried dough stand, where he worked with two brothers who traveled with the fair. They were men in their forties but looked much older. They were about as unhealthy as a person could get, short of being dead.

The bubbling oil and the sweet smell of fried dough appealed to Twerp. He enjoyed grabbing the finished pieces out of the fryolator with the metal tongs that he would clap together a couple of times just because he liked the noise.

"Do you guys eat a lot of fried dough?" Twerp asked the brothers after sitting quietly in the stand, wondering why they needed a third person to operate something so simple.

"Sure do," one of them replied. Twerp noticed his face had as much acne as a fifteen-year-old boy's.

"It must get unhealthy after a while," Twerp said, shaking confectionary sugar onto his own piece of hot dough before taking a bite.

The two brothers exchanged glances and began giggling in a "bad-guys-in-a-creepy-movie" way, which made Twerp's smile fade. It also ended the questions.

Regardless, it was a sweet gig—working a food stand—since it came with all the free fried dough he could eat.

Martin was assigned to work with the "Repair Team," a group of mostly men tasked with fixing the endless mechanical issues with the fair rides.

He had made it clear upon receiving the assignment that he had no experience working with mechanical devices and did not have a penchant for fixing things. He reiterated this to the woman in charge of job placement during orientation. They put him there anyway to assist the full-time carnys, exacerbating Martin's longstanding concern that fair rides might not be that safe.

Twerp visited Martin on his first official work break, bringing him a piece of fried dough wrapped in cellophane.

"That's F.O.C., by the way—free of charge," Twerp told him, though Martin was already aware.

"Thanks," he replied.

They sat outside the repair trailer where Martin was stationed. It was a long camper that had been gutted and filled with tools for fixing broken things. Spare parts, broken pieces, random gadgets, and various oddities were crammed into nearly every inch of space in the trailer. Martin wondered how they found anything.

The boys sat at a picnic table.

"What do they have you doing?" Twerp asked.

"Nothing, really. I'm just moving stuff around, doing manual labor—lugging crap from here to there. What about you?"

"I'm running the fryolator."

"Already?" Martin said, a pang of admiration in his voice.

"Yup. It's not that hard. You just drop the dough in the basket for sixty seconds, then take it out, shake it off, and plop it onto a paper plate."

"That sounds fun."

"It is. Plus, I can eat as much of it as I want. I've had two already this morning, but now I feel like I have to poop."

"What an interesting story," Martin said with some derision.

"What's that over there?" Twerp asked, pointing at a blue board tossed off to the side. He could see it was a solid plastic, rectangular piece about three feet long and two feet wide.

"It's a seat from 'The Zipper'—that big green ride that spins around? That piece broke right off and went flying."

"Was anyone on it?" Twerp asked, alarmed.

"No. It happened yesterday during the trial runs, so that ride is closed until further notice," Martin told him. The two boys looked out at the rides, loaded with screaming people whirling around in all directions.

"I wonder if any of the other rides are ready to break?" Twerp pondered.

"That's a good question," Martin replied. "Anyway, I get off at three. Let's play some of the games and check everything out then."

"Yeah, for sure," Twerp said. They had free access, and they were going to enjoy it.

"Hey, little one, let's get back to work," a plump carny called out to Martin through the trailer window, his face barely fitting.

"I gotta go," he told Twerp, taking his last bite of fried dough and tossing the cellophane into a trash bin before disappearing into the trailer.

Twerp took a minute to examine the blue plastic seat. He could feel how solid it was—thick but light.

"Glad I wasn't on that ride," he said.

None of the foursome had ever held actual, paying jobs. They were too young to legally work anyway, so this was a new experience for them. Somehow, the school was able to circumvent the laws regarding the age of employees, allowing them to put students to work for the five-day stretch.

When Martin finished his first shift, he felt a sense of accomplishment—the feeling of making it through the first day at a new job. He tracked down Twerp, and they met up with the girls. They now had free reign at the fair. They ordered food and sat on a park bench, eating cheeseburgers and fries while talking about their respective jobs and the carnys for whom they worked. They also people-watched, observing the crowd.

As he sat there, it occurred to Martin that this was the first time he felt like the girls were true friends. He and Twerp had graduated from being annoying tag-alongs to genuine companions. This was especially true with Emily, who regularly engaged Martin in conversation. He felt less and less awkward chatting with her; until now, he would blush every time he spoke to her.

Gia was less engaging. She kept the boys at a distance, especially Twerp. She would look at Emily ninety percent of the time she spoke, glancing at the boys only as a crumb of acknowledgment. They took what they could get, especially Twerp, who seemed to become more enamored with Gia with each dismissive gesture.

"Let's try some games," Martin suggested as they finished their food. The group gave tacit approval by crumpling their paper plates and following him through the maze of wooden booths.

"Check it out," he exclaimed as he spotted an attraction he'd never seen before. It was a photo booth called "Age Yourself," where someone could pay to have a computer-generated photo of themselves at any age they selected.

It claimed to use government-style software that would extrapolate into the future to show what they would look like in ten years, twenty years, or however many they wanted. It could make an old person look young or a young person look old. Judging by the line length, the gimmick was popular.

"What is it?" Twerp asked.

"It shows what we'll look like in the future," Martin explained, already pulling out his money. The rides were free, but he'd have to pay half-price for the attractions.

"That's cool," Twerp said.

The line moved along nicely, and Martin and Emily got their pictures taken together first. They stood in front of the computerized camera as it scanned their bodies, then created an image that looked like a photograph of them at age twenty-five. It took a few minutes for the final product to appear, but when it did, they weren't disappointed.

"Whoa," Emily said, seeing her future self—a beautiful, shapely young woman.

"That really does look like you," Gia remarked. "You're hot!"

"I know," Emily replied with a big laugh.

"Wow," Martin said, looking at her picture before glancing at his own. "*Wow!*"

he exclaimed, suddenly brimming with optimism for the future. "Look at me."

He was handsome—tall and thin, but not gangly. He had a nice shape, helped by being imaged in fashionable clothes. Emily raised her eyebrows at the picture of Martin, trying not to reveal how much she liked it.

"Not bad," she said with a little smirk.

"Come on," Twerp urged Gia as he paid for them to get their images taken together. This was as close to a date as he would get with her, and he looked thrilled.

The two of them got scanned and waited for the results. Gia's image came through first.

"Nice," Gia said, admiring herself as a full-figured woman, busty and cute with nice hips. "I look like I have a great butt," she laughed to Emily.

Twerp's photo came next, the last of the four.

"What the hell is this?" was all he could say. The others saw the image, which looked exactly like the current version of Twerp—just taller.

He was skinny and hairless. He looked twelve.

"This thing's broken," Twerp shouted.

"It worked for everyone else," Gia pointed out.

"Maybe you're stuck that way," Martin joked. "You know, like the little girl in *Interview with the Vampire?*"

"Say it to my face, Martin," Twerp retorted, holding up a clenched fist, prompting groans from the others.

The group lingered for a while, listening to music and watching the throngs of people milling about before Gia brought it up.

"We need to get him out in public—Baghead. I think we should use the Ouija board here and see if we can get him to show himself in a crowded area," she suggested.

"That's a good idea," Emily agreed.

"Then what?" Martin asked.

"We steal the mirror," Emily proposed. "It's probably his source of strength, right?"

"It's the key to destroying him. It has to be," Gia said as she nodded.

"And what if you're wrong?" Martin asked them.

"I don't know, Martin. But we have to try," Gia insisted.

Gia had gone to her room alone to retrieve the board. Twerp went to the fried dough stand to find his cell phone, which he realized he had left behind after his shift ended. Martin and Emily were now walking together at the fair. It was nice for him to have some alone time with her. He felt a bit less pressure without anyone else around listening to them talk. He could be a little corny if he thought the moment was right without worrying about someone rolling their eyes.

As they walked along the sidewalk that ran the perimeter of the fairgrounds, Martin tried to think of something witty to say to avoid any awkward silence. He had hoped they had moved past that point. They hadn't.

And so, the two of them shuffled along the old, broken-up cement sidewalk—broken the way sidewalks in historic southern towns always seem to be—when Martin's foot scuffed an elevated patch of cement, jamming his leg and causing him to stumble awkwardly. Emily noticed, which made Martin feel silly. He tried to think of a joke to make about it, but it took too long; he couldn't be clever under pressure, so he just kept walking.

His knee hurt. It felt like a tendon or something inside had jammed from the impact of his foot scuffing that stupid piece of sidewalk. *Don't limp,* he thought to himself.

"Hey," he heard Emily call out to someone, breaking the long silence.

He saw Gia had arrived carrying her Ouija board in a box.

"Hey," Gia said back to Emily. Then she looked at Martin and asked, "Are you limping?"

"No," he replied immediately, making an awkward snort in an

attempt to convince them both that the question was absurd.

A tiny snot-bubble popped out of one of his nostrils when he made the sound, further embarrassing him.

Had they seen it? How humiliating!

His nose felt a bit moist now, but he wouldn't wipe it. He didn't want to call attention to it. So, he stood still with a moist nose and an aching knee.

"Come on," Gia urged, and they all began walking again. The fair noise and the sound of their clopping shoes on the sidewalk were all Martin could hear.

He saw Gia glance at him, noticing his gait. He tried to walk normally but couldn't.

"You're definitely limping," Gia pointed out.

Emily noticed.

"Oh, for fuck's sake," Martin exclaimed as he abruptly stopped.

His strong reaction caught the girls off-guard.

"What's wrong?" Gia asked.

"I jammed my foot back there on the stupid sidewalk while I was trying to think of something interesting to say to Emily. Why can't they just make the sidewalks level? Right?"

The girls just stared as he continued.

"So, the sole of my sneaker caught a raised piece of cement and it jammed my knee, not to mention I did one of those goofy moves we can't help but make whenever that happens. So now my freakin' knee hurts, and I'm limping."

"Why didn't you just say that?" Emily asked.

"You really don't know why?" Martin countered.

"No," she replied.

"Because I felt stupid," he admitted. "I always feel stupid, uncoordinated, awkward, small, or inept when I'm around you. I get tongue-tied. My face gets flushed. My voice cracks. I get a boner."

"*Whoa,*" Gia interrupted, holding up her hand. "T.M.I. there, buddy," she said.

"We talked about it earlier—being honest with ourselves," Martin told Emily. "The truth is, the whole reason Twerp and I came to Ashley Hall on that first night was that I wanted to try to find you, Emily," he said, staring down at the ground, too shy to look her in the eyes.

He continued, "I've always had a crush on you, and I don't know what's going to happen to us now—if we're going to die or what. So, if we do, I want you to know that I like you. A lot," he said.

The three of them stood there in silence for a few awkward seconds until Emily did her best Twerp impersonation and said to Martin, "Say it to my face."

The joke made Gia and Martin both break into laughter, Emily as well. It eased the awkwardness, and when they were all done laughing, Martin looked her right in the eyes and said, "I like you, Emily."

It felt good to say it right to her. It took more guts to tell her that than it would have to fight Ricky Rude, and he'd done it. She looked moved, maybe even flattered. She nodded at him but didn't reply. Then he turned to Gia.

"And yes, Gia, I am limping," he concluded.

"Wow. All righty then," Gia said with a smirk.

It was right then that Martin spotted it: a dunk tank. A clown sat on a wooden board over a small tank of water, microphone in hand, taunting people who paid money to throw baseballs at a target to try to sink him. Martin stared at the tank filled with water.

"Be like water," he whispered. The girls were confused.

"Are you okay?" Emily asked, snapping him out of his trance.

"I think I just got an idea," he told them.

They all began walking again, headed toward the fried dough stand to find Twerp so they could set up the Ouija board, have a séance, and draw Baghead to them. Martin wasn't limping anymore, either. His knee suddenly felt better.

The foursome came together over a free piece of fried dough for each of them, compliments of Twerp's new job. This would be his fourth serving of the day.

"It's so good," he kept whispering between bites.

"Are you all right?" Gia asked him, annoyed with his continual commentary. He nodded at her and kept eating.

"My stomach does hurt a little," he admitted to the group.

"I found a trailer out back," Gia said, transitioning the conversation. "It's for the animals from the petting zoo, but it'll be perfect for a séance."

"Are we gonna get in trouble?" Emily asked.

"I hope not. I doubt it," Gia replied as she stood up.

They all followed suit, glancing at each other anxiously. They began walking together slowly, no conversation. There was no rush. Playing with the Ouija board wasn't a game anymore; it had become nerve-racking. They could all read in each other's expressions that everyone was twisted up with jitters, even Gia.

When they arrived at the trailer, Gia pulled open the back like she owned it. The stench of wild animals hit them hard, so they had to let it air out for a minute while scanning for any carnys.

They climbed in and pulled the doors closed. Gia went to work setting up shop. She laid down a blanket, lit a few candles, and then opened the board. Emily's face was pale; she had dark circles under her eyes. She looked unhealthy.

"Why don't we just use your room?" Martin asked Gia.

"He has to come out in public, around people. We can use it to our advantage," Gia explained. "If there's a lot of activity around, we can distract him and steal his mirror."

"Then what?" Twerp asked.

"We'll figure it out from there. I'm not sure yet," Gia said.

Martin shook his head with doubt and said, "That doesn't sound like a very well-laid-out plan."

"You have any better ideas?" Emily snapped at him, her eyes bulging with stress. She looked overwhelmed. Martin slouched a bit.

"I'm sorry," he said to her.

"No, it's okay," she said apologetically. "I'm nervous, too."

They nodded at each other in support.

"We'll get through this together, as a team," Martin reassured them. "Besides, I think I might have a plan."

"What is it?" Gia asked, all eyes turning to Martin, which made him feel pressured.

"I have to flesh it out first," Martin replied.

"Well, don't wait too long. There's a lot at stake here," Gia warned him.

The foursome gathered around the Ouija board and held hands. Their arms stretched further with just four participants, a sad reminder of their missing friend.

"I wish Betsy were here," Emily said.

"Me too," Gia agreed. Then she began her opening ceremony, closing her eyes and chanting the Voodoo incantation: "Hounkou Bolokou Djavohoun Bohoun."

Martin opened his eyes and noticed that Emily's were open too. They both looked around for signs of anything unusual. There were none.

Gia continued, "I am searching for the spirit of Baghead. We call upon you to join us here tonight," she said, placing her fingers on the "floaty thing." Everyone else followed suit.

There was silence, broken only by the distant sounds of the fair outside. The candles remained still, the wind didn't blow, and the planchette didn't move, even slightly. A palpable sense of relief settled amongst them.

Martin silently prayed nothing would happen. He wanted this to end once and for all. Gia tried again and again, but nothing came of it.

Then, Emily spoke.

"He's here for me," she said in a loud, clear voice. They all looked at her, knowing she was right. Taking a deep breath, she closed her eyes and spoke with all the bravery she could muster.

"I know I'm the one you want. I'm the girl who saw you in the old folks' home when you killed that man. I'm the one who stabbed you. Come out, come out, wherever you are," she declared.

Her last words sent a chill through Martin, and just as that feeling hit him, the candles blew out and the rear door of the trailer was ripped open, prompting Gia and Emily to scream. Outside lights flooded in.

"What the hell is going on in here?" yelled a man standing outside. He looked unhappy, a carny with a few missing teeth and filthy overalls.

"I'm sorry," Emily quickly replied, taking charge of the situation. "We thought this was the medical trailer. My friend hurt his knee," she said, gesturing at Martin.

"That's right," Martin added, seamlessly going along with her.

She was so quick and convincing that the man didn't think to doubt it.

"The medical tent is up front by the entrance. It has a big red cross on it. Now, collect your belongings and get out of here," he instructed.

They were already packing their things as he spoke.

"I'm so sorry," Emily told him as she stepped down from the back of the trailer. She and her three friends walked briskly away from the man.

"That went well," Martin said as they made their way toward the bright lights of the fair. The wind rustled the trees, and a warm autumn breeze blew, making it feel like rain. And just like things often do in the Deep South, the sky opened up, and before anyone knew what was happening, it started to pour.

They scattered, hands above their heads in a futile attempt to stay dry. Without thinking, Martin reached out to Emily, and she grabbed his hand. They broke off from the group and ran together toward his nearby work trailer, losing track of Gia and Twerp in the downpour.

There was a van belonging to the woman in charge of the Repair Team, used for breaks. It had an air mattress in the back and was kept reasonably clean.

Martin pulled open the back doors of the van and jumped inside with Emily, shutting the rear doors behind them. The rain was pouring down in sheets now.

"Whew," Martin exclaimed, wiping the raindrops off his face with his hand.

"You don't happen to have a towel in that backpack, do you?" Emily asked, squeezing her hair between her hands and chuckling at her own question.

"No, but there are paper towels in the van somewhere," Martin said, raising his index finger as if he'd made a discovery.

He scrambled to find them to accommodate her, and when he did, he pulled off a long strip for himself before handing the remainder of the roll to Emily.

"Thanks," she said, pulling some off as well. They began patting themselves dry for a minute until Emily finally asked, "What *do* you have in that backpack, by the way?"

"I have a slingshot and some binoculars," he said with a shrug. "Oh, and one marble."

"That's kind of random. Why the marble?" she asked.

"In case I ever need to use the slingshot and don't have a rock nearby." He crawled deeper into the van. "We can lay back on this air mattress if you want. The woman makes anyone who uses it spray it clean afterward, so it's in good shape," Martin suggested as he slid right up to the front seats and laid back. Emily did the same.

They rested there, listening to the rain pelting off the roof and windows.

"I love the sound of rain," Martin said to her. "Especially when I'm in a car. The way it patters on a flat roof is so soothing."

They both laid back a little more now, almost lying right next to each other.

"Is it okay that we're in here?" Emily asked.

"Yeah, the boss is a nice lady. She likes me."

"I can see why," Emily said.

The comment made Martin feel good. The two of them listened to the storm for another moment before Martin spoke again.

"I remember when I was a kid, my dad lost his job for a while. My parents were in financial trouble, I guess. They're not anymore, but they were back then. We had to move out of our house and lived in a trailer park for a year or so. My mother was upset about it, but I thought the whole thing was pretty cool," he said with a reminiscent smile.

He continued, "The RV park was like its own town where everyone lived nearby. When it rained, the droplets were so loud bouncing off the roof of our camper. I'd lie in my bed listening to it.

"I know it sounds dramatic, but it felt like a giant baptism," he added, glancing at Emily to ensure he hadn't embarrassed himself with that statement.

She just lay there, listening. So, he continued.

"Anyway, sometimes I'd pray that it wouldn't stop raining. I wanted it to go all night long. So comforting. I'd try to stay awake to keep listening, but I'd end up falling asleep without realizing it. And when I'd wake up, it would be over, and I'd be bummed out," he said with a little chuckle.

"I've done that," Emily said, looking up at him.

"You have?" Martin asked. She nodded as he shuffled his body on the air mattress to get more comfortable, now lying flat.

"Sometimes I wish I was still living there, with my parents, in the camper. I think we were happier back then—*I* was, anyway," Martin admitted.

He caught himself getting unexpectedly emotional about the memory. He could hear it in his own voice and felt self-conscious, wondering if Emily had noticed. He worried he looked wimpy.

Clearing his throat to regain composure, he finished, "Anyway, I really like the sound of rain, is all I was trying to say."

He felt Emily nuzzle up to him. Her clothes and hair were moist from the downpour. She stretched her arm across his torso and laid face-down against him, her head resting on his chest. She smelled like vanilla.

She was exhausted, that was clear. Weeks of chaos and stress had taken a physical toll on her.

She'd admitted to Martin in a text exchange that she was relentlessly fatigued, yet still couldn't sleep for more than a few minutes at a time without her body jolting awake in a futile attempt at self-defense against her demon.

Martin felt bad for her. He also liked her pressing up against him like that. A good kind of nervousness washed over him. He needed to play it cool; he didn't want to blow it.

Did she want him to kiss her? He couldn't tell. Her eyes were closed. It would be an awkward maneuver; he'd have to stretch his neck quite a distance, and even then, he might not reach.

He'd never kissed a girl before, not in any meaningful way. It would have to be done right, or it would ruin the experience.

So, Martin lay there without speaking as the rain pelted the van. The sky outside was dreary, visible through the rear windows. The clouds were multiple shades of gray—the most relaxing color in the world—blending into one another.

With each passing moment, he felt himself growing more comfortable. His body felt heavy and safe. Emily was so warm against him. He couldn't stop inhaling her scent.

She was sleeping, Martin realized. He could hear her wheezing softly through her tiny nose, which was utterly adorable.

He pulled her more tightly into his body. It felt so right. She instinctively reciprocated, hugging his torso like a body pillow.

If they ever did get married—and that was a big *if*—he'd tell their kids about today. He'd remember every detail, too. This was their first date, or as close to one as he'd ever had. And it was a great one.

He wanted to stay awake for it. He fought against the urge to fall asleep. He didn't want to miss one second of this.

But the sound of the rain was his kryptonite. So sedating. He was tired, too, just like her. He decided to close his eyes to rest.

Just for a minute, he thought to himself. *Just for a minute.*

Something woke Emily up. She knew she wasn't in her own bed as soon as she felt Martin's body. She didn't know what time it was or how long they'd been sleeping, but she felt a wave of anxiety wash over her right away. It had become an uncomfortable reality she'd grown to expect, as much as she hated it. But even within the realm of anxiety, this was a higher degree of discomfort. She *felt* something. She also heard something.

A scratchy, bothersome noise was coming from the front of the van. It took her a few seconds of focus to realize the radio was on. She could hear it, but she couldn't tell what was being said. It sounded like murmurs, feedback, and hiss. The volume was low.

The moon was on full display through the clouded van windows. It felt much cooler than it had earlier. She had a chill, her clothes still damp.

Emily pushed herself up onto her elbow and squinted at the old-fashioned radio, which was lit up. There were two knobs—one for volume and one for tuning. She'd only seen them in old photos of cars from the 70s and 80s.

She sat up completely and crawled to the front of the van, squeezing between the two seats until she could see the radio. She reached for the volume knob to shut it off, but paused. She could hear it more clearly with the speakers on the door panels.

Amidst the feedback and crackling of poor reception, she heard human voices talking over each other, as if there were many of them. Some whispered with a sense of panic, while others moaned in distress.

The language was garbled and impossible to parse, but she caught snippets—two or three words at a time. They were in pain. They were scared and uncomfortable. The periodic feedback was cacophonous, and Emily tried to adjust the channel tuning, but it made no difference.

Then she heard him: Professor Joe. His voice was distinct, but she couldn't make out what he was saying. His words were obfuscated by the moans of others, layers of background chatter, and the hissing of poor reception.

She felt alert now, wide awake, looking around the van and noticing the windows had all fogged up. She could see her breath, too.

She reached toward the radio and turned the volume up, trying to focus on Joe's voice amidst the chaos, but she couldn't. She sensed he was trying to communicate with her. He had something to tell her but was being purposefully drowned out.

She raised the volume again and leaned toward the steering wheel, trying to get closer to the driver's side door where one of the speakers was located. The feedback grew more profound, but Emily zoned in on his voice, drowning out the noise around it, which took concentration.

She turned the volume up a tick louder, the radio practically crying in a jumble of electric hissing and unpleasant feedback.

"…the van," she heard him say, missing the first part.

"What?" she whispered as she leaned closer to the speaker, trying to single out his frequency amidst the noise.

She heard it this time—enough of it, anyway.

"…outside the van," he said urgently.

Emily filled in the blank as she whispered to herself, *"He's outside the van."*

Her chest burned from the realization; it felt like sulfuric acid. The radio then *screeched* in the most painful burst of feedback she'd ever heard, piercing her eardrums.

She snapped off the radio and fingered her ears to ease the sharp pain.

Martin sat up, alarmed.

"What happened?" he called out, still halfway asleep. Emily looked at him; his figure was almost purely a silhouette against the blackness of night. Behind him, at the back of the van, she could see the two square windows on the doors, clouded with moisture. In one of them, she could see the outline of his head. She recognized it.

"Oh God," she heard herself say.

"What?" Martin asked.

With a swipe of his hand, the moisture was gone, and Baghead pressed his odious face to the glass, peering in, uglier than she remembered. He smiled.

"He's here," was all she could say, her voice drenched in fright.

There was a split-second pause, the kind that happens right before two cars collide. Then, with the same awful noise of a crash, Baghead punched through the window, reaching inside. With his long arms, he grabbed Martin by the leg and began yanking him repeatedly against the doors of the van, slamming him against the metal.

"Martin!" Emily screamed, watching helplessly. Martin kicked at the monster's wrist and face, whimpering with sheer terror in his first encounter with the beast.

He managed to land one solid shot to Baghead's chin, which seemed to stun him for a moment. Baghead angrily grabbed the van doors and ripped them off the hinges, flinging them aside before diving into the van.

"Holy shit!" was all Martin could say as he scrambled for his life toward the front of the vehicle. Baghead grabbed him by his belt and flung him like a small toy, sending his body tumbling out of the back of the van and across the wet grass.

Baghead scampered on all fours at Emily, taking her by the neck with one hand and squeezing.

She'd never felt anything so powerful. The corners of her mouth pulled down involuntarily, her eyes bulged, feeling as if they might pop from her skull. Saliva streamed from the corners of her mouth as her eyes watered profusely.

Her body became stiff and incapacitated, unable to even make a sound. This was the end. She was going to die.

Martin scrambled back to his feet. He could see Baghead's massive body hovering over something in the van. He knew what that something was.

He ran toward the van and jumped inside, grasping at anything that could be used as a weapon.

The van was filled with tools, and the first thing he laid his hands on was a thick pair of metal locking pliers. They were solid steel and heavy. Hitting Baghead with them wouldn't do much more than make him angrier.

Martin could see the monster's ankles were exposed. He was kneeling, squeezing Emily's neck. His pant legs had slid up, revealing his Achilles tendon.

Knowing it might be his last action on this planet, Martin took the pliers and clamped them onto the thinnest part of the monster's Achilles, *squeezing* with all his might, using both hands. The monster wailed in pain, grabbing at his ankle. He made a noise like an elephant.

"Run!" Martin yelled.

Emily scuttled right past Baghead and leaped out the back of the van. Martin didn't wait around, either. As soon as she was gone, he let go of the pliers and took off. He knew he had hurt the monster; he could hear the disconcerting *snap* of his Achilles when he squeezed those pliers.

Baghead chased them, enraged but compromised, lumbering behind the faster kids.

Martin caught up to Emily and grabbed her hand as he passed, pulling her along. She could hardly keep up, still coughing from the choking she'd endured.

They sprinted toward the dorms. The fair was still open, but the rain had ruined the night, leaving few guests. Even so, there was comfort in seeing people. And Lord, did they need help.

Twerp was asleep. He'd lost Martin and Emily when they broke off during the storm. He tried to keep up with Gia, but she was too fast and headed toward her dormitory. So he ran to his workstation and took shelter under the awning of the fried dough stand, munching on a treat. That was the last thing he remembered before falling asleep.

He heard someone yelling, which woke him up. His neck ached from sleeping in a sitting position with his head forward on his chest, and a little circle of drool had darkened the front of his shirt.

As soon as he opened his eyes, he realized Martin was the one hollering. A moment later, Martin and Emily ran past the stand fast, looking terrified.

"Whoa," Twerp mumbled. Then he looked to see what they were running from and, for the first time, saw him.

Baghead was lumbering along in the distance, running with an injured leg. He was massive and gruesome.

"Holy shit … he's real," Twerp whispered, his heart racing.

The monster was getting closer. Twerp wasn't going to take any chances that he might stop to introduce himself, so he took off running behind Martin and Emily. He saw them duck into a building—an attraction from the fair called The House of Mirrors. Twerp barreled into the structure right behind them. Emily and Martin gasped when he entered, but then sighed with relief when they saw it was him.

"Jesus Christ, Twerp! You scared the crap out of us," Martin yelled.

"*I* scared you? What about the monster?" Twerp yelled back, pointing outside.

"He's coming," Emily said, looking out the door.

Martin and Emily pulled the door closed tight and locked it. There were no windows in the building to see out of; inside was nothing but a maze of rooms lined with mirrors.

"What happened?" Twerp asked, breathless from his sprint, shaking from his first exposure to the beast.

Martin didn't answer him. Instead, he stood frozen, raising his hand at Twerp to hush him. All three of them remained motionless and silent, hearts pounding. They heard it now: someone was inside the building.

There were footsteps, and they sounded heavy. Opening the door and risking Baghead being there wasn't an option, so they stayed still, quietly waiting, unsure for what.

A moment later, he turned the corner: Ricky Rude. He looked at the three of them.

Martin's shoulders slouched as he let out an exasperated sigh.

"Jesus Christ," Martin said. "I can't pay this kid to fuck off."

"Who is he?" Emily asked, as if Ricky wasn't right there in front of them.

"Ricky Rude," Twerp whispered to her. "He's the guy who's gonna beat up Martin."

"Are you happy about that?" she asked Twerp, noticing his tone.

Twerp looked guilty as he turned to her and said, "No. But I don't want to miss it either."

Emily looked at Ricky.

"He's kinda cute," she whispered.

"Are you kidding?" Martin replied. She shrugged.

"You are a dead man," were the first words Ricky spoke as he pointed at Martin.

Martin didn't run this time, though he could have. He estimated he could beat Rude to the door and dash back out to the people, or to Gia's dorm. Not this time, though. He was scared, but compared to Baghead, Ricky Rude was like Richard Simmons.

He wasn't going to allow this knuckle-dragger to humiliate him again. He'd laid sleepless in bed, squirming to the memory of that night, reliving it again and again. The way it made him feel—so inadequate and weak. Ashamed. That wouldn't happen again, especially in front of Emily. He'd take the beating if he had to, and he'd do it proudly.

"Get lost, loser," Martin said defiantly.

There was a moment of silence. Twerp's jaw literally hung open. Ricky looked almost as if it might have hurt his feelings.

"Whoa," Twerp said aloud, "You've got *balls*, Martin."

Ricky slid off his leather jacket and hung it on the back of an empty chair at the entrance before walking toward Martin. Halfway across the floor, the entrance door shook. Someone was trying to open it.

Ricky looked back, and a moment later, Baghead plowed through the cheap wood, splintering the door into fragments.

He looked at the group and headed straight toward Emily, dismissively pushing Ricky out of his way. Ricky stumbled for a moment, but then shoved Baghead back, prompting the monster to turn and confront him.

"What the hell is your problem, bro?" was the last thing Ricky Rude would ever say. Baghead laughed as he grabbed Ricky by the head with both hands, lifted him in the air, and slammed him to the floor.

Ricky wasn't unconscious, but he was close. Baghead pulled him off the floor by his hair like a WWE wrestler and thumped him into the chair at the entrance. He whipped out a roll of duct tape from his back pocket and bound Ricky's hands to the arms of the chair. He took out a clear plastic bag and pulled it around Ricky's head, tightening it. Ricky's face lit up with fear. He was wide awake now.

Emily, Martin, and Twerp were in shock. Everything was happening so fast. There was nowhere to run, other than deeper into The House of Mirrors. Baghead was blocking the only door they could see.

Ricky bucked and kicked a few times in a panicked frenzy. His eyes grew wild with urgency as he twisted left and right, trying with all his might to free himself, to get a breath of air.

Baghead stared at him through the plastic, his face mere inches away. He was smiling, giggling like a psychopath. Just as Ricky's body went from stiff to faltering and then to limp—all the fight gone from him— Baghead took out his hand-held mirror.

Still holding the bag taut around Ricky's neck, he raised the mirror up to Ricky's face, showing him his dying reflection.

Ricky's eyes bulged for one instant of horror as he saw his own waning image.

He wilted right there in front of them all. His eyes drooped shut, his body going flaccid. He looked sad and feeble more than dead. But Martin had no doubt he was no longer living.

Emily doubled over and threw up, splashing it on the wooden floor. The trio didn't move, as if they were watching a horror film. They felt paralyzed.

Baghead then turned and looked at them, breaking into laughter, exposing his gnarled, discolored teeth.

He looked like a gigantic, mentally deranged, 300-pound baby— rotund and menacing. His laughter sounded like a high-pitched machine-gun giggle, fast and repetitive and piercing, so much so that all three kids covered their ears with both hands. His giant belly reverberated with it, too.

Twerp was getting his first close look at Baghead, noting the stitching around his skull, the severely cleft lip, and the sweaty gleam of his blubbery face.

"Holy crap," Twerp heard himself utter.

It wasn't clear who moved first, but someone twitched, and when they did, the trio scattered like spooked deer, running as fast as they could through the maze, bouncing off the walls—and off each other—as they scampered their way to the back of the building where they mercifully found an exit.

Martin kicked open the door marked EMERGENCY EXIT ONLY. This qualified.

Emily and Twerp were right behind him. Nobody needed to look back; they could feel the monster giving chase. He was a mountain of molten lava rolling downhill behind them. His feet thumped as they landed on the ground with each long stride, like the giant in *Jack and the Beanstalk*. Whatever damage Martin had done to his Achilles had apparently been insufficient.

Martin's gimpy knee buckled on him, the same one he'd jammed earlier. He fell to the grass, face-planting into some dirt and smashing his nose. He rolled over onto his back, clutching his leg. The colossal monster didn't stop for him; he looked straight ahead at his true target.

He didn't know how it happened, as it transpired so fast, but Martin stuck his foot out just as the disgusting creature was running past him. Baghead tripped over it, like he'd clipped a rock in the earth. He fell harder than Martin anticipated he would, his monstrous head bouncing violently off a tree stump. He looked dazed, shaking his head as if he was seeing stars.

Martin took advantage of the pause, pushed himself up, and took off running again, adrenaline coursing hard enough to keep his knee from stopping him.

His skinny legs whirled like a cartoon character. He'd lost sight of his friends. Everyone had scattered. That's when he heard Twerp yell to him.

"Martin!"

Martin stopped running when he saw Twerp hiding behind a wooden food stand, panting and out of breath. Martin joined him, both boys gasping for air, ducking down behind the counter, looking around for the monster. He was nowhere to be seen, but surely still nearby.

"Where's Emily?" Twerp asked him.

"I don't know. I lost her," Martin replied.

Twerp took a long moment to try to catch his breath. He then looked at Martin and said through his gasps, "Welp, it doesn't look like Ricky Rude will be bothering you anymore."

"Yes," Martin said. "That problem seems to have resolved itself."

Emily was alone. She'd lost the boys, but she knew Baghead was trailing her. She ran toward the crowd at the fair—get out in the open, she figured. She glanced back just once. He'd fallen behind, but she could see he was still pursuing her.

She ran to an adult couple and grabbed the man by his arm, clinging to him as she looked around for Baghead. She couldn't see him now; he was enveloped in darkness.

"Are you okay?" the man asked Emily with a concerned look on his face.

Emily couldn't speak. She was out of breath and terrified. She squeezed the man's elbow hard enough that he was pulling it away from her. Emily wedged herself between him and his wife, nestling into their bodies, hiding.

Then she saw him. Baghead was walking in her general direction, moving through the crowd, looking for her from high above the sea of heads he towered over. He looked demonic. *Would he kill her in front of everyone? Could anyone stop him if he tried?*

"Help me," Emily pleaded with the man, her eyes full of desperation. He and his wife looked back to see what she had seen. Something had spooked the daylights out of her. They saw Baghead in his blue jumpsuit walking toward them. A random carny stopped him.

"There's a cleanup in The House of Mirrors, near the entrance. A kid must have puked," the carny said. Baghead paused and looked at him. "You're a janitor, right?" the carny asked, glancing over the uniform.

Baghead nodded and turned around to walk toward the entrance.

"What's wrong, dear?" the woman asked Emily, clearly concerned for the girl.

"Nothing," Emily said as she saw Baghead walking away. "I'm so sorry I bothered you. I'm fine, really. I just got scared."

Emily broke away from the couple, who tried to get her to come back, but she walked off quickly while they watched her leave.

She headed back to Gia's room, hoping everyone would be there. As she walked, she heard a familiar voice.

"Hey," Gia called out. Emily looked over and saw her friend standing there.

"I got it," Gia said, holding something up. It was his mirror.

Inside Gia's dorm room, the foursome gathered around the small mirror.

"He must have dropped it when I tripped him," Martin said.

"Yes. I was watching you guys. I tracked Emily's phone to The House of Mirrors. I saw him chasing you," Gia explained.

"Don't look at it," Emily cautioned her.

"I already did," Gia replied, glancing again into the mirror before flashing it at Emily. "See? It's literally just a cheap mirror."

"Let's smash it," Twerp suggested.

"No," Emily insisted, rejecting any prospect of breaking it. "We're going to use it—to trap him inside."

They all looked at one another.

"That's a good idea," Martin said, nodding. "But that means we'll have to kill him."

"We'll do it tomorrow," Gia said resolutely. "It's Halloween. Perfect day to murder a monster. We just have to figure out how."

"I know how," Martin said, commanding everyone's attention. He nodded at them. He'd been thinking about it. He had a plan. "I know exactly how."

12

"**G**rab it," Twerp said to Martin as he looked around to ensure nobody was watching. Martin picked up the blue plastic ride seat that had been lying alongside the repair trailer. The plastic was solid, designed for two riders, with small handles at each end for those who were scared stiff, which was most of them.

"It's perfect," Martin said as he slid it into a long gym bag. He doubted anyone would come looking for it, but he couldn't help feeling nervous. Stealing was never his thing, yet he made an exception this one time. Today was a big day: Halloween.

They also had a ten-foot-long chain and a padlock. They hadn't stolen those, though; they belonged to Twerp for locking up his bicycle. Martin stuffed them into the gym bag as well.

Twerp was dressed as Rocky Balboa for the holiday, wearing yellow satin boxing shorts, black wrestling shoes, and a cheap gold belt secured with Velcro around his waist.

Martin had to give him credit—he went shirtless despite his cringeworthy lack of muscle. His legs dangled like two strands of dental floss with a bump in the middle where his knees were.

Martin himself was dressed as Bruce Lee, donning black karate pants with white trim and a black shirt. He carried a set of plastic nunchucks to avoid breaking the school's rules about carrying real weapons. He also wore a wig that resembled Bruce's black Dutch Boy hair.

"Your head looks like a paintbrush with that wig on," Twerp teased, clearly enjoying the moment.

"Shut up, Twerp," Martin replied, struggling to come up with a better comeback. Virtually everyone had to ask him who he was supposed to be. Most people could tell who Twerp was dressed as, and he even had a few strangers shouting, "Ay' *Rock-o!!*"

The boys made their way to the front gate, where the fair would be opening soon. Halloween was always the biggest day of Fall Fest, featuring face painting, costume contests for children, and a trick-or-treat area cordoned off where kids could go from stand to stand collecting candy from the staff.

Emily was dressed as Barbie, along with half the girls in the place. She looked good, and Martin noticed. Gia was with Emily at the entrance, unrecognizable as Pennywise, the evil clown from the Stephen King novel.

On the front of her costume, she had stenciled in black ink the words: "My Pronoun is IT".

Not surprisingly, hers was the best costume at the fair. She had worked on it for weeks leading up to her favorite holiday. Today was her personal Super Bowl.

Twerp tried to flatter Gia for her choice of costume, pointing at the front of her shirt.

"My pronoun is *It*. Clever. I like how you're poking fun at the current social mores regarding pronoun politics, yet it's benign enough not to hurt anyone's feelings. That's a hard balance to strike. Plus, the double entendre, because the movie title is 'It.' Well-played," he said, nodding at her with a big smile.

She gave him the middle finger and slowly moved it closer and closer to his face until it touched his nose.

"I'm going looking for him," Gia said to Emily as she turned to walk away. Martin laughed to himself when he heard her speak; he wouldn't have recognized her without hearing her voice.

"How do you know he's here?" Martin asked Gia.

"It's Halloween," she replied.

"So, what does that mean?" Martin inquired.

"Halloween is the day when the veil between the worlds of the living and the dead is thinnest," she told him. "He's nearby. I know it."

Her confidence was infectious but also unnerving for the rest of the group. She had a few hours to kill before her shift began. The students only worked four hours at a time.

She walked off alone as the gates opened and people began pouring in. The weather was warm for autumn. It would be a busy day and an even busier night; the teenagers would come in droves when the sun went down.

Gia passed by all the games, stands, and rides. She knew them by heart already. The fair seemed so big at first, but after a couple of days, it felt tiny. She recognized all the faces of the carnys by now—where they worked and what stands they ran.

She passed the strongman sledgehammer game and then walked by The House of Mirrors, where Emily and the boys had witnessed Ricky Rude being eliminated from existence by Baghead. His body hadn't been recovered, and there was no word of him missing.

Looking up at the towering Ferris wheel, she realized it appeared less intimidating from the ground than it had when she was in one of those little buckets staring out at the town as far as the eye could see. They had all been on the ride twice.

"It makes my balls tingle," she recalled hearing Twerp yell to Martin as their bucket reached the highest point. "Does that happen to you too, Martin? Do your balls tingle when you're this high up?" he continued unabashedly.

Gia hated to admit it, but it made her laugh. She and Emily could hear the two of them as they rode together in sequential buckets, just a few feet apart.

She also thought about Twerp in his Rocky costume. *He wasn't a bad kid,* she mused. He had grown on her, she supposed—not that she liked him in that way. He was more like an annoying little brother than the turd she initially thought he was.

As she passed the dunk tank, her heart did a little flip-flop. It would be part of their plan for the day. She stopped to watch patrons throw baseballs at the target, trying to dunk the obnoxious clown perched atop the wooden board above the glass water tank.

The clown was taunting them as they took turns attempting to dunk him. When he noticed her, also dressed as a clown, he gave her a respectful nod. Professional courtesy, she presumed. She nodded back. They were paisan today.

Continuing her walk, she became distracted by the smell of food—burgers, fries, and the sweet aroma of cotton candy being spun. She caught a glimpse of plump sausages sizzling on a hot grill. She stopped to buy a bratwurst with peppers and onions. Using her employee badge, she got a fifty-percent discount and sat at a picnic bench to eat it carefully, mindful not to smudge her makeup, which had taken so long to apply.

When she finished, she crumpled her paper plate and napkins and walked to a trash barrel to toss them in. As she turned to leave, she bumped right into him. He stood there in his janitorial jumpsuit, towering above her.

Looking up at him, her sphincter tightened. She felt weak, as if she needed to sit back down. Their eyes locked—she didn't want to look away for fear of revealing herself, but she couldn't sustain the gaze. She needed to calm down to quell her instinct to run. This was her first face-to-face encounter with him, the closest she'd ever been.

He couldn't recognize her through the makeup, *could he?* Finally, she broke the stare as casually as she could and walked away, careful not to quicken her pace. Unsure whether to look back, she resisted the urge for several steps.

As she walked, she felt awkward, overly deliberate. The more she tried to appear natural, the more unnatural she felt.

Eventually, nearly hyperventilating, she couldn't take it any longer and turned to look back. He was staring right at her.

With all the scary books she'd read, she had never felt so petrified, and there was nothing fun about it. She felt unsafe, even in the midst of the crowd of people. *Don't run* was all she could think. *Don't run. Don't run.*

She didn't.

When the first work shift ended, Gia approached Emily at the front gate. She didn't hesitate and went right into her story.

"He looked straight at me," Gia said as Emily affixed wristbands to the folks coming in.

"What are you talking about?" Emily asked.

"Baghead. I saw him. I felt like he knew it was me," Gia continued. Emily stood up from her stool to face her.

"How could he? Your face is completely covered."

"I don't know. But he did. When our eyes met, I could feel it. He recognized my energy from the séances."

"Maybe you should be the bait then," Emily said bluntly. Gia's expression melted away as an uncomfortable rush of adrenaline coursed through her chest and throat.

"We'll be right there, watching," Emily assured her in a hushed voice, trying to comfort her friend. Gia nodded, looking down at the ground.

"Did you text Twerp?" Gia asked a moment later.

"Yes. Everything is in place. You can't miss, though," Emily replied.

"I won't." Gia said.

That night, after the fair closed to the public at ten o'clock, the only people left were the carnys and any staff remaining to clean up the trash and secure the games and food stands.

Martin, Twerp, and Emily climbed on top of a wooden shack—about twelve feet high—that housed a game whose front shutter was now pulled closed. They lay flat on their stomachs. Martin retrieved his binoculars from his backpack. They had Gia in their view.

Twerp seemed uneasy about something as he lay there, so he whispered to Martin beside him.

"Martin," he said in a hushed voice.

"What?" Martin replied, glancing away from his binoculars to look at

Twerp.

"Listen," Twerp said, his expression filled with real concern. "If anything happens to me tonight—like, if I don't make it…" He paused for a moment before continuing. "Please make sure you log onto my laptop and delete my browsing history."

"Oh, for Christ's sake, Twerp," Martin said, returning to his binoculars.

"My poor mother!" Twerp exclaimed. "I don't want her finding any—"

"I'll take care of it, Twerp," Martin interrupted before he could finish.

"Thanks," Twerp whispered, seeming more at ease with the possibility of dying tonight.

Gia was stationed on a park bench near the food stands, alone and out in the open, pretending to do inventory for the game she was in charge of. She knew he would come for her. She could feel him. She could hear the moans of the spirits, the painful howls, like a pack of rambunctious wolves. He would be here, in the flesh. She could smell his rancid spirit.

The warmth of the day had faded into a clear, chilly night. The moon shone bright, illuminating the sky.

The fair lights were off, leaving only the emergency lights to see by. There were no more kids screaming on rides, no live bands playing, and no announcements over the PA. Just silence.

Her eyes scanned the landscape. She was on high alert and felt surprisingly confident. Gia knew the others were watching, and she was certain they would do everything they could to help her if things didn't go as planned.

On the roof of the wooden shed, Martin continued to peer through his binoculars while Twerp and Emily observed with their naked eyes. They weren't seeing anything out of the ordinary.

"He's got to be here somewhere," Emily said.

She was right.

Behind the three of them, atop the rickety wooden shed, a creaking sound impinged upon the silence. On any other night, it might have gone unnoticed. Not tonight.

"Oh, crap," Martin whispered as he barely pulled his eyeballs from the binoculars without looking back.

Emily had heard it too, as a distressing warmth washed over her. She turned to look back.

Against the blackness of the night, she saw a huge figure. From her prone position, he appeared to be seven feet tall, smiling that same hideous grin, exposing a newly fractured incisor that must have been cracked when he face-planted on the tree stump.

His portly, baby-like face seemed more menacing than ever—*closer* than ever. Summoning all her strength, she screamed, "Run!"

He was on her before she could stand.

Martin and Twerp were already in mid-air, having leapt off the structure in an instant. Twerp never looked back, sprinting for his life into the night as soon as his feet touched the ground. Martin was right behind him, glancing to see if Emily was following. She wasn't.

On the roof of the shack, Baghead lifted Emily's body as if picking up a sleeve of Styrofoam cups. He planted her on her fanny and held both of her hands together with one of his—the monsters fingers were as long and thick as a bunch of bananas.

With his other hand, he wrapped a plastic bag around her head, pulling it taut on her neck, all the while giggling like a lunatic, taunting her with a manic stare. His belly jiggled with each burst of laughter that echoed through his corpulent frame.

Emily was paralyzed, unable to fight back. There was no point, anyway. The plastic bag around her head filled with her own warm breath, fogging it up with every desperate attempt to inhale.

Her mind went to the mirror and the thought of being trapped inside. *Does he have another one?*

She wasn't ready to die, and the reality of it made her lose control of her bladder as she felt her pants grow warm from escaping urine. It soaked her inner thighs and buttocks.

She was limp, terrified, and fading. She knew her mouth was wide open, but no air was coming in or going out. Then she saw a flash of movement on the roof. The figure grew larger, and she recognized it was Martin. She'd never been so relieved to see anyone in her life.

He charged from behind with a screwdriver in his hand and plunged it into the lower back of the monster, who howled in pain, letting go of the bag and spinning around. He smacked Martin on the side of the head with a violent backhand that sent the boy soaring off the shack, landing with a thud on the dirt below.

Emily was already on the move. As soon as she felt the vice-like grip of the monster loosen, she rolled away, tumbling right off the roof and landing on her side onto the earth below. She saw Martin and ran to him, grabbing him by his hair and yanking him up.

"Come *on!*" she shrieked, panic filling her voice as tears streamed down her face while she ran into the night.

Martin pushed himself to his feet and took off with her, placing a hand on her back to urge her to run faster. Baghead was in close pursuit. He was injured from the attack, but his rage fueled him.

"Go!" Martin shouted as he felt the warmth of the monster gaining ground on them.

He was still seeing stars from the blow to his head, while Emily gasped for breath after nearly being suffocated to death.

Despite their exhaustion, they held onto each other's hands and ran as fast as they could until Martin's legs began to give out from the dizzying impact. He felt himself stumbling and broke off to the right, redirecting Emily toward the dunk tank by pointing in that direction. He then fell to the ground and vomited water.

Baghead didn't acknowledge him, or perhaps he simply didn't see him. Either way, he stayed on Emily's trail as she sprinted toward the rendezvous location, which was now in sight.

Martin pushed himself back to his feet and followed as best he could, still unsteady. He needed to get there—the plan required all four of them.

When Emily arrived at the dunk tank, she was still crying, overwhelmed with hysteria as she glanced back at Baghead, who was closing in on her. She quickly climbed the side of the structure, over the glass tank filled with water, and up the telephone pole that held it all in place.

Baghead was right behind her, beginning to climb as well, swiping at her feet. Emily whimpered and kicked down at him. His large, cumbersome frame struggled to keep up. She fought to maintain her composure, suppressing the urge to become hysterical.

Over and over, she kicked at his head as he drew closer. One kick landed squarely on top of his skull, causing him to awkwardly stumble down the pole. He managed to find his footing on the wooden plank above the water tank.

Emily looked down at him and then at Gia, who was standing at the helm of the game. She held a baseball in her hand, reared back, and pitched it at the small target with all the force she could muster. She knew she had to hit it—and she did. Bullseye.

The wooden seat thumped loudly as it buckled under Baghead's weight. He yelled something unintelligible as the support fell away from beneath him, and he dropped with a mighty splash into the tank of cloudy water.

Twerp emerged from behind the tank and slapped the blue plastic seat over the top, blocking Baghead in where the wooden plank had been.

Martin scrambled to the other side, gripping the handle. Both boys hung on, using all their body weight to keep it down. Martin threaded Twerp's ten-foot bike chain through the hand grip on his side and tossed the rest over to Twerp, who did the same.

Baghead pounded the plastic seat with his fists, causing the boys to lift a few inches, but not enough to free him from the tank.

"Lock it!" Martin screamed at Twerp, who frantically attempted to click shut the padlock. He struggled as the monster repeatedly slammed against the plastic seat, yanking the chain tight again and again.

Gia climbed onto the blue plastic seat, standing on top of it to add more weight as the creature furiously punched at it from below. His power was compromised, having to swing his fist through water.

On his fifth try, Twerp managed to sink the shackle into the body of the lock. He felt the click of the locking mechanism and shouted, "I got it!"

Again and again, Baghead pounded on the plastic seat, trying to free himself from the water tank. With each attempt, he grew weaker and more panicked, closer to losing consciousness. He flailed as he struggled for air, kicking at the glass walls of the dunk tank, trying anything to escape. The glass cracked but didn't shatter.

Emily scurried down the pole and made her way to the front of the tank, watching the monster through the glass. His face was contorted in horrible pain as he began to inhale the water, his body involuntarily trying to breathe despite knowing it was futile.

His lungs filled with water, causing hemorrhaging in his respiratory muscles, which triggered cardiac arrest.

Blood began to flow from his mouth, floating in the water like thin pink oil. Then it turned red. Then dark red.

He stopped fighting and began to wither, sinking to the bottom of the tank. They all watched in disbelief, witnessing a beast this powerful wilting before them. It almost felt like a ruse.

But then his eyes grew distant, still open but fading, filled with the reflection of horror and fear at his imminent demise. His massive body settled at the bottom of the tank, his face pressed against the glass.

Emily took out the hand-held mirror and knelt down next to the tank. As the last bit of life was about to leave the manifested body of the horrible spirit, she showed him his own hideous face.

His eyes bulged at the sight, as if they might pop right out of his head. His expression was so disturbing that Emily had to look away.

And then—he died.

Gia did not feel the same pang of sympathy for him. She gave Baghead the middle finger through the glass tank and said, "Happy Halloween, *asshole.*"

She then placed a hand on Emily's shoulder.

"Let's get out of here. All of us, let's go now," she urged as Twerp and Martin hurried to collect their things.

13

Inside Gia's dorm room, the foursome stood in a circle, speaking over one another about what had just happened. Things hadn't gone exactly as planned, but it had worked anyway. They had successfully captured him in the mirror, which now rested on the bed.

The conversation was frenetic and unhinged; they were all still buzzing with adrenaline, speaking as if they were wired on speed.

Emily was overwhelmed with emotion after witnessing the death of Baghead, the monster who had tormented her since childhood. *Was he really gone?*

Seeing his face up close, spewing blood into the water, was a horrific vision she would never forget. Her pants were still soaked with her own urine, her face wet with tears. Her voice was hoarse from all the screaming, whimpering, and mewling. The events were so overwhelming that she felt a bizarre sensation of calmness, a sort of paradoxical effect.

"There are spirits in that mirror with him," she said to the group. "We have to try to free them without letting him out. Professor Joe is in there."

"How?" Gia asked. "How do we get them out?"

Emily walked to the window of the dorm room and stared out at the fair in the distance. She could see it in the darkness—the sign: The House of Mirrors.

"Do you remember when you told me to look for the signs? You said there are coincidences and signs, and people often get them confused."

"I remember," Gia said, nodding.

"Grab the Ouija board. I'll get the mirror," Emily instructed.

"Can't we wait?" Twerp offered, exasperated.

"No. Let's finish this tonight," Emily replied, almost dismissively. Twerp pushed back.

"I don't want to. I'm done here," he said, his voice quaking with stress, fear, and pressure.

They all became quiet. He looked like he was about to cry, as if he could no longer hold it in.

"We just killed someone. Don't you get that? I want to go *home*. I don't want to do this anymore. I want to go back to my dorm room, go to sleep, and wake up to find out this was all a bad dream. I don't care if you think I'm a geek. I don't care about hanging out with you girls. I'm finished with this!"

Gia could see that he was trembling. They all could. His eyes were watery, and his face was flushed. She took a moment to talk to him like a friend. Lowering her voice, she placed her hand on his shoulder, looked into his eyes, and spoke kindly.

"Hey, I'm shaken up too. We all are. We couldn't have done this without your help. Thank you for that. You're really brave," she said.

He nodded and looked down at the floor, emotional. "But Emily is right," she continued. "We need to close the books on this tonight, and we need you with us. You're part of the team," she said, glancing around at everyone before looking back at Twerp.

He appeared calmer. Then she sealed the deal by saying, "So, what do you say, *Rocky?*"

Twerp's face visibly reacted to being called that name. Like the Grinch, whose heart grew three sizes on Christmas, Twerp's spirit expanded like a gummy bear in a glass of water.

His eyes lit up with pride. It took him a moment, but he nodded at Gia and said, "Well, when you put it that way…"

Emily walked over to him and said, "There's no more danger. The monster is dead."

She believed she was telling the truth. Unfortunately, she was wrong.

The foursome met no resistance as they slipped inside the fenced-off area where the fair was being held. This wasn't Fort Knox. A couple of security guards were on duty somewhere, probably sleeping or watching videos on their phones. The carnys didn't seem to care about much after work other than getting stoned or sleeping.

"Where are we going?" Martin asked after they had been following Emily for several minutes.

"Here," she said as she came to an abrupt halt. They saw the familiar structure: The House of Mirrors.

"I don't think we should go back in there," Martin said, shaking his head with certainty.

"It's closed. It'll be fine," Emily said without explaining how she had connected those dots. "Come on, Martin," she urged him with a wave of her hand.

It didn't take much convincing. He would have followed Emily into the gates of hell if she asked him to.

Inside the attraction it was dim, but not pitch dark. The emergency lights provided a hint of illumination.

They sat down in the middle of a room surrounded by mirrors on every wall. Emily lit a couple of candles while Gia set up her Ouija board.

"Great, we're doing the Ouija again," Twerp said sardonically, covering his face with his hands. Martin gave him a quick pat on the back.

The group formed a circle and held hands while Gia went through her pre-séance ritual with her eyes closed. When she finished, Emily took over.

She held the mirror and spoke in a clear voice.

"Are the souls trapped in this mirror with us right now?" she asked.

There was no response. She hesitated before looking into the mirror, still nervous to do so. She saw her own reflection and nothing more. She passed the mirror around, and others did the same. Nothing happened.

"I had a book," Gia said. Everyone looked at her as she remembered. "My grandmother bought it for me when we were on vacation in Maine. She was cool—my grandmother. She was into Wicca, too, and she took me to this little Voodoo shop, just the two of us, without telling my parents. It was funky. The name was '*Reverend Zombie's House of Voodoo.*' They stocked a lot of touristy crap, but people in-the-know could sniff out the real stuff," she said proudly.

Breaking away from the séance to tell a personal story was something Gia rarely tolerated, so the group knew it must have been important.

"She agreed to buy me a book, so I picked one called *The Wicked Good Book of Wicca for Wicked Purposes*. Kind of a funny title. I guess it's because they say 'wicked' up there to mean 'very.'

"Anyway, the weird thing is, when she died, I lost the book. It's as if it disappeared when she passed on. A coincidence, I guess. Or maybe not. But the book had a chapter on mirrors and what they meant. It asked, 'What would be reflected in a mirror if you put another mirror in front of it?' There would be nothing to reflect but the reflection of a mirror reflecting off another mirror."

Emily said, "It's like if a tree falls in the woods and nobody is there to hear it, does it make a sound?"

"Yeah," Gia said with a nod, "kind of like that. It's an abyss—just one continuous vision into nothingness. It warned against looking at the back of a mirror unless you're ready to confront your own demons. I remember that from the chapter on self-reflection."

"What's your point?" Twerp asked.

"Maybe if we put the hand-held mirror against the wall mirror, we can see inside it? Maybe through the back?" Gia proposed.

Emily stood up and carried the hand-held mirror to the wall, which had a mirror glued to it like every other wall. She leaned the hand-held mirror against the wall mirror, facing it. Balancing it was tricky, but it worked. When she did, they all gasped audibly.

She stepped back to see for herself. Through the back of the hand-held mirror, they could see the spirits trapped inside.

The room they were confined in was dank and difficult to make out in detail, but there were human souls in there. They appeared as people, albeit more translucent, imprisoned in a sort of concrete jail.

The room was a harsh, cold shade of gray with tiny flecks of blackness. The occupants were naked, sitting on the floor. They looked pale, skinny, and scared, hugging their knees, many of them crying into their hands.

Emily could see their breath puffing in the cold air of their quarters. They all appeared so tired, hopeless, and forlorn. She could barely hear some of them moaning in occasional pangs of distress while others just sat and shivered. They looked as if they hadn't slept in months.

After a moment, Emily located Professor Joe among the people.

She sat down at the Ouija board with the others, and they watched the mirror like a television.

"Can you hear me?" Emily asked in a shaky voice, clearing her throat, embarrassed by her own feebleness.

"Professor Joe, can you hear me?" she said with more clarity and determination.

The planchette began moving without anyone touching it, and they all noticed.

"Has that ever happened before?" Martin asked, his eyes wide.

"No," Gia replied.

The planchette landed on the word "yes."

Gia gasped, her eyes watering with emotion. "Oh my God," she said.

"No way," Martin whispered, shock written across his face.

"Can you see us?" Emily asked.

The planchette floated to the word "no."

Twerp picked up a lit candle and carried it to the back of the hand-held mirror, placing it beside it. "Tell him to look for the light," he said.

"Can you see the light we're shining?" Emily asked.

The planchette floated to the word "yes."

"What's keeping you there?" she inquired.

The planchette moved from letter to letter, spelling out: HIM.

Emily leaned back as far as she could, trying to get a different angle on the mirror. When she did, she was finally able to see him—Baghead. He was the only one standing.

Emily looked at Gia. "Do you remember what he said in class?" she asked.

"Who?" Gia replied.

"Marcus Aurelius. 'What stands in the way becomes the way,'" Emily said. Then, raising her voice, she declared, "The obstacle *is* the way, Professor Joe. Go to him."

Through the reflection in the mirror, they watched as Professor Joe looked scared. He appeared fragile and borderline lifeless. Even so, he found the courage to push himself off the floor while the others looked on in stunned silence.

He wobbled like a baby deer standing for the first time on its spindly legs, moving toward Baghead. The foursome could see him more clearly as he got closer. When he stood in front of the monster he had created, he tried to speak but faltered. He tried again and again. Finally, he managed to say, "I'm sorry."

They stared at each other—Professor Joe and the odious creature towering over him, weighing more than he did by 200 pounds.

"I know this may sound strange to you," Joe continued, "but I created you. Then, I left you alone to navigate this cruel world. No parent should ever do that," he told him.

Baghead remained motionless. Emily thought her eyes might be playing tricks on her, but she swore she saw him shrinking. A moment later, there was no doubt: the monster was changing. First, he transformed into a man. Then, he became a teenage boy. Finally, he shrank to the size of a child—much smaller than Joe, only reaching the middle of his thighs.

"I'm sorry," Joe said again, this time to the child. He knelt down and hugged the boy, who hugged him back.

Emily whispered, "Tell the souls to walk toward the light."

Inside the cold, cement room, she watched as Joe waved at the spirits with one hand while hugging his son with the other. He gestured for them to walk toward the light, but they were too scared at first, too weak to move.

Finally, a woman pushed herself up from the floor, steadying herself on weak legs. She hobbled toward the mirror, and a moment later, she emerged from it into The House of Mirrors.

Her face broke into an expression of elation as she transformed into a beam of bright light and ascended, disappearing through the roof of the structure.

The foursome felt her joy so intensely that they began to shed tears.

They watched as the others followed her—one by one, they hurried past Joe and the child, exiting through the mirror, each transforming into warm rays of light and ascending skyward.

The remaining spirits helped each other stand. They hooked arms for support and shuffled along together, escaping their horrible prison. Each transformed into positive energy, lifted upward until no one was left.

Only Joe and Baghead remained, hugging each other tightly. The boy had his eyes closed tight.

"Joe, get out of there," Emily urged him. He looked at her and shook his head.

For the first time, she heard him speak directly: "The captain goes down with his ship."

The young boy opened his eyes and looked around to find the room empty. He appeared deceived, and then angry, causing him to grow large once again, transforming back into the menacing monster he had been.

In a fit of rage, he grabbed Joe by the throat and lifted him into the air, strangling him. Professor Joe was physically compromised—weak and sickly. It was a quick death.

A moment later, Baghead laid Joe's body on the floor and stood over it, peering down. He dropped to his knees beside the corpse, placing one hand on his father's chest, filled with sadness and remorse.

The group watched as he began to cry. It was the most awful sound anyone had ever heard, echoing off the walls of the room—a wailing of pain and anguish that conveyed endless sadness and hopeless heartache.

All four of them covered their ears as the sobbing became unbearable. Baghead hunched over the body of his creator, tears pouring from his eyes like a fast-dripping faucet.

Then he turned toward the mirror, toward the light. Baghead stood up and charged at it, his face filled with venomous rage.

"No!" Emily screamed, louder than she ever had in her life.

She saw a small object flash past her. It hit the mirror and shattered just as Baghead was about to break through.

The dense rubber wall behind the mirror stretched with a massive thud, as if a tank had collided with it from the other side. The impression of Baghead's body charging forward was captured in the wall, like the carvings on Mount Rushmore. He hadn't broken through.

Emily looked at Martin, who was holding his slingshot having just fired it at the mirror.

"I knew that marble would come in handy," Martin said.

"Holy crap," Gia whispered as she exhaled. She stood up and walked to the wall, touching the hard rubber impression of the monster's body. "It's warm, like a body," she said.

"Nice shot!" Emily said to Martin, who looked a bit stunned himself.

"Thanks," he replied as he broke into a smile.

They all stood up and hugged one another, catching their breath and collecting their things. They blew out the candles and packed up their possessions. The joy amongst them was palpable. The nightmare was over. They'd won.

They felt relief and happiness. Twerp high-fived Martin, and they hugged.

"You're the Bruce Lee of slingshot shooters," Twerp said, and they both broke into laughter.

Twerp even hugged Gia, and she hugged him right back. There was jubilation and triumph. They were alive and free from the burden they had been carrying for so long.

Martin noticed Emily had stopped what she was doing and was standing with her hands on her hips, facing the wall, her head down.

"Are you okay?" he asked her. She didn't turn around. Gia noticed and walked to her, gently placing her hand on her shoulder. Emily turned and they could see she was crying.

"I'm so sorry," she said. "To all of you."

"You don't owe us an apology," Gia told her, choking back tears. Emily hugged her. "It's over, Emily," Gia assured her.

"How do you know?" Emily asked, looking into Gia's eyes. "Places aren't haunted; people are, remember?"

"I didn't know what I was talking about," Gia said, offering as much comfort as she could.

"I guess we'll find out," Emily replied, her tone laced with fatalism. Still, she managed a sigh of reprieve as she glanced at the figure of the beast stretching out from the wall. It was creepy. "Let's get out of here," she said, not wanting to be anywhere near it.

They grabbed their bags and headed out of The House of Mirrors, back to the dorm.

Martin and Emily were on the pedal boat together, cruising along the pond that connected Ashley Hall School to Porter-Gaud School for Boys. Two days had passed since she texted him, asking him to come see her to help with something.

Emily had the mirror with her, along with the video cassette. She'd placed both in a small carry-on travel bag, along with a ten-pound weight from the school gym.

"Did you watch the tape?" Martin asked her.

"It's blank," she replied. "I watched it all the way through."

They pedaled some more until they were about halfway between the two schools. Emily took the travel bag and pushed it off the boat into the pond. They watched it disappear from sight.

"I feel bad for Professor Joe," she said.

"He saved them all in the end," Martin replied. "I guess some mistakes are built to last."

They sat in silence on the boat, looking out at the beautiful shoreline. This was the first semblance of real peace either of them had felt in many weeks.

"I really like how you're going to turn out," Martin said. "I mean, according to that age-yourself photo booth," he clarified with a shrug.

"So, what are you saying? You don't think I'm cute now?" Emily said with a look of faux shock.

"No," Martin said in a panic. "I just meant—"

"It's okay. I'm just messing with you," she said, smiling. "I like the way you supposedly turn out, too. *If* it's accurate."

"Maybe we can stay in touch," Martin said, his voice trembling slightly, silently praying it wasn't a mistake to suggest it. He never would have thought to do it two months ago. Things were different now. He was different.

"Yeah, let's do that," Emily replied, nodding. "I need someone I can count on."

She then reached over and took his hand, like good friends do, and together they pedaled the boat back toward Ashley Hall School.

AUTHOR'S NOTE

I was always embarrassed to tell people I was a writer. Not because there's anything shameful about the vocation—not at all—it was just that I didn't think I'd earned the right to call myself one.

Yes, I did write, but not for a living. So, when people I would meet for the first time would ask, "What do you do?" I would feel obligated to tell them I worked in a factory processing American passports, or in the mailroom of a finance company, or as a repo man for a rent-to-own store; all of which I did at some point. I didn't feel like I'd achieved enough public recognition to claim I was a writer.

I was wrong for that. I was a writer—a professional one at that. I didn't make any money from it, which is the most committed kind of artist you'll ever meet. Earning a living from 9 to 5 and then coming home to open a notebook and craft stories over an untold number of hours—thousands of them, maybe tens of thousands spanning the many years—qualifies you as a professional.

Writing is hard. Trust me, I know. It's harder than going to the gym, or eating healthy, or quitting drinking. It's harder than studying for a test, or going outside to shovel snow in the cold, or cleaning the bathroom.

Whether you do it every day, or every week, or every once in a while, it's hard. The more you do it, the harder it is. The act of writing on a consistent basis takes extraordinary discipline, so if you do it, embrace it. Talk about it. Be proud of it, and don't apologize for not being famous. You are a writer, just like William Shakespeare or John Grisham or Charles Bukowski.

And after you finish writing, you type it, you edit your work, you email agents, managers, producers, anyone at all in the industry who might be able to help advance your project up the line. Mostly, I wouldn't hear back at all, or when I would, it was a form letter saying, "No thanks, but good luck."

Putting in the work every day is what professionals do. We do it over and over, despite disappointment, or rejection, or that awful sense of hopelessness that occasionally whispers in our ear when we're alone.

Refusing to quit, knocking on the same doors that have been closed in your face a hundred times before, and finding a reason to try one more time means the ink is in your blood. It's who you are.

I am a writer, and I have so many people to thank for the help they've given me. Sometimes it was an encouraging comment, or in the form of advice or guidance. There are too many people to list, but there are a few that I cannot NOT mention, and these are them. I apologize if I have forgotten anyone who should be included. I'll surely miss a few.

ACKNOWLEDGMENTS

My siblings Joe, Steve, Matt, and Betsy for their friendship and encouragement. Also, their spouses and children: Linde, Gayle, Amy-Beth, Big Dave, Marcus, Mia, Gabriella, Matthew, and Henry.

Daniel M. Rosenberg for taking a chance on me and the years he invested in teaching me how to develop a proper story.

Michelle Shepard for her friendship, creative input, and steadfast belief in me.

My Junior High School English teacher, Edna Dufresne.

My high school English teachers, Jimmy Kelleher and Thomas Flangheddy.

Beth Ludden for being my first official fan.

Tim Grabarz for telling me long ago that an overnight success is just a guy who worked his ass off for twenty years before getting discovered.

Kris "Mudd" Meyer, YNWA.

Gabe Napolitan.

Ben Eads.

Timmy Sullivan for being there to toast with me the night I finished the novel.

Everyone at my gym who was rooting for me, including the owners, Tres and Shannon Bennett, for their enthusiastic support.

Joe Mynhardt for giving me the break I needed.

Monique Snyman for being patient and guiding me through the process.

My cats Siegfried, Toonces, Marvin, Clyde, Oscar, and Wanda.

Bob Ross for being Bob Ross.

ABOUT THE AUTHOR

Jim D'Andrea was born and raised in New England, the last of five kids. After graduating from Fairfield University, he spent a year in San Francisco running a clinic for the homeless population as a member of the Jesuit Volunteer Corps.

After a stint in New Orleans where he made his living as a Repo-Man, Jim landed a gig on a film crew, working as a production assistant on movies such as Kingpin, The Ringer, and Fever Pitch.

He taught himself to write screenplays by reading them as often as possible, focusing on comedy and developing multiple projects with various producers. He earned representation from WME and Paradigm on separate low-brow romps.

His passion for horror—specifically in the form of prose—took hold, compelling him to write his premiere novel The Haunting of Ashley Hall School, an Adult/YA gothic horror story.

Jim's favorite show as a kid was Tales from the Crypt. He was also heavily influenced by movies, books and tv shows like The Twilight Zone, Creepshow, The Shining, Rosemary's Baby, Abbott and Costello meet Frankenstein, Bram Stoker's Dracula, Burnt Offerings, Silence of the Lambs and The Lost Boys.

His favorite writers include: Mario Puzo, Hunter S. Thompson, Franz Kafka, Charles Bukowski, and Elmore Leonard. Favorite books: Frankenstein, Fight Club, The Trial, Animal Farm, The Godfather.

He prefers Jason Vorhees over Michael Myers, and can never turn down the opportunity to watch House of 1000 Corpses.

He currently resides in Charleston, South Carolina, in a 300-year-old home that is gently haunted. He has two cats for protection. He never works on Halloween, and rarely on other days.

Readers…

Thank you for reading *The Haunting of Ashley Hall School*. We hope you enjoyed this novel. If you have a moment, please review *The Haunting of Ashley Hall School* at the store where you bought it.

Help other readers by telling them why you enjoyed this book. No need to write an in-depth discussion. Even a single sentence will be greatly appreciated. Reviews go a long way to helping a book sell, and is great for an author's career. It'll also help us to continue publishing quality books.

Thank you again for taking the time to journey with Crystal Lake's Crystal Cove Press.

You will find links to all our social media platforms on our Linktree page: https://linktr.ee/CrystalCovePress.

MISSION STATEMENT

Since its founding in August 2012, Crystal Lake has quickly become one of the world's leading publishers of Dark Fiction and Horror books. In 2023, Crystal Lake officially transitioned into an entertainment company, joining several other divisions, genres, and imprints, including Torrid Waters, Crystal Lake Comics, Crystal Lake Games, Crystal Lake Kids, and many more.

While we strive to present only the highest quality fiction and entertainment, we also endeavour to support authors along their writing journey. We offer our time and experience in non-fiction projects, as well as author mentoring and services, at competitive prices.

With several Bram Stoker Award wins and many other wins and nominations (including the HWA's Specialty Press Award), Crystal Lake Publishing puts integrity, honor, and respect at the forefront of our publishing operations. We strive for each book and outreach program we spearhead to not only entertain and touch or comment on issues that affect our readers, but also to strengthen and support the Dark Fiction field and its authors.

Not only do we find and publish authors we believe are destined for greatness, but we strive to work with men and women who endeavour to be decent human beings who care more for others than themselves, while still being hard working, driven, and passionate artists and storytellers.

Crystal Lake Publishing is and will always be a beacon of what passion and dedication, combined with overwhelming teamwork and respect, can accomplish. We endeavour to know each and every one of our readers, while building personal relationships with our authors, reviewers, bloggers, podcasters, bookstores, and libraries.

We will be as trustworthy, forthright, and transparent as any business can be, while also keeping most of the headaches away from our authors, since it's our job to solve the problems so they can stay in a creative mind. Which of course also means paying our authors.

We do not just publish books, we present to you worlds within your world, doors within your mind, from talented authors who sacrifice so much for a moment of your time. There are some amazing small presses out there, and through collaboration and open forums we will continue to support other presses in the goal of helping authors and showing the world what quality small presses are capable of accomplishing. No one wins when a small press goes down, so we will always be there to support hardworking, legitimate presses and their authors.

We don't see Crystal Lake as the best press out there, but we will always strive to be the best, strive to be the most interactive and grateful, and even blessed press around. No matter what happens over time, we will also take our mission very seriously while appreciating where we are and enjoying the journey.

What do we offer our authors that they can't do for themselves through self-publishing?

We are big supporters of self-publishing (especially hybrid publishing), if done with care, patience, and planning. However, not every author has the time or inclination to do market research, advertise, and set up book launch strategies. Although a lot of authors are successful in doing it all, strong small presses will always be there for the authors who just want to do what they do best: write.

What we offer is experience, industry knowledge, contacts and trust built up over years. And due to our strong brand and trusting fanbase, every Crystal Lake Publishing book comes with weight of respect. In time our fans begin to trust our judgment and will try a new author purely based on our support of said author.

With each launch we strive to fine-tune our approach, learn from our mistakes, and increase our reach. We continue to assure our authors that we're here for them and that we'll carry the weight of the launch and dealing with third parties while they focus on their strengths—be it writing, interviews, blogs, signings, etc.

We also offer several mentoring packages to authors that include knowledge and skills they can use in both traditional and self-publishing endeavours.

We look forward to launching many new careers.

This is what we believe in. What we stand for. This will be our legacy.

Welcome to Crystal Lake Publishing—Where Stories Come Alive!

THANK YOU FOR PURCHASING THIS BOOK